MW00709326

K. B. PELLEGRINO

A PREDATORY CABAL

WORM IN THE APPLE

©2020

Livres-Ici
PUBLISHING™

On Sado-masochism by Eric Fromm

"In the authoritarian philosophy the concept of equality does not exist. The authoritarian character may sometimes use the word equality either conventionally or because it suits his purposes. But it has no real meaning or weight for him, since it concerns something outside the reach of his emotional experience. For him the world is composed of people with power and those without it, of superior ones and inferior ones. On the basis of his sado-masochistic strivings, he experiences only domination or submission, but never solidarity. Differences, whether of sex or race, to him are necessarily signs of superiority or inferiority. A difference which does not have this connotation is unthinkable to him."

Erich Fromm, Escape from Freedom

MAIN CHARACTERS

<u>West Side Major Crimes Unit Detectives</u>
Captain Rudy Beauregard
Lieutenant Mason Smith
Lieutenant Petra Aylewood-Locke
Sergeant Ashton Lent
Sergeant Ted Torrington
Sergeant Lilly Tagliano
Sergeant Juan Flores
Sergeant Bill Border

<u>Other Recurring Characters</u>
Captain Chilicot
Chief Coyne
Attorney Norberto Cull
Sheri Cull
Mona Beauregard
Mayor Fischler
Jim Locke
JR Randall
Luis Vargas

CONTENTS

1

The Scene

West Side MCU Lieutenant Petra Aylewood-Locke's eight-month baby belly just fit under the pull-out keyboard on her stand-up desktop. Major Crimes Unit Captain Rudy Beauregard accommodated her condition with the stand-up, which was the central item of envy in the West Side Major Crimes Unit. They all understood that Petra's condition guaranteed an issue with typing from a sitting position; thus, creating stress which may not be in her best interests, and certainly not in her colleagues' best interest. Petra could bitch at a level far exceeding the other detectives' ability to endure. Milly, the admin assistant for the unit, insisted that Petra receive this extra help, quipping, "Now that she's assigned to desk duty, Mason and I are the ones stuck here listening to her. I hate it, Captain, when you take one of your over the top action detectives and confine her to desk duty. Hell, you punish everyone when you do that."

Beauregard just gave her the look and she exited the 'Pit', commonly known as the main office room surrounded by all the little cubicles; each allowing just a modicum of privacy. Beauregard had been known to comment, "Privacy, what do you need privacy for; this is a tight knit family, and like any family, we're supposed to be thrown together."

No one countered his statement, despite the fact the Captain enjoyed his own private office, as did Lieutenant Mason Smith the computer go-to guy in the unit. Sergeant Lilly Tagliano, relatively new to the unit, would often say to Mason, "You're just hiding from the world, Mason. You have so many sisters and aunties, your mother, and your wife telling you what to do at home, they make you closet yourself into this nonhuman environment and then come out to the 'Pit' to present words of wisdom to us. You then retreat before we're able to counter your brilliant but stupidly timed remarks."

Tagliano's partner, Sergeant Juan Flores, asked Petra how she was doing today saying, "Didn't you see your OB yesterday, Petra? Did he say when you're expected to have the baby?"

"You think she'll tell me. It's now all this nicey, girlie talk when I go there, and she never, never tells me a date. I get her to say, 'Petra, the baby's doing nicely. Don't worry. Everything is as it should be at this stage.' What freaking stage am I at? At the last ultrasound, I saw a picture and a week number stage. Nothing since then. They don't know. I asked her if I ran some laps would it help move things along. Did I get an answer from her; no, no answer, just that the baby will come when the baby's ready. I'm really mad at Jim too. Apparently, according to him, husbands don't want to know the baby's gender, saying whatever is fine with him. Well, I'd like to know. He's got that psychologist's mentality of whatever is, just is. These nice people are driving me bonkers."

Juan turned to Sergeant Ashton Lent, always just called Ash, and said, "I should know better than to ask a pregnant woman a question about anything. So how are you doing in the relationship area, Ash? You and Martina doing well or should I not ask? It's just that nothing's going on for me and I look to others for confirmation that connected happiness exists."

"Stop feeling sorry for yourself, Juan. How old are you; you're a kid?"

"Ash, I'm almost thirty and I haven't been seeing anyone seriously since my high school girlfriend married another guy at seventeen. Mind you, she was dating him while she was dating me. My mom said that she was just in a hurry to get married and have kids. She's probably right, Marcy now has four kids. I wasn't ready for that, but I might be ready now."

Sergeant Ted Torrington, a very happily married guy, told Juan, "Don't go looking for someone to marry. It will end in disaster. Just be open to the nice people around you. Be nice to them. Some lovely young thing will be there right in front of you; in fact, there's probably one already glancing your way. You just don't see her. You're focused on the social media concept of the perfect girl appearing in a bikini with a bank account who will fall at your feet and say you're perfect. Get rid of that thought, Juan, it doesn't work that way. She's there already; you have to look and see her."

Ted's words ended the detectives' banter and they returned to work on some domestic assault cases and a home invasion by two local roughneck kids looking for some drugs. There was nothing exciting and Ash thought, *it's as it should be. The trouble is we had a run of horrible serial murders and drug related murders. That was crime activity that did not belong in a small city like West Side, Massachusetts. Still, the world is changing. There are more people, instant communication, a culture that supports immediate fulfilling of wants, and a cultural diversity that confuses people. Top it all off with ads on television that encourage kids to think they can have everything. It's amazing we don't have even more crime. The job is never boring when we have really bad guys to chase. What's wrong with me; I get a little breather and I miss the chase?*

Almost in answer to Ash's thoughts, Millie barged in looking for the Captain who had stepped out to do an errand. She had news. They all knew she had news, but she would not share it with them, and further, she was annoyed that Beauregard did not tell her where he was headed and when he would be back. She said, "That is not like the Captain. Just where would he be going that he wouldn't check out with me?"

The detectives agreed it was not at all in the Captain's behavior pattern to disappear quickly; mainly because the Captain rarely moved quickly. It wasn't crime related or he would have told them. In their discussion, they concluded that it must be personal about his family, or that he was ripped about some administrative or political issue that would affect the unit. Try as they might, they could not get Millie to join the discussion. That alone gave them the signal; the problem emanated from the chief's office.

Captain Rudy Beauregard headed for the Italian bakery in Agawam hoping he would not see anyone he knew there. It was early in the morning and he expected most of the people he knew would be working. He needed to be alone, as he was fuming at the news he had just received and he knew he had only himself to blame.

Rudy ordered his breakfast sandwich which included bacon, and some coffee, and attempted to be friendly to the very attentive clerk. He certainly fooled her into thinking he was there for the social interaction, because she just talked incessantly about the weather and world affairs, which in her mind, were a disaster. When he finally seated himself in the big adjoining dining room, he was able to think through the issue bothering him in what his wife Mona insisted was his own personal manner of self-therapy. *it was okay for me to take my choices without their input when I had Lilly and Juan join the unit. Well I didn't choose to have Ted, the Mayor's brother-in-law join the unit? The*

Chief gave me no choice on him; although he is one of the best detectives. It is a lack of respect when he texts me that Sergeant Bill Border is joining MCU. No question about whether I think he's right for the team. I don't know anything about him and I don't understand why he would put him in MCU. Chief Coyne gave me some gobbledy-gook that I need more help. When has the Chief ever worried about my lacking a position. The last position I filled in the legitimate detective route was with Ash. Good decision making on my part and a good result. What have I heard about this guy, Border? Not much. He's a former marine and walks around like one. Not in itself bad, but detective work is laborious and often requires subtlety. Who am I kidding, some of my detectives have to work at being subtle. If they can do it, a marine can do it. He's only been in the department for a bit more than three years. He came in as patrol, funny he was a transfer from Holyoke's department. That in itself is weird. Holyoke's police department is a lot bigger; most ambitious cops would stay there, and not come over here. Although, maybe he left Holyoke PD because he saw no future as a white guy. Could be he's not white; I've never met him. He could be impatient; that won't work for me. I never saw him here on patrol. Millie says he's connected with the DA and the drug task force; that I should ask Captain Chilicot. I won't ask him, yet. I'll call Luis, my Holyoke police contact. He'll tell me what he knows.

He had to go through a few connections before he was given Sergeant Luis Vargas, who greeted him in his special way, "So how's the Greek, French, and Irish and who knows what, serial murderer's arch enemy? How you doing, Superman?"

"Cut it, Luis, I need some info on a cop who was on your force for a very short time. He's now headed for my unit without my input. His name is Bill Border, a former marine. Do you know of him?"

There was a protracted moment before Luis answered. "Rudy, I'm not sure what to tell you. He's noted as 'Rambo' in the field, quiet around the higher ups, doesn't drink with the guys, has an eye for the badge bunnies, and lives well; and I'm talking about his career here as a patrolman. Don't know anything else except no one cried when he left for the West Side force. I heard he was undercover at your department and maybe you didn't meet up with him. I'm told he got top grades on the sergeant's exam over there with you recently. If it wasn't for his Rambo behavior as a patrolman here, the task force would never have tapped him. He chose to go over to your department because there was a lot of hell raised in your city about drugs. West Side is a ritzy area and the brass wanted the drug situation quieted down. Then you go and interfere and create havoc."

Rudy said, "Enough talk about my solving police assault cases. I want to know more about Border."

"I'm telling you, Rudy, he was perfect for undercover. He can convince anyone of anything. Our chief was happy to have him leave. He doesn't want a guy who makes waves as a patrolman; I heard he thought it just meant a future big control problem. I hope he won't be a problem for you."

"So, he's trouble; that's what you're telling me?"

"I didn't say, Rudy, but he is not easy; awfully smart, but not easy."

Rudy made a few more comments and they said their goodbyes leaving a thoughtful Rudy sipping the end of his cappuccino, which had cooled.

Leaving the bakery, he called Millie and was surprised that she had already been informed by paperwork forwarded from the Chief's office about Billy Border joining the team. It meant that the appointment was now public leaving no opportunity to persuade Chief Coyne to change his mind.

Rudy wondered, *what was the pressure put on the chief for him to shove Border down my throat?*

He asked Millie to keep the detectives inside until he came back

6

saying, "I'm scheduling a meeting before the new detective arrives. I won't be too, too, long, Millie. I've just got one stop to make."

Forty minutes later, as Beauregard attempted to pull into his allotted parking spot, he saw an ambulance in front of the station loading a patient. He was too far away to see clearly who it was, but surely saw half of his detectives standing by the ambulance. By the time he got closer the ambulance had left and so also were the detectives leaving to return to the building. He yelled, "What's up?"

He moved quickly, for him, toward the building. Ash Lent responded, "It's okay, Captain. Petra suddenly went into hard labor and we called the ambulance; mostly because she didn't want our help although it was clear to us that she needed it. I think it's early for the baby, but hopefully they'll be alright."

Lilly discoursed on the incident telling the Captain that Petra's water broke and she had severe pains. "She was really stressed, Captain, and told us that she was afraid she was going to lose the baby. She cried and wouldn't go with me to the hospital. We all tried to convince her but she was embarrassed about the mess. We called Jim and he called the ambulance. He was meeting her at the hospital."

It was just a short while later that Beauregard overheard Ted talking to Mason telling him that Petra recently had a urinary tract infection. When he told his wife Charlotte about the early labor, she said that a UTI could have been the trigger. Beauregard thought, *things are not right. Maybe getting her that stand-up computer station kept her on her feet too much.*

When he voiced his thoughts, the other detectives made him feel like a jerk; but that didn't last long. He got a call from the medical examiner that changed the tenor of the office conversations.

The M.E. said, "Rudy, I'm over at 97 Wood Valley Road at an unattended death. I was called by a member of the family. The woman is thirty-five years old with no negative health history and according to her relatives had not seen a doctor in three years. They called her doctor and he was not willing to come. That just means that he won't sign the death certificate, because he had no current information on her. The scene leaves me uncomfortable and I'm not certain why. Before it's further disrupted, can you take a look?"

"Aren't there cops there already, Johan?"

"Nope, the family member here called the doctor, refused to call the cops; said that they didn't need any notoriety. The doctor, who's a friend, called me. Said he was left no alternative, call me or the cops, and the family agreed to have him call me. He wants off the hook. Says the woman was extraordinarily difficult to handle as a patient, but she was in good health. He says she argued over any suggestions made. Please, just come and look. I've told them there'll be an autopsy unless I get additional medical information that explains this death. It's a funny scene, Rudy, and this family, as represented by a cousin, is off."

Rudy and his detectives took eight minutes to get to Wood Valley Road which he noted was a wooded area housing thirty mostly semi-detached and other individual high-end condominiums. He'd never been in the neighborhood before. He thought the landscaping deserved a design award. He muttered, "Outstanding, the landscape beats the high-end country club's grounds nearby."

Pulling in the U-turn driveway, Rudy saw outside the condo a welcoming committee of two. Johan Devon, the medical examiner, greeted him and introduced Leonora Sontin as a cousin of the deceased Eleanora Captreau. Rudy didn't often see Johan at a site. Normally his assistant would be there.

When Rudy entered the exquisitely designed and decorated condominium, his first glance caught nothing out of order; in fact, to him it looked like a showcase design for a furniture store. All normal with the exception of a stunning looking beauty lying dead on the eggplant colored velvet couch. There was something odd that he noted. The woman's right arm was raised up high on the couch. Before he could fully analyze just what was in front of him he heard voices arguing at the front door. He went to check and was accosted by three people, not including Leonora who had stayed outside. The group was told to stay outside, but they clearly had difficulty taking orders from Juan, Ash, Lilly, and Ted. Approaching the group, he asked his detectives why they had not been driven to the station for witness statements. He was told they refused to go and would give statements here. Ted, Ash, and Juan had each taken a witness aside to keep them separated while Lilly was talking to the cousin.

The Captain asked if any of the witnesses lived in the neighborhood and if so, would the neighbor allow the police to interview the witnesses in his home. Eric Shulman, a neighbor from across the street was amenable to the use of his home. Beauregard told the witnesses, "Please follow Sergeant Lent to Mr. Shulman's home. We need witness statements. He will direct you and this should not take long."

With some low muttering, they did what he asked. Leonora was the last to go saying, "There is much that I can tell you about this, Captain Beauregard. Please don't form any conclusions until we talk."

Beauregard harrumphed to Johan saying, "You need uniforms on a death scene like this to control things. I'm calling it in. Doesn't matter what you promised them, Johan. Just blame me. I'll try to have them arrive without fanfare; get your folks in here too."

He made the call. Johan questioned him. "Rudy, you've already made a decision on what evidence? You haven't given but a cursory look at the scene."

"Johan, she's in full rigor and her arm is above her head. It's not a natural pose. I don't care if she was poisoned, or choked, or died of natural causes, that arm up is fishy. Also, Johan, was the television on when they found the body and who found the body?"

"Leonora found the body and said the television was on. Why do you think it's important, Rudy?"

"Television's on but she can't see it from where she's laying. She's on the wrong end of the couch. The pillows are piled up on the other end for someone to be propped up to watch TV. Why is she on this end lying flat with the exception of the arm standing in attention? If she wanted to lie down flat, wouldn't it be more likely to just move the pillows off the couch and stay in place? Another thing is that she's wearing a dressy work suit; granted it's beautiful, but most folks take something that special and confining off the minute they come home. Time of death is going to be important. We'll also have to talk to the witnesses to see who approached the left side of the couch. Did you go to that end of the couch, Johan?"

"No. The couch is over nine feet long. You know I'm careful how I approach a death scene, even when it's supposed to be from natural causes. Rudy, this group appeared to be uncomfortable and wouldn't even come in the home to look at her let alone go near her with the exception of Leonora who found her and said she stood at the right-side head of the couch looking down on her cousin and crying."

"If no one did, then that footprint I can see, in the lush pile of the area rug by the left side of the couch, may be important. I need it photographed."

Rudy continued to look around while the Medical Examiner greeted his team. Johan started taking pictures before he did further examinations. Rudy called Johan's attention to a large exotic plant with a vacuum nearby, but completely visible, which interfered with Rudy's assessment of the victim's sensibilities. These thoughts he verbalized with, "Johan, what do you think? The room is in impeccable condition, but she's left the vacuum out for everyone to see. My wife Mona puts the vacuum where it belongs the minute she's finished and our house doesn't measure up to the perfection of this one."

Johan answered, "I'm with you on that, and Rudy, I'll bet she doesn't clean this place. She has help. Every resident in this neighborhood has some sort of cleaning service. I've been here in the area before on a call and saw two professional cleaning service trucks. It's like Longmeadow when, during the travel hours in the morning, all the residents are rushing from the town for work while all the service contractors are going the other way to work in the homes."

Rudy continued to view the scene from what he often called the 'outlier view.' He made several notes including one of two chips in painted wall corners which he thought did not fit with the otherwise perfection of surfaces all around the room. The chips were not at vacuum damage level; instead they were around four and a half feet from the floor. Another observation included damage to the surface of the console table upon which the enormous television sat. The damage looked new to him. The marks may have been made if the TV had almost fallen and been saved by someone; his thought arose from scrape marks on the table causing him to think that the weight of the TV made the scrapes. Had there been a struggle was one thought. The window blinds in the front of the home were shut tight while none were shut in the back of the room which opened out onto an enormous room of all windows decorated in a rustic New Hampshire style of dark wicker and glass furniture and vivid paisley upholstery. He thought, *I would live out here if this were my home.*

There were two French doors at one end of what he would call the 'summer room' and it was obvious that a table by the door had been moved. The intricate almost Arabic designed tile floor showed rubber track marks, and the table, which was heavy, had rubber coatings on the bottom. Rudy thought, *enough already; there has been a struggle here and an investigation is in order.*

Johan agreed with Rudy's assessment that the death was at least suspicious, just in time before greeting the police. Johan asked the police to assist him in the overall markings for analysis and photos, and measurements of the scene. He had already checked the body for full rigor and determined that death had occurred sometime between six and twelve hours before; but he would need to use forensic techniques such as 'Liver Mortis' to hone in on a more accurate time of death. He then suggested that Rudy make the call to the District Attorney's office to inform the attached state trooper. He said, "Rudy, you'll have time to get your case and arguments together before they get here to try to talk you off a homicide or even a suspicious death. Better call your chief first. You know he won't want a homicide. It might help to tell them both that we're in agreement, so they don't start with the usual political claptrap. They drive me crazy sometimes with their political agendas."

Clearly not concerned with this detail, Beauregard asked, "Johan, who are the witnesses in the kitchen and what is their relationship to the victim?'

"Well in addition to her cousin Leonora, there is a neighbor from across the street Eric Shulman, Judith Wallace who says that she is the victim's best friend, Otto Walder who had had dinner with her last evening at the Casino in Springfield and dropped her off at ten o'clock, and a co-worker Mildred Ryan."

They were interrupted by a uniform who informed them that an insistent neighbor from next door had pertinent information on the victim, reporting, "Captain, he says there are always goings on from midnight to three in the morning on some Wednesdays to Thursdays; that if Eleanora died of suspicious causes, that's the reason. He is certain the parties are important. Should I bring him in? He's annoying and is not taking 'no' well. He says that we should talk to him now. If we don't he's just going to the station and make a report."

Rudy asked his name and was told that it was Reggie Sutten and that he looked about fifty years old. Reggie was let in.

Beauregard informed West Mass Police Chief Coyne about the suspicious death, who with a sigh, said, "Don't take an accidental death and invent it into the first of a string of serial murderers, Rudy; we've had enough of those in West Side," and he clicked off. Rudy thought that the Chief must be at a public function to let him off so easily without a little debate. Knowing he was lucky for the moment and being absolutely certain that this was a case of a single crime, Beauregard went about his business.

2

The Witnesses

Beauregard assigned Sergeant Ted Torrington to do his, separate from Johan's, analysis and photographing of the death scene and the rest of the condo using one of the uniforms to assist. He was certain that Ted, famous as a detail guy, would preserve every piece of potential evidence. Also, Ted was a good photographer.

Ash and Lilly would be helpful to him. He thought, *Ash has much more patience than I have with people behaving emotionally, and Lilly is a genius in getting people to tell her private details. Both remember everything that's said and document well. I'm surprised that a musician would be that disciplined. I know they hear stuff in their head, but I didn't know that one would be so good at writing reports. Lilly is not as attentive in her reports but has greatly improved. She'll want to show me that improvement today.*

The witnesses, each separately, had formed their own conclusions, and from each witness' body language Beauregard observed, that in addition to being annoyed with the police, each had issues with other witnesses; each fought to be the first witness interviewed. They had been instructed to sit separately in the adjoining den area under the watchful eyes of two uniforms. Ash interviewed in one section of the home, a small area off the kitchen, and Lilly in another section called a mud room. He had a uniform sit with the witnesses confined to the den.

Ash interviewed Leonora Sontin who was still crying. She stopped after five minutes when she realized that Ash was willing to sit for an extended period until she gained hold over her emotions. He took care of the details getting permission to record the interview. Leonora told a tale of two cousins, daughters of sisters, born within weeks of each other, who attended the same schools, and were socially connected at the hip until several years before. She said, "Detective, Eleanora was the risk taker. She took over a room when she entered it. Our mothers named us these names because they are two versions of the same name and versions of their own names; Ellen and Leah. Our mothers were so close and they envisioned their daughters would also be as close to each other. There, however, is a difference. Our mothers, maybe because of their strict upbringing, were very much alike in personality. Eleanora and I were very different. I'm a conservative in dress and actions, while Eleanora was not. The differences didn't seem important until later when I met Lawrence, my husband. We married last year. Eleanora wouldn't stand up for me. She didn't approve of my marriage; said that I was settling when I didn't have to settle."

"Was she jealous? You are a good-looking woman."

"Jealous of me, are you kidding? Did you see her? Every man who ever met her tried to date her."

"I imagine that you never had a problem keeping your own boyfriends to yourself. Despite my opinion, what about your husband Lawrence, did he try to date her?"

"Detective, Lawrence is an IT engineer. He's about machines and machine language. He thinks I'm gorgeous because I'm his. He'll never look further. Like I said, I'm conservative and I play it safe. Eleanora thought I was afraid of life. She thought I married Lawrence just to keep me out of trouble. I'll tell you I was afraid of the life Eleanora was leading. My husband thinks Eleanora is a sociopath which he describes as having no consideration for anyone but herself."

"How so, Leonora? How so? Is Lawrence correct in his assessment?"

"From the time we were in nursery school, I knew enough to let her win at everything. She almost always did win because she was better at most things than me or others. Eleanora had a mean streak, Detective. I think she enjoyed hurting people. She left me alone because she was afraid I'd tell my mom, who would then tell her mom. My Auntie has passed, but when she was living, she could keep Eleanora in check. Aunt Ellie died four years ago. It was sad; her passing was so unexpected. Soon after, Auntie's husband died of a massive heart attack. I think it pushed Eleanora's mean streak further. I was happy I was not in the party scene any longer, I can tell you."

"Leonora, do you think that her being mean made enemies for her? Is that why you don't think she died of natural causes."

"Detective, Eleanora was the healthiest person I know. She was an athlete and she taught occasional nutrition classes at her wellness center. She did have a problem with something called GERD, which made her pay attention to what she ate and drank. Although she was a partier, she wasn't a drinker and never did drugs other than occasionally at a party. The way I found her lying on the couch didn't look right. I never saw her lie on a sofa before; she'd sit, and always sit up straight. She said the symptoms from GERD were much better if she didn't lie down. In fact, you'll notice that she slept on a slant cushion in her bed. She believed in order and neatness. She would not commit suicide. Something's off, I just know.

"And the outfit she's wearing, well I question that; I do. Unless she died right after coming home from work or maybe a dinner after work, she would never stay dressed like that! She has the most wonderful lounging clothes; like a movie star. She'd change into those on any day and especially on Wednesdays when people would be coming over."

"You didn't answer my question, Leonora. Could there be someone, an ex-boyfriend out there who would hurt her? Who are her boyfriends?"

Leonora put her head down and cried saying, "I don't know. I've not been out with her lately. But I heard she had an argument with a client at work that got loud. Most of her boyfriends were short-term; her relationships never lasted more than six months and they were never exclusive. Eleanora kept us all at a distance."

Beauregard watched Lilly's first interview with Eric Shulman. Eric stated he had lived across the street from the victim for ten years. He did not see Eleanora go to work that morning. When he went outside to bring his trash barrels in, he saw Leonora and Eleanora's best friend Mildred Ryan talking outside the house. He knew something was wrong and walked across the street to find out. Eric was divorced, but said that his ex-wife was friendly with Eleanora before the divorce. She would go to clubs with her, and one time she went to Eleanora's Wednesday night parties. After that she never went out with her again. In fact, he thought that his domestic difficulties started right after that. Eric, in Beauregard's thoughts, did not appear to hold it against Eleanora. "Detectives, I don't know what goes on across the street many Wednesday nights, but there must be parties to end all parties. Most cars leave around two a.m., with only one or two cars staying until five a.m. She leaves for work at about eight o'clock looking ravishing. I mean she's one good looker and staying up all night doesn't seem to bother her."

When Eric was questioned as to whether he had ever had a

relationship with Eleanora, he said, "Nope, I know trouble when I see it. In fact, I told my wife Dorie to stay away from Eleanora and look what happened. Dorie would never talk about her experience. She left me and is not running around; in fact, she is almost a recluse with the exception of work. We never had children. Dorie thought she was too young at first and later said she didn't think she was cut out for motherhood. I think kids would have made a difference. I don't know what happened that Wednesday night, but Dorie was never the same after."

"What about last night, Eric? Did she have a party last night?"

"I wasn't home last night. I'd played golf and had dinner and drinks with my golfing partners. I got home around eleven. The lights were on across the street, but there were no cars parked outside."

Lilly's next interview was with Otto Walder, who was a high-volume residential Springfield real estate broker. He'd been Eleanora's dinner escort on the night before her death. Walder described his dinner with Elenora. They'd been to the Typical Sicilian Restaurant in Springfield and then stopped by the Casino for a half hour of gambling and a couple of drinks, after which he dropped her off at home at about ten in the evening. Lilly asked about their relationship, whether it was romantic or business. His reply was that it was both, or at least he was trying for both. He'd been seeing Eleanora for three months, but had to admit that she did not let him get close to her. He did think there was some progress being made when she agreed to go to the Long Meddowe Days in Longmeadow and dinner afterward this coming weekend. It was new for her to go out with him all day and then dinner. He thought her joining him to Long Meddowe Days, Longmeadow's annual fair, was a sign of her wanting him to share in everyday fun; he said it'd never happened before. She told him her life had changed and she might now be ready for a mature relationship. He hoped it meant a future for them. He appeared upset and kept saying, "She was so gorgeous -- to die so young."

"Otto, have you ever been invited to her Wednesday nights' soirees?"

"Oh no, Detective, I wouldn't be invited to those parties. They were cosmetology events. Eleanora said that everyone's schedule is so busy, that she had a professional friend, an esthetician, who was willing to come as long as Eleanora could guarantee five or six clients. You know, they do Botox and other injectables; she said everybody does it, but you need a professional who knows the product or the results can be disastrous. I can tell you I certainly don't think she needed Botox or any beauty product. Maybe she got a percentage of the sales and free samples for herself. She is – oh my God – I mean – was pretty smart about business."

Beauregard gave Otto the standard ending he'd given to all the witnesses that his detectives may call him in later when they learn more about the victim's death, while thinking, *this guy is a numbskull if he believed that story. Cosmetology parties going until three and maybe five in the morning.*

Mildred Ryan, Eleanora's co-worker and, according to her, one of her dear friends, cried constantly, making soft whimpering sounds. It required Lilly to wait periods of time between her tears for an answer to each of his questions. Beauregard found it distinctly annoying but tried his best to be understanding. Mildred's work was in commercial real estate where she was an office manager while Eleanora was the lead sales figure and partner. Her view was stated forcefully, "Eleanora was so special. Men asked for her. She was one of the best sales brokers in the industry. Other firms constantly tried to woo her on a regular basis."

Mildred explained that this geographical area was not a top commercial market, but Eleanora was known throughout the larger geographical area and had more listings than any other commercial agent. In fact, she recently was recognized by a national commercial real estate brokers association as one of the top brokers in New England. Eleanora told Mildred, "Why would I ever leave here for Miami even if the market would make me extraordinarily wealthy. I'm wealthy already and best of all I'm in complete control of my life."

Mildred reported that she and Eleanora had lunch at least two days a week and always at the best places. Occasionally, Eleanora would invite her for a drink at a martini bar. She got lots of attention from the bartender who clearly was mesmerized by Eleanora. Mildred thought Eleanora to be absolutely brilliant and a loyal friend who enchanted all who met her. When Beauregard questioned her about Eleanora's boyfriends and nightlife, she looked uncomfortable, responding, "I'm not in that league, Captain, and I don't normally go to bars, although she invited me several times. I did go to the martini bar, but it was after work for 'happy hour'."

Beauregard invited Judith Wallace in for the next interview. She sat down with a grace that reminded him of the British Royal Family, wherein she slowly lowered her body without touching any side of the chair. He thought she was stunning. Judith answered all questions as if she were testifying in court. If a 'no' or 'yes' would do, that was her answer. Lilly found it difficult to see beyond her exotic looks until she asked, "Were you invited to Eleanora's Wednesday nights' soirees?"

Her eyes almost closed up at the question and she did not speak for an elongated period, finally saying, "Sergeant Tagliano, I've known Eleanora for years. We were roommates in college, but Eleanora needed to be in charge. If she couldn't control the venue or what we should all wear for the evening, then she'd put you in a position where she had some other kind of control. She was into dressing when we went clubbing; you know costuming, like fifties' style or the twenties, or punk. Eleanora insisted on being center stage and we mostly let her, but I have limits and I know her well. Wednesday nights were not for me. I would never attend and never did."

Lilly asked how she knew what was happening on Wednesday nights if she never joined in the party. She looked at her with what Lilly and Beauregard both thought was a glimmer of fear and told them that she had heard rumors and that she didn't need a map to keep herself safe. Try as Lilly might she had nothing more to say. When she asked why she came to Eleanora's house today, she said, "I tried calling and texting this morning. She didn't answer. She always answers. It hit me immediately that she was in trouble and today is Thursday, Detectives, the day after Wednesday night."

Lilly could not budge the lady into disclosing any information or into giving insight into Wednesday night activities. She was dismissed.

Ash joined them asking for a minute aside saying, "Captain, it's taken all this time to interview these witnesses. Who's left to interview?"

Beauregard said, "We have the vociferous next-door neighbor, Reggie Sutten. Let's do this one together. You'll be effective, Ash; I'm bushed from listening to the stories Lilly has elicited that say almost nothing. Our victim was an operator but nobody wants to give details."

They brought Reggie in and before they could ask a question, Reggie started rambling. They let him. "Captain and, uh, Detective, there is so much to tell, I almost don't know where to begin. It took me a long time before I realized what was going on in Eleanora's house. She looks beautiful, but I always felt that there was something off about her; you know what I mean."

Beauregard felt that he should get an award for patience as Ash prodded and directed Reggie to tell his tale in intelligible prose. The detailed story told was a testament to the public image of a neurotic and nosy neighbor. Reggie was a web designer for a high-end and well-known New York City marketing firm which allowed him to work from home three weeks out of four. He loquaciously described his typical day at his computer with breaks every ninety minutes. He insisted that in addition to his workout at six-thirty in the morning, his body needed to move regularly away from his chair. The detectives listened as Reggie detailed what he could see from his kitchen windows; he knew most of all the goings on at Eleanora's home. His kitchen windows happened to face Eleanora's great room and adjourning glassed-in space. His view of the house from the kitchen included a view of most of her rear yard and the only rear exit door other than from the garage. He insisted that the detectives should walk over to see just what he could see from his yard saying, "I saw much more than I bargained for."

Eleanora's life, according to Reggie, was rather well structured. She would leave for work early in the day and return home generally around four in the afternoon with the exception of Wednesdays when she was home by noon. A few months ago, her scheduled varied a little; in fact, on one or two nights she didn't come home at all. He thought something was up.

Reggie said he concluded she must have taken naps on Wednesdays to fortify her for Wednesday nights' escapades. Ash asked Reggie to stay on only what he saw, that conclusions could not be made until facts were established. It was at this point that Reggie became excitable. He almost yelled, "You don't understand, Eleanora looked normal, but she works hand in hand with the devil. Wednesday nights were spent in Eleanora doing evil; she hurt people. Sometimes I heard a man or two men telling her to stop. Stop what? Well, you use your imagination. On several occasions I could even hear her say something to the effect of, 'I'll stop. Do you really want me to stop? You may leave anytime. You know that, but what do you really desire? You just can't come back, and I would so miss you.'"

He relayed that on one evening, he walked over to her yard to see what was going on because the blinds in the big room were partially open. A light outside turned bright, and before he could go back to his own yard, she shouted through a speaker, that he did not know was installed there, "'Come in, Reggie, I'd like a try at you.' She was cruel and a sadist with men; of that I'm certain."

Ash asked him if that evening was in the winter or spring and was told it was in the winter. Reggie said that last night, she was out in the backyard for a while around eleven o'clock, maybe a bit earlier, but the lights didn't go on. He heard lots of noise around her water pond.

Reggie had never been in Eleanora's house. He'd not been invited before and felt that her saying what she said that winter night just demonstrated how twisted she was. He was certain that she was not afraid of the police. He saw several police go in there on Wednesday nights and once he saw an unmarked car there on a Thursday afternoon. It had been parked outside waiting for her. The cop, who was not in uniform, was a tall guy and seemed angry. "Well she made short shrift of him, I can tell you," said Reggie.

It took the detectives about fifteen minutes before they were successful in extracting Reggie from the home without incident. He promised to visit them at the station with more information he had documented in his daily notes, leaving Beauregard to sigh and say, "Nosy neighbors are valuable, but God save me from them."

Laughing, Ash said, "Captain, you know that I'm the one who will be stuck listening to him after this, and helping him understand why the Captain is too busy to speak with him. You know, when he has such important information. I'm going to suffer, Captain; your suffering Reggie is over today."

"Don't be so sure, Ash. These little stage plays tend to bite me in the ass."

Ted entered the room and introduced State Police Lieutenant

Forman from the SPDU or State Police Detective Unit, formerly called CPAC or the Crime Prevention and Control unit, was attached to the District Attorney's office. He was new to his position and neither detective had met him before. Forman, although friendly and the presenter of good news, shared his news in a position superior manner that annoyed all three detectives. He announced that the District Attorney would support West Side MCU in gathering all the evidence and send it to the state lab, if necessary. MCU would report on the ongoing investigation, which from Forman's perspective looked like a natural death, and therefore would be closed shortly. He said that the District Attorney was most comfortable with Captain Beauregard's efforts, who was known in policing circles as the prince of solving serial murders. He added his own opinion that the death may be at most, a suicide. Forman had, upon entering the scene and based on his quick observation, determined previously it was a suicide. He then left without any glad handing. As far as police protocol, he was a dud. West Side police would always be in charge of a murder in West Side and didn't need permission to proceed into investigations from outsiders. Ash commented, "What a jerk! He doesn't know anything about process, just his own importance."

The two detectives decided to walk the perimeter of the house's exterior focusing mostly on the rear area. There was a large fish pond with a bridge enveloped by a quarter acre of woodland offset by the pristine lawn. On the bridge lay a woman's lace panties. Beauregard texted Johan and asked if the victim was wearing panties. The returned text said, "No."

Near the French doors in the rear of the home, they could see broken branches from an evergreen that had been allowed to grow large enough to infringe upon and partially obstruct the exit path. Ash said, "There has to have been some action out here last night.

The panties are new and there was no rain last night. These broken branches mean that at the very least, someone was careless in walking through the doorway."

They toured the area and noticed that the security motion lights did not activate. There were rocks around the water that had been turned over to one side and Beauregard determined that forensics should examine the area. There was a partial man's footprint on the dirt where a large stone had been moved.

Before leaving they went back into the home to check the bedroom for the slant board that Eleanora supposedly slept on, and it was there. Across from the king-sized bed was a large portrait or Eleanora in see-through lingerie leaving nothing for the imagination. Ash said, "At the very least, she's an exhibitionist."

The detectives were ready to leave the scene when both of their cells signaled a text. The text read, "There is news: a healthy baby and mother." Nothing else was said.

3

New Baby and New Detective

Petra Aylewood-Locke and Jim Locke were as happy as Beauregard thought was possible for what he called 'earthlings,' his term for ordinary people. Petra held an absolutely healthy seven-pound little lady named Carlotta Catherine Locke. Carlotta was so quiet and so pretty. They all wondered whether she would remain that way given that Petra had never been able to sit still. Ash said, "Do we have a miniature 'Bolt' here or a talkative psychologist, Petra?"

As her nickname suggested, Petra bolted and said, "You have Carlotta here, Ash. She is a person in her own right. She is going to be a lot cooler than her parents, I can tell that right now. Look, she has five detectives staring at her and she won't even wake up to welcome you. There are no tears or faces made. She's going be cool."

Lilly's reaction was the best, they all thought, when she said, "I guess this is a moment in life where everything is perfect. I think I'd like to be here someday."

Juan chimed in, "Never heard you even mention kids in this way before. I like this softer side, Lilly, keep it up."

Beauregard said, "Thank God that Mason's not here; he'd make you suffer for months for that remark, Lilly."

"Wouldn't have said it in front of Mason, Captain. I know better and he has a memory that never quits. He's also a softie and tries to hide it with sarcasm and cynicism. He says the job has made me cynical; must have made him cynical too."

The crew shared some sandwiches Juan brought in, insisting that hospital food would not do for a celebration. He then tried to schedule a christening party; but the parents were not to be rushed and said they would celebrate but needed six weeks of parenting before sharing Carlotta with the world and bringing her to God. The nurse visited their room twice; once to eat a sandwich and another to tell them to quiet down. Finally, Ted arrived, and his first response was to take the baby out of the baby cart and hold her. He did not ask permission which surprised all the other detectives, but did not bother the parents. Ted looked down at Carlotta saying, "A good looker, sweetheart, but with those parents, what could anyone expect?"

Beauregard, amidst the gaiety, received a text from Mason saying, "New detective, Sergeant Bill Border is here and is taking charge. I told him not to go to the hospital. Better get back here. He needs guidance."

Beauregard could feel the tension when he entered the station, first from the Desk Sergeant who just nodded at him with no 'What's Up, Captain' and second from Millie whose Southern roots always took hold when she was under stress saying, "Finally, y'all come back from visiting. Y'all better take care of business as Elvis would say, Captain. The new detective is a piece of work."

He moved towards the noise which came from the conference area where murder boards were posted. There, on the board was a complete set of pictures of the morning's scene, with Lieutenant Mason Smith arguing with Bill Border. "We haven't determined if it's a murder investigation yet, Border. The Captain has protocol before we assign a board to a case."

"How the hell can you know if it's a murder, if you don't do the preliminary work to investigate and that requires posting. You guys have gotten sloppy over here."

Beauregard spoke up in a clear and controlled voice. "Sergeant Border, welcome to the Unit and now, if it's agreeable to you, please join me in my office."

Mason tried explaining to Beauregard just what had happened, but a raised hand silently instructed him to relax. The motion could not prevent Mason from thinking, *I don't know how the Captain's going to handle this detective; Border doesn't listen well and thinks he knows everything.*

The Captain walked more slowly than usual to his office requiring Border to change his normal take-charge walk in order to stay behind his new superior. Protocol was required, yes, even for Sergeant Bill Border. Finally, the two sat opposite each other and made eye contact. Border's eyes dropped first, when, finally, Beauregard said, "This is my unit, Sergeant Border. Nothing happens here without my absolution. Do you understand? You have a history wherever you've been. You were sent here, probably for the brass to test my patience and not theirs. If I hear, just once, that you talk to the press or any outsider, you are gone; and don't think I can't do it. Now, why don't you tell me just why you, as a sergeant in a new unit, would not listen to a lieutenant and senior detective's instructions. Think carefully before you speak."

To his credit, mused Beauregard, Border's face reddened slightly and he looked uncomfortable saying, "Lieutenant Smith told me that there was a possibility that the death was not accidental, nor a result of suicide. Seems to me I was just getting a jump start on things by starting the murder board. Mason seems a little slow to me; almost reluctant to move forward."

"You think that a senior detective in my unit and a lieutenant wouldn't know when and what action to take; is that what you're saying?"

"Captain, he does move slowly and talks slowly. He seemed to need my assistance."

"You ever been in the South of the U.S., Sergeant Border? They move and talk very slowly. Doesn't mean they don't know when to rush, and I can tell you right now that if you continue to jump to conclusions without facts, you will be gone. You will be gone. Get it?"

Putting his head down slightly, Border questioned, "Is this the kiss of death for me in this unit, Captain, because I want to be in MCU."

"No, Sergeant, but if you don't show respect for the other detectives in the unit, then I can't help you. They are a savvy bunch. Don't try to put one over on them, nor on me. You'll rue the day you do. Now go in there and make amends. Review our other work. We've not met on this morning's events, therefore it's out of bounds for you. That also means that you don't touch what you've already done. Okay?"

"Yes, sir."

Before he could exit, Beauregard added one more piece of advice, "Sergeant, my mother once told me to be the last to speak in a group; how else will you know what the others really think. You are quick on the trigger and a quick leaner; try harder and build for substance and background for your statements. If you don't you'll be left behind and I know you're ambitious and don't want that."

Mason walked in a few minutes later and asked if he should remove the evidence from the murder board. He was told to leave it. He replied to that, "Good thing, Captain, he did a good job and the scene does look suspicious. Chief Coyne is waiting for you in the murder room.

He was wild when he saw the murder board and asked Border why there was a murder board when at this time the ME hadn't given a report."

"Border said, 'Can't tell you, Chief. First thing is that I'm new here. Captain Beauregard is in charge; you'll have to ask him.'

"Chief Coyne was sputtering when I left, but was busy reading the stuff on the board. Border didn't feel the need to explain himself for disobeying MCU's rules. Told you he was smart."

Two minutes later brought Beauregard and Chief Coyne together in a review of the murder board. Coyne said, "I thought you told me you'd inform me if the investigation reached a point where it wasn't accidental or suicide. Now I see a thorough view of the scene. There may be questionable issues, but we don't even know yet if she died of a sudden coronary. What made you jump the gun, Rudy; that's not like you."

"One of my detectives got overly ambitious when he saw some of the issues. It's not a murder yet, Chief, but just a little early preparation in case of doubt. We're waiting."

Beauregard then spent some time going over the scene with Coyne. When finished, the Chief said, "Okay, something is not right. Don't parlay this into something more. This city doesn't need another notable case."

Five minutes later the other detectives returned and were introduced to Sergeant Border. They moved to the murder room when Border was asked to explain his work on the board. Border looked surprised but the detectives did not; for there was no reaction. Every picture in question from the crime scene was posted on the board. Sergeant Border pointed to each one summarizing why it was chosen and what possible implications it presented: murder, accident, or suicide. Lilly said, "It may have been an accident, but it's not suicide. This is one lady who has taken care of her looks; she's gorgeous. If I cared that much about my looks and my perfect home, I'd be laid out on my bed in a designer outfit before taking the deep sleep. She would have cared about how she would look when she was found. There's no evidence so far that she was under the weather by drugs or booze. She didn't fall over onto the couch. She's all dressed up and lying on the couch that way and all. Nope, it's not suicide."

Ash said, "Great visuals, Lilly, can't wait for that offing scene; but please don't do it, my black suit is at the cleaners. I do agree with you for your reasons and the fact that the victim is most likely OCD. I ask why, if she were suicidal in her perfect setting, would she leave the vacuum cleaner out. Talk about a non-fit to perfection."

Ted piped in, "That arm up in the air is not a natural pose. Even if I throw out the fact that she's not lying in the normal direction of a home owner who would be watching TV, it doesn't make sense from the sheer lack of comfort for her to lie with her arm up like that. She'd have to die quickly or be exhausted. The autopsy and blood tests should help, but not a suicide!"

"Not accidental either," announced Juan. "Unless she took an overdose of something and just laid down in that spot and died, it doesn't look right for accidental death. That hand up high is just odd. It's not natural. As Lilly pointed out, she didn't fall over. She's not on her face. She's not lying the right way for comfort."

Bill spoke slowly. The others listened to him, while Mason just stared thinking, *Captain is not good enough to change the leopard's spots in an hour, but maybe he's had some effect.*

"It's murder for sure. I don't know how and I don't know why, but nothing about these pictures seem to make sense. Panties in the backyard; and the victim was not wearing panties though dressed in a business suit. I think this is murder and I haven't even read the interviews."

Beauregard, not agreeing or disagreeing, instead said, "Ash, write up the interviews from our notes. Call me when done. Distribute them and tomorrow at nine, sharp, we'll meet here."

The next morning found the detectives and Beauregard discussing two new armed assaults. The Captain asked, "Mason, what have you got?"

Mason summarized the assaults which each by itself would not have been quite so alarming. The two together, along with witnesses' statements, presented a pattern, both for similarity of victims and description of the assaulters. He read from his report. "Neighbors in both assaults said that a man, whose face was half covered with a kerchief mask, attacked the women pulling her, in each instance, to the ground. In both cases, he was fumbling with a needle attempting to inject the women. In one instance a dog attacked him and in the other a neighbor who was putting out his barrels saw him and screamed. He got away, running. He was described as being over six feet, well built, dressed in black jogging clothes, and was probably a runner. He escaped very quickly. They had no information yet on whether the women did know each other, but because the attacks were so similar, there must be some connection."

Beauregard assigned Ted and Bill to interview the first victim, named Leslie Hosman, while Juan and Lilly were to interview the other, Alison Brunder. Both women lived in West Side and the attacks were near their homes.

Meanwhile, Ash was to review notes from the scene of the suspicious death and attend the autopsy which Johan had said he would do immediately. Beauregard said he would be gone from the office for the afternoon and asked Mason to research Eleanora Captreau. Mason had taken her computer with him after logging it in as evidence.

4

Absolutely Murder

Beauregard's brain was buzzing. He'd seen Eleanora before; but just where or when? She could not have appeared in his daily life, a stunning woman like that; she would be remembered by all the cops if she appeared at the station. He realized she would not be at the playing fields when he was watching his kids' games or his nephew and niece's games. He knew he may not remember at all, despite her good looks, if he just passed her on the street. Yet he was certain he had more than a passing view of her. Just, what, and where was it? Rudy called his wife Mona knowing she would remember if he had met any beautiful women, good looking enough for him to remember. She was surprised that he would call her in mid-afternoon, but understood his purpose when he questioned her.

With a burst of laughter, she said, "Hmm, do you want me to fix you up with someone? Rudy, you are a piece of work, calling your wife to find out if you've ever met a beautiful woman. Now let me see, do you have a description. We know a lot of beauties, Rudy, I need help."

"You would remember her, Mona, she was something, and I only saw her dead body. Five foot seven, long blonde and brown streaked hair, slim, perfect features, and described as always in charge."

"Oh, Rudy, she's one of your victims. I don't think I want to know who she is. Let me think, and I'll call you back, okay?"

Rudy was comfortable now knowing that Mona's memory would be able to give him a long list of ladies he'd met and he was convinced that he had met Eleanora. His phone rang and Juan was talking too fast. He thought maybe he was jumbling his Spanish with his English, which he sometimes did when he got excited. Juan's ability to switch back and forth between two language astonished Rudy. Rudy's mother Lizette had taught him French, but the Canadian version, which frustrated his French teacher at Holyoke High School. He ended up speaking passable French, but could never go back and forth easily between two languages. He did have a working knowledge of Spanish which had been helpful to him. "Slow down, Juan, what's going on?"

"Lilly and I are at Alison Brunder's home and she's not answering. We talked to a neighbor and he said Alison was there half hour ago when she let a man in. He left five minutes later and she did not leave the house. Look, Captain, Lilly has that feeling that something's up."

"Do we have any contacts on the police report?"

"Says that she didn't want her parents to know. She's divorced and she didn't take her name back. She refused to give the cops her maiden name last night. The report says that she wouldn't do it because she doesn't want her parents to worry. I checked the DMR, but her middle name is not a surname. She told the neighbor that she was accosted last night. He is worried."

"Have you checked the garage door or the rear door?"

"All are locked, Captain; after all, she would be worried about security after last night."

"Call me when you find her and like Lilly thinks, this makes me uncomfortable."

Rudy called Ash at the station and got Alison's address, informing him that he forgot to get it from Juan. Ash said, "It happens, Captain. Where are you?"

"Well, now I'm on my way to Alison's house. I hope it's a wasted trip. Have Ted and Bill left yet for Leslie's home?"

"They just left, Captain, Ted had a call that took him forty-five minutes to resolve."

Beauregard felt that mounting anxiety that often appeared when bad things were happening. He thought, I'm *like an old man, always fearing the worst. One fact, she was assaulted, and I think the guy's coming back? Nonsense! I've got to stop thinking that trouble comes in threes. It's just plain childish!*

Five minutes later, Beauregard pulled alongside Juan's car. The front door was opened and a man was standing there who said, "You can't go in there, Sir. The detectives said that there's trouble inside. I saw her let a guy in earlier. He left pretty quickly. He didn't look like trouble to me."

Beauregard introduced himself to the neighbor, Dick Lyons, who explained that his neighbor Alison Brunder was a good neighbor, who had been assaulted last night, and thought maybe she had knocked her head and was out or something. Dick was questioned whether he was available in the next two hours for an interview from the police. He was happy to wait for them.

Upon entering the home, Beauregard knew Alison was dead; he could feel it. Lilly said, "Captain, her neck is broken, and it wasn't accidental. There's no furniture near her that she could have hit. It looks like a professional job; you know the guy knew what he was doing. She let him in. She knew him."

Beauregard's reaction was to call Ted and Bill. "Get over to Leslie Hosman's house now. If she doesn't answer, enter. Call me ASAP."

Hearing his call, Lilly said, "You don't think that Leslie has met this fate? Captain, what's going on?"

"I don't know, but call the ME's office. I'll call Chief Coyne. Get some uniforms over here. I don't want any sloppiness. My gut says that we have a bad situation that implies more trouble."

Beauregard made his call to Chief Coyne, whose exact words were, "What the F--- are you doing? Inventing another serial killer, Rudy. Let me know how the District Attorney takes this. I'll ask him to help you. He really won't want to, so don't worry, there'll be little interference. Keep the info flowing on this, Rudy. Now you have two young women who are dead. Right now, only one is a sure murder. Keep your thoughts to yourself. Hell, I don't have to tell you that. You're the friggin' sphinx."

Happy that the Chief wasn't making too much of the investigation at this point, Rudy was smiling when Mona called. The smile got bigger and he answered, "You remembered something, didn't you, Mona?"

"Worth dinner this weekend if I have?"

"Hell, you're like the Mayor, tit for tat, every single time. What is it, Mona?"

"You talked with a woman named Ellie, another guest, when you picked me up at a shower that Ronnie Wyberg held for her daughter. I didn't come out quickly enough so you came in to get me. You're always so impatient. Ellie is the only knock-down beauty I can remember with whom you held a conversation. Does that refuel your memory, Rudy?"

It looked like it did, since Rudy slapped the side of his head and said, "How could I forget? She's my dead body. Thanks, Mona and dinner's on for Saturday. You choose. Okay?"

It was okay with Mona. What was not okay with Rudy was the fact that he could forget a person, who clearly was exceptional in her looks. He'd even had a five-minute conversation with her. He thought, *what did she say? We talked about girlie parties and showers. She did say that*

Susan Wyberg was stupid to marry. She had everything, but now would lose her freedom. When I said that marriage had worked out fine with me, her response really cooled me; something about my being a cop and for that kind of life maybe marriage was all right. Hell, she was off, I thought at the time. I guess when I'm turned off by someone, then I don't think about them; I just don't remember them.

His cell rang. He knew it meant trouble. He thought it may be that kind of day. Bill said that Ted had used a set of burglar's entry keys commenting, "Captain, those quiet ones really can fool you; Ted would make a great thief."

The story told was that Leslie Hosman was dead in the entry hall; strangled as was Alison. She'd only been home for forty-five minutes. According to the lady next door, Leslie had checked into work to explain that she needed a couple of days off to recover from the assault. She had what the doctor at the hospital said was a stress headache. The neighbor lady did not see a car in front and she did not see anyone go in the home, but did explain that after she spoke with Leslie, she vacuumed her first floor and would not have heard if Leslie had a visitor despite the fact that all her windows were open. Rudy informed them he would be there in a few, but directed Bill to call uniforms in saying, "Get community police in from that area. She's over by the high school playing fields and that group of officers know everything. Have them interview all the neighbors for info on a tall male walker/runner within fifteen minutes of her getting home. Tie the time down. I'll call Johan, and get his guys out. It'll be awhile before he finishes processing Alison Brunder's scene. He'll be thrilled with three bodies in such a short time. Stay there until I'm able to be there and hold the fort. Tell the uniforms to keep mum until the end of the shift. I'll have to make another call to the Chief and the District Attorney."

Less than an hour later, Beauregard pulled up to Leslie Hosman's condo. It was in a group of twenty condos built last year, after all kinds of negotiations with City Hall. Apparently, a neighbor who didn't want the development found some sort of salamander; he wanted to say it was a marbled or blue-spotted salamander, but he couldn't remember which. On top of that, the neighbor also found a mountain winterberry. This triggered investigating the neighbor, who had been trying to buy the land for conservation before the developer came in with more money. The neighbor lost his credibility, after two people told the state officials that he threatened to find some rare species and the neighbor's photo of the salamander and winterberry were found to be stock photos doctored up to fit in a section of the land.

Entering the front hall, Beauregard looked at the body of Leslie Hosman thinking, *another perfect woman strangled within an hour of the other woman. Both were assaulted last evening. Not serial murders. This makes three murders, but where's the connection? What's with the reason for the difference between the assaults and the murders? In the assaults, the perp did not try to strangle them; more like, tried to inject them. As I recall, the perp had a needle in his hand, and was trying to inject them. Murder weapons are different from assault methods. The ladies both knew the perp; else why let him in the house. This time he didn't wait to be invited; he probably strangled her the minute she turned to shut the door. Maybe she thought she could shut him out. There's no storm door. All the condos have the same massive, ornate, but charming front doors that were not to be covered by storms and screens which would have faded their beauty. No struggle except one of her perfect nails is torn in half. Maybe I can find the broken piece; if so it happened during the strangling. There it is, just two feet away. I'll have Johan's guys check her fingers more closely before they move the body. Could we possibly get DNA; nah, he would have worn gloves. This guy is a planner and the plan called for these two ladies to die right now. Why?*

Within ten minutes the scene was active. Uniforms interviewing neighbors, the ME assistant noting the scene, and the detectives searching the grounds outside while they waited for CSI to photograph the scene. Beauregard asked Bill and Ted to go through personal effects. He insisted that they check all photos and notes for Leslie's connection. He quipped, "We could be lucky and find they knew the same people."

The detectives laughed at the thought with Ted quizzing the Captain, "You really think it would be that easy? Didn't you say the Perp was a planner?"

A uniform who had been stationed outside the front door to prevent spectators from entering motioned for the Captain. He went outside to see an older couple, assumed to be Leslie's parents, crying and insisting they must see their daughter.

Beauregard noticed an Infiniti parked on the curb with the vanity plate saying "trees 1." He knew then that they were the Porgorski's who owned one of the largest tree removal businesses in the county. He'd met Jake Porgorski years ago before he was first appointed to major crimes. He tried to introduce himself but Jake said, "If you're here, Captain, it means she's dead, doesn't it?"

As her husband spoke, Mrs. Porgoski started wailing, "My little girl, my poor baby. First, they try to hurt you and not even a day later, they kill you."

Jake insisted they let him see his daughter and he was none too happy when Beauregard said it was a crime scene and that it would be better for them both to identify the body later. He would call Jake to schedule.

Ted exited the house allowing Beauregard to tell the couple to follow Sergeant Torrington to give statements. He did not want the couple staying in the condo. The three retreated to the couple's car which with the air conditioning on, was more suitable for interviews. Leslie's mother continued to cry, actually almost wailing. Her dad said he was surprised Leslie let any person get close enough to strangle her. She tended to keep her distance from most people.

"Detective, Leslie was not a people person except on the telephone or online. She never let anyone in her space including her mother and me. And for certain, she would have been on guard from the guy who tried to attack her last night. She had to know her killer, but what bothers me is she's never been close enough to anyone, like a boyfriend or lady friend to incur that kind of anger."

Ted left the car shortly later, stressing he or another detective would schedule an interview soon.

At the crime scene, Beauregard saw Bill discussing the state of the body with Johan. There were no fibers under the body's fingernails. Johan said the site was too clean. "Rudy, the guy was in here for seconds. She was dead almost immediately. The perp is strong enough so the body did not move far in fighting back plus the victim is not very tall. She is well muscled; probably works out diligently. He was, my best guess, over six feet, outclassing her in size; she was a little gal. I wish she'd dug into his face, but maybe she couldn't reach it."

"That's your guess, Bill, then document why you and Johan think that." Taken back a bit as shown with a frown on his face, Bill agreed.

Johan had some items in his hands and offered Leslie's diary, cell phone, and a laptop. "Captain, I've checked the diary and something's funny. Do people who have cell phones also keep a physical appointment diary, because this one is filled."

Beauregard scanned the items and right in front Leslie listed her passwords for the cell and laptop. He looked at the cell and saw that all her business appointments were documented. The ones in the diary were different, written at a different time and seemed to be written in code. Her computer showed no personal appointments. He thought that it was strange saying aloud, "Some computer files with interesting names have password controls that are not in her diary. Looks to me that the lady had secrets. Mason needs to work the computer."

The detectives worked the scene for a couple of hours. Johan and CSI had left earlier. Ted stayed behind to secure the site.

MCU was jumping when Beauregard returned. He'd made a stop to grab a lunch bringing it back with him. He should not have bothered. Millie had ordered pizzas from the nearby B-Napoli Italian restaurant in West Springfield. Not allowing himself to be disappointed he placed his bagged sandwich for a later snack in the fridge, recalling that ten years ago he would have felt guilty about the possibility that the sandwich would not be eaten. Not now, he knew, with this crew, someone would always be hungry.

Lilly said, "Geez, my family never made pineapple and ham pizzas; and this other veggie with peppers, salsa, and guacamole; Millie, these are not Italian. There's only one pizza that I recognize and it is good."

Mason, the acknowledged gastronomic omnivore said, "Stop complaining, Lilly; you Italians stole spaghetti from China. It's all fair game. I don't care how or where you get these recipes, the test is: is the result good? Man, I've tasted them all and they're good."

Munching away for almost an hour the detectives discussed the murders with Juan saying, "Well, we know for certain the two murders are by one perp; that's not enough to call them serial murders. The similarity of victims suggests serial murders, but you don't get them normally murdered within a couple of hours of each other. These ladies were murdered because they knew something and saw something; that's what speaks to me."

Ted asked Juan and Lilly if they found anything interesting at

Alison Brunder's site. Lilly and Juan had brought back a cell phone and her laptop, but she kept practically no paper. Both items were password protected.

Lilly said they had tried to contact Alison's parents but they were on a trip to South America and, according to a neighbor, they wouldn't be back for a week. Lilly was working at identifying a tour agency that booked the trip. The neighbor said that Alison booked it for them, because they weren't that computer savvy. He didn't know Alison's parents' surname and said that she kept personal info to herself. She'd heard through the grapevine that Alison had gone through a difficult divorce. The pressure was now on Mason to access emails. Lilly personally thought, *take your time, Mason. Give these folks a few more days of contentment.*

Mason said, "I'll work on her computer first. Parents have the right to know."

The Captain charged Bill Border with setting up murder boards causing Mason to laugh and say, "Shouldn't be so fast in showing your skills, Bill. You're the point man for murder boards now."

After the Captain retreated to his office, Bill grumbled, but started his work, leaving the rest of the detectives smiling. Ash said, "Bill, don't worry it's all in the Captain's training. You'll be a better cop for it. Lilly will tell you that." And Lilly nodded a yes.

5

Dead Guy in the Woods

Two days later, and there still were no results on the unexplained death of Eleanora Captreau despite several calls made to Johan. He said he was waiting for test results. The medical examiner did find an injection mark under Eleanora's earlobe. There were no other injection marks apparent on the body. Just what was injected had not yet been determined; it would take more time. The time of death was narrowed down to the interval between eleven p.m. to five a.m. the next morning.

Ash's scribblings noted that the boyfriend said that he had gone to a local bar in Springfield after leaving Eleanora that evening, explaining, "I was really happy; just couldn't go home yet. Met up with some friends at Theodore's bar in Springfield."

"Pretty quick with an alibi for at least part of the time span for death. Don't like it when they're so quick on the trigger. He could be the perp if he found out what she was about."

Lilly was quick to say, "He could also be innocent and naïve about women."

She was about to discourse on men when the Captain rushed in from his office and said, "Over to the West Side Country Club, both of you. Where's Mason, Ted, Bill, and Juan? There's a dead body in the woods on the eighth hole."

Lilly replied, "Mason's out for an hour. He should be back any minute, Captain."

"And the other three?"

Ash responded with, "Captain, look on the board. Ted will be here in another hour, and the other two are redoing interviews of Eleanora Captreau's neighbors."

Beauregard made the call for Bill and Juan to meet at the eighth hole of the country club and told Millie to send Ted immediately when he returned, but only after Mason was back to hold down the fort. Grumbling under his breath, the captain was heard to say, "Lots of detectives now, but who knows where they are from one minute to the next."

Beauregard drove his golf cart to the eighth hole leaving a host of club members questioning what had happened over there. The club's invitational weekend would start the next day and so lots of members were on the putting green or finishing the last hole when he hooked up with this vehicle. No one was allowed to start the play. He heard one tough older guy tell the Pro, "Can't be just a normal heart attack or death, they'd let us play all but that hole. It's more than that. It's trouble, I can tell you; that cop is Captain Rudy Beauregard. He's been in as many stories as the mayor with all those serial murders he has solved."

Rudy thought, *funny that I'm famous for all the wrong reasons, famous in my own backyard. If I'd done something really important, then I'd be known nationally and ignored in my home territory.*

It was a dazzling sunny morning and the course was impeccably maintained for the June Invitational. Beauregard didn't think that it really could be murder. Why would anyone take the chance to kill someone on the course when there were so many club members out and about? The first-person Beauregard encountered, by the woods to the right in the middle of the eighth hole, dressed in the latest high-end golf statement with what he thought were G/Fore golf shoes at over $200 a pair, was the infamous defense attorney, Norberto Cull. He groaned inwardly noticing also that the medical examiner Johan was present alongside CSI and his uniforms roping the area. There were also a half dozen others dressed in golf digs, one of whom he could see and who waved, was his own brother-in-law JR Randall. Rudy groaned. He by-passed the larger group and drove over to Norbie and said, "Counselor, just what the hell are you doing here? Do you already have a client? I don't know yet if this is even criminal."

Cull replied in a low voice, "Oh, Captain, you have a crime. Take it from me, and I'm the one who found the body. His neck is broken. Go check it out and come back with your questions. I'll wait. With my cell, I can do business here just as well as I do from my office. I want to see your take on this. Johan has had a few minutes with the body to give you some thoughts. It's too late to chase whoever did this. He or she is gone, a fleetfooted soul. Gone before I found the body or I would have heard rustling in the woods. The woods are next to that short dirt path that connects to the major artery to the mall."

Beauregard was annoyed with Norbie. *He inserts himself in everything. Not enough that he gets involved when he's pursuing justice for his clients, now he's a witness and one who I'm certain will involve himself in solving this case, if it is a case.*

Beauregard slowed his cart bringing it to a stop at the edge of the yellow tape. Johan welcomed him with, "Another one, Rudy. At first, I thought maybe the guy had a stroke, but he's only mid-thirties and then, well, look at the bruises on his neck. It's broken. I asked Norbie

Cull, who'd been playing in a foursome with the deceased, if there were bruises on his neck before he went into the woods. He said, 'no.' There is also petechiae in his eyelids and on the neck. I'll need to do a full autopsy, but it does not look like accidental or normal death. The woods are dense but mostly evergreens with a few deciduous trees; there are no hanging vines or anything. If he was strangled, I can't find the weapon. I'll know later what the weapon might be, other than just manual choking, after I look for fibers or whatever. Got yourself another one, Rudy. You're on a roll. Oh, one other thing, the guy is in great shape, so think about that, Rudy."

Rudy walked around the site and saw no evidence of footprints. The woods were covered with pine needles and the day was dry. He looked for broken branches but thought, *I never went to camp and learned about bent twigs. Still, when I look around I don't see broken branches.*

He heard sort of a gasp, looked over, and saw Sergeant Lilly Tagliano standing near the body. She was staring at the body, then looked at Rudy and said, "I know him, Captain. He lived near me. He was a hunk, although about five or six years older than me or maybe more. I can't believe he's dead. He was a Don Juan, and in perfect shape. I'd see him at the gym working out shaming the rest of us."

She wiped a tear from her eye. Then, looking more closely at the body, she swore, "Look at the neck, Captain. It's not right. Do we have a murder here? Who the hell would murder Josh Cantor? Josh was our body fitness idol, and was still available."

Rudy mused, *that's the problem with a small city police force. Our detectives often know stuff and so I have to filter how reliable will their input be as we work the case. Why do I worry about every little association?*

Juan watched the drama in front of him; he did not comment. Instead he started searching the immediate area to the left of the body.

The Captain approved and said, "I only went towards the main road, Juan. I found nothing to show recent movement. The perp, if it's a murder, had to get away somehow. I'll do an in depth with the other players. I'm sure Norbie will be an astute witness. It does seem to me that the exit would most likely be by the main road if the perp wanted to ensure not to be seen."

"Yeah, I agree, Captain, but over here are bent branches following the course. Bizarre choice, don't you think, if your objective is to get away unnoticed?"

Ash, who had never played this club, had walked the eighth hole to look for anything off-kilter. Near the eighth green he saw cart marks dug from the turf and not replaced. Knowing that this was a 'no-no' for golfers, he took a photo. He then responded to Juan, "He may have gotten out on a golf cart near the end of the hole. There are turf divots, well more like turf rivets there."

Juan discussed various possibilities with the other detectives. Finally, the Captain said, "Ash and Juan, follow the broken branches and see if the person walked all the way to the end of the eighth hole. Lilly, you start interviewing the Pro. See who's been playing today. Get the times and names down. Get who used golf carts belonging to the club or regularly parked at the club. I know that some are privately owned. Check if any belong to the condos over there. I want to know if some of the residents drive around the course or to the clubhouse, but don't play golf. Pin all their schedules down! Lilly, you come with me."

Lilly and the Captain started the interviewing process dealing first with Rudy's brother-in-law, JR Randall. JR wanted out of there saying, "Rudy, after what my family's been through, I want you to know that I know nothing; do you understand me?"

Lilly stepped in with, "JR, this is not a drug case and we don't know if it is just an inconvenient natural death. I know you went through hell with your wife and son assaulted before. Just tell us about your day. Johan said that there was a foursome that included Josh. Were you in the foursome?"

Looking relieved and assured by Sergeant Tagliano, JR said, "We have a foursome about every two weeks. Sometimes Norbie's court schedule screws up his attendance, but this time Jay Adams was sick. He couldn't get a substitute, but this young guy, Josh, and I can't remember his last name, asked to join us. He's a decent golfer, but tense. You know the type who's over in the corner taking a bunch of practice swings and is never happy with the result. He had a lousy tee shot on eight and then a hook to the right that went into the woods. Instead of letting it go, the guy said that it was his lucky ball and he was going to get it. He told us to finish the hole and he'd meet us at the tee for nine. I told him he was nuts to chase the ball over there. Everyone loses a ball in that area once in a while, but he said that he's never lost a ball before and today would not be the first time."

Beauregard asked each of the witnesses where they were on the course during the time Josh was in the woods. They all answered that they kept playing. Each of them was seen by the others. When they finished the hole, Norbie told the other two he was going to find Josh. There was a twosome behind them that wanted to play through. He told them to start the ninth. Grant Lawson, the last member of the foursome said that the other two could start, and he'd wait for Norbie. Norbie and he were in the same golf cart, but he said he had no interest in arguing with this kid over reclaiming a ball in the woods when there probably are five hundred balls in there. Lilly, as requested by the Captain, took over noting all contact information and reviewed the details of all but Attorney Cull. The Captain took Norbie aside and said, "What gives here, Norbie? You normally would have just yelled that the foursome was going on or told the twosome to play through. I've never seen you do a search and find on the course before. You allot only so much time to the game. Something bothered you; what is it?"

Norbie laughed, saying, "Rudy, I didn't know you did behavior analysis on me while I was golfing. You calm quiet guys are really soaking up what everyone's doing or you're just plain nosy. I applaud you in this case. You're right. It was not my normal reaction to someone who chases a damn ball when he had about six in his bag; most were Tiger Woods Bridgestone tour balls. He also had a few Titleists. He had to show me. I didn't know him well enough to give him shit about being cheap or OCD."

"So, you thought he was a pretentious braggart, right?"

"Yeah, Rudy, and maybe, I just assumed it because I see many acting this way from his generation. They're often show-offs which could be a symptom of their insecurity. I should be kinder, but the guy didn't deserve to die because he was acting like a clown today. Good looking guy who presented himself well; still, he did appear to me to be very tense. Something made him look for that ball and I don't think it was the need to retrieve it. His behavior was off, even for my pre-judged concept of him."

Rudy laughed. "You're telling me, Norbie, that in eight holes of play that you were able to conclude all this info. The only time you talk on the course is when you're in the cart or commenting on a bad ball. Yet, the defense attorney in you formed some conclusions. You just can't stop that grey matter from forming new ideas every minute, can you?"

"Seriously, Rudy, it's my training. I study potential jurors for what could be patterns in their decision-making. It's my profession. This thinking carries over into my non-working life. Sheri rebels every time she catches me crossing my work thinking to my home, but it's a valuable tool. Even in this case, I think we should talk about what I think. It's not evidence, well most of it is not evidence."

"Defense counsel, let's start with what you heard that could be considered evidence from a witness."

"Two things, Rudy, maybe more, come to mind. Josh was looking around carefully watching his surroundings, even on his drive at the first hole, enough so that I asked him whether he was expecting a girlfriend to save him from his bad shots. He had a few dumb shots, just like the one that went into the woods. Sounds like I'm concluding too quickly, doesn't it? To answer my own question, I don't think so. He was a decent golfer. Some of his shots were pro level. The guy was nervous."

Rudy's answer was a put-down when he said, "That's not evidence and you know that."

"No, but take it home, it's truth. Evidence is that I heard a noise in the woods just before he took that shot, and I saw a white cap moving. I think he heard the noise too. I think he dummied his shot, so he could go into the woods. He knew someone was there and he expected that person to be there."

Rudy reacted with, "The noise you heard and the white cap you saw is evidence; the rest is you again playing with my mind to direct me. What else?"

"I played the hole through and came back. I saw the white cap moving going to the eighth green and yelled, 'Hey, Josh, over here,' because Josh also had a white golf cap on; which as you can see, is not on, or near the body. He wore a NIKE cap, what I think they call the 'swoosh' cap. I'm not that into caps. I have a couple of favorites."

"You're sure he was wearing a white NIKE cap?"

"Absolutely."

"None of the other members of the foursome even mentioned it as missing, Norbie."

"I never allowed them to see the body, Rudy. They don't need to see a dead golfer they knew. JR certainly doesn't need that. He already shows signs of PTSD when he hears a car backfire; all since his family was shot. The guys only saw an image of someone lying there. They're amateurs, Rudy, why ruin their day?"

If a grump could be heard, Rudy grumped, not because he didn't agree with Norbie, but with his dissatisfaction that it was part of his life to view murder victims. He asked Norbie, "Did you see a golf cart up near the green when you finished the hole?"

Norbie thought for a minute and then said, "There was one over by the woods. I didn't think about it then. I saw it before I went back to chase Josh from looking for his ball in the woods. But now I have to conclude that there was no reason for a cart to be there, unless somebody had played the hole before us and the cart wasn't working properly. That sometimes happens. It happened to me once, but that was before the new owners took over. They're pretty good with the carts. I'm thinking now that it was one of the older carts. Maybe that's why I didn't think it was unusual. Cripes, I must be losing my investigational skills, Rudy. Sorry."

Beauregard told Lilly to find Ash and Juan at the pro shop, saying, "Go chase info on all the older carts and question if the Pro ever let private users have them. I want all info on older carts."

"What else can you remember or are you able to infer? That's the right word, infer, I think, for your legal intuition."

"Josh took his shot before I took mine. I was right there when he did and I'm pretty certain he pulled his shot to hook. I saw another white cap in the woods before he took his shot. Chances are if I saw it, he saw it. He then adamantly went after the ball in the woods. I think it was unusual because I'd previously noticed he avoided walking too much on the previous holes. He was one of these guys who drive their carts as close to a shot as was allowed. Many of us, you and I included, like a little walking and leave our carts in the same place, only moving the cart when there is a good distance to walk. He may have been in good shape, but he was not a walker. That's why his willingness to search the woods seemed odd to me. He also insisted that the rest of us play through. I don't think he wanted us near the woods."

"I'll keep your ruminations in mind, Norbie, but that's all they are. I'll not run an inquiry on them."

"No concern of mine, Rudy, but as a witness, it's my duty to tell you what I saw and interpret it. I'm off, now. Call me if you think of something."

Rudy noticed that Norbie drove to the end of the eighth hole slowly scanning the woods, before he cut over to the cart storage area. He thought, *he's not done with this. Norbie can't leave a puzzle like this alone, even if there's no money on the table for him.*

After taking some further notes on the body in site and questioning Johan, Beauregard was about to drive back to the clubhouse, when Sergeant Bill Border arrived, gleefully driving his golf cart at an indecent rate. Beauregard reminded his detective about the club's rules on speed, but Border was not to be chastised. Instead, he said, "Captain, this is the fun part of the job. No one's going to stop me today, because we're on an investigation. What do you need me to do, now? It looks like you're done here."

The Captain instructed his detective to hit the clubhouse, the pro shop, and any area where there were groups and take photos. Also take photos of the cars in the lot. After that he was to tell the other detectives on site at the pro shop to talk to employees, including the greenskeepers for their take on unusual activities that morning. He directed them to write their reports and have them on his desk before the end of the day.

Driving back to the clubhouse, Rudy called Mason Smith and

instructed him to get what information he could on Josh Cantor concluding with, "I want his social life, his work life and any home life history. I think he was a player and I don't know which playpen he worked, but I think it got him killed. Oops, I forgot to ask Norbie Cull how aggressive Josh was in asking to be the fourth in his golf match. Confirm with Norbie."

6

A Reverie

Beauregard reminisced on the events of an evening that he didn't want to remember. That time was close to thirty years before when he knew he was an innocent; well as innocent as his childhood history allowed. Certainly, he thought maybe he was just clueless about society and women. He was a graduate of Holyoke Community College and Westfield State College's Criminal Justice Programs and was quite proud of himself for finishing both programs with honors. Later he would pick up a Master's degree in CJ. However, at that time he had just finished the Academy and taken the Civil Service exam, both of which he scored at or near the top for achievement. He was feeling his oats, which was how his dad Roland would describe him. He met a really nice-looking girl at 'The Bud' in Holyoke. It was a college and young twenties bar and she sat down next to him initiating a conversation.

He remembered how he felt at that time, *I was so surprised. No girl had ever done that before. She was pretty and lots of guys looked at her. I felt so lucky. I had no trouble talking with her, so much so that I thought I had arrived and she thought me charming as well.* It was only later he realized, he was her mark. That evening ended with him giving her his telephone number. She couldn't give hers, because according to her,

her roommate would not write down who called. Later he would discover that her roommate was a he not a she. A week later she called him and suggested they meet at Callahan's Pub in West Side. They did and she gave him more attention than he'd ever received from any girl he dated. Her name was Jean; supposedly she was named for 'Jeanne D 'Arc,' which meant that she was a savior of people. Later he would remember the conversation. Savior was not a word he would later use for her. At eleven, she had to leave, but promised to call him. He said, "I'll pick you up the next time. It will be like a real date."

"No, Rudy, I don't know you well enough yet. Let's see how far this relationship will go by itself. I like you. Let's give ourselves some time."

He remembered that he never questioned her. Whatever she wanted was okay. He thought he was lucky. She was always touching him. That was new to him. She would hug him in public. This went on for close to three months. They met at every bar catering to college students from Septembers in Chicopee to Points East in Westfield. He knew he was smitten, and he hadn't had more than an occasional deep kiss. Rudy thought at the time that it was okay, that she was not going to let a guy get close until she trusted him. At the time he had expressed to a friend that he couldn't understand why she never let him near her apartment or gave her phone number. The friend said that it probably related to trust issues and that in time she would come around.

Several months later she invited him to Thanksgiving at her mom and dad's house. He was elated that she was thinking about him as a serious relationship. He was on third shift in the police department then. Jean was never available for an afternoon day trip; this holiday dinner was the first time he would see her in the daylight.

Mr. and Mrs. McCarthy were welcoming to him. They appeared to him to be pleased Jean brought him home. Jean had a brother who was stationed in Georgia and could not be there for the holiday.

Mr. McCarthy commented, "It's nice to have you here for dinner. You're not a replacement for our Dennis, but I enjoy someone who appreciates football. These two don't." He caught a funny look in Jean's eyes when she heard what her dad said; the look he thought then had implications. Since Jean had her own car, he could not drop her off after dinner, but instead just said thank-you and good-bye. Her parents enthused over his visit and welcomed him back again. Mrs. McCarthy thanked him for the apple pie he had brought and remarked that she was pleased Jean was seeing a police officer, saying, "At least I know you are a sensible and good companion for my Jean."

Again, Rudy was left to drive home by himself to the warmth of Lizette and Roland's home where he was fed turkey for a second time. It was apparent they had waited for him to return before celebrating Thanksgiving Day which gave him some guilty qualms in his gut. He chastised Lizette for waiting only to be met with, "It didn't seem the same without you, Rudy, and now isn't this very nice?"

He couldn't argue but did wonder, *someday I will leave for good. I'd better make sure that they are always included. This always feels homey; this house of theirs always makes me feel I belong.*

Jean called him on the Saturday after Thanksgiving and invited him to a party at her friend's house. She said it would be wild and lots of fun. She also said she had some special friends she wanted him to meet. The party was at a private home in South Hadley owned by an older guy who loved to run with a younger crowd. He asked how old the guy was and she said that he was about fifty. He questioned her about what was wrong with a guy who wanted to hang with college and working people in their twenties. She told him not to be such a fuddy-duddy continuing with, "Sometimes I wonder if you weren't born an old man. I know you're a cop, but don't you sometimes want to tear my clothes off me and rape me?"

In his naivety he said that he would never think about raping a girl. She laughed and teased him again, but he agreed to meet her at the party.

When he arrived at a very modern style, mainly glass home, he found the middle of three front doors wide open noticing a group of well-dressed guests partying up when he entered. Liquor flowed along with beer and the man behind the bar was dressed in a smoking jacket and an ascot, a type of dress Rudy had only seen in movies before. His name was Dr. Wendell, at least that was how he introduced himself, while he poured a beer from the keg for him. Jokingly he said, "I have a keg for this crowd but in a bit, they'll graduate to better stuff and then the show begins. I love hosting these parties filled with young studs and good-looking fillies looking to see what's possible in life."

Dr. Wendell continued, saying, "I heard that you're a young cop, but Jean promised me that you are, as she put it, just plain sweet, and I think her judgment is excellent. You and I are going to get along."

Rudy took his beer in hand and threaded his way through the crowd. He did not see Jean, so he found a corner where he could lean against the wall and watch the goings-on. Almost an hour later and yet, Jean had not arrived. He could not call her to see if she was going to show. He decided, instead, to wait one more hour. He noticed that couples were disappearing into some other rooms. It did not at first seem that unusual, until he noticed that three of the couples when they joined the party again, switched partners and went back into whatever the other rooms were. He assumed they were bedrooms. Then he noticed that threesomes were going back there. He knew enough then to decide to exit since he thought, *I'm not into the interchangeable sex scene. It scares me.*

He had nursed that one beer despite Dr. Wendell walking over from the bar several times to push another beer on him. He took two more but dumped them in a ten-foot plant or tree or whatever that was next to where he was standing. The tree had served as great coverage for scanning the scene. He put down his beer on the floor planning to escape at the closest of the three adjacent but separate doors, all glass and all oversized, that were part of the front entrance. The lights went down, and entering from another bedroom wing, at least he thought that, with a spotlight from the squared off balcony opposite was a woman in a nude see-through dress with her hair flowing decorated with sprays of gold ropes. She carried gold ropes in her hand and motioned to him to join her. He was mesmerized by her body and presentation until he realized she was Jean, and that everyone was watching them as if they knew it was going to happen. At that point when he did not move, Dr. Wendell took Jean's hand and said, "Rudy, you are in for the night of your life."

He shook his head in a no, and holding back tears, he left the party. He never called Jean again. The experience jaundiced him in his relationships for a while afterwards, until the thoughtful and understanding Mona forced him to take a chance. Much later he ran into Jean, and she acted nonchalantly as if there had been no incident. He could no longer see any beauty in her. She appeared very hardened and wore tons of make-up. Further she said, "I guess being a cop was always good enough for you. Cops don't have imaginations. I must go with my dreams."

He remembered he did not respond. Later, he heard through the grapevine that she had a contentious divorce from her older and wealthy husband and received a decent settlement, although as she told anyone who would listen, it wasn't enough. Then she married his best friend who was even older and wealthier.

Rudy rarely thought of this experience, buried deep in his sub-conscious, but he was aware that his early background as a child, however sad it was, saved him at that pivotal time in his life. He thought, *being tied to a chair as a child was the teacher of patience and reflection. What else can you do if you can't move? I also believe it's the reason I'm so slow to move, as I was that night. I did learn early to observe. The golden ropes she carried as if she would hit me or tie me with them, well I think that could have struck fear in my head. I remember Jean in my image of first impression with her cute ponytail, collegiate dress, and brilliant smile. She was charming. At least she cultivated me with her charm to seduce me later and shatter my self-esteem. I was so damn innocent; I was there for the pickings. When I realized at the party that I had been groomed to be a patsy for an audience in the play of innocence lost, I was devastated. Little did Jean know that my experience with her, a sociopath, would lay the groundwork for some of my professional success.*

Rudy talked aloud while driving, saying, "Sociopaths, who have not been grounded in moral teachings, have no controls on their narcissistic goals, whatever they may be. For Jean, expressing herself sexually for an audience while being in control of me and my innocence, seemed to her, okay. It fulfilled her needs and the hell with my being smitten. Sociopaths don't always murder and maim, but they always manipulate to get their way, always, despite the cost to others. I'm frightened for my boys. What if one of them brings home a 'Jean.' "

Rudy stopped for a sandwich at a local grinder shop. The owners were a Mr. and Mrs., who had their kids sometimes working. They were a happy family, always talking and laughing. While chomping on his Italian special that included Soppressata, his favorite cold cut, Rudy thought about Jean as an example of uncaring sociopathy in action and the devastating pain she could have caused for him if he were even more vulnerable, before the light bulb glowed and lit his brain with a thought -- just as was happening now. *Eleanora could be a 'Jean.' I know that if Jean had worked her manipulation on another type of guy, she could have been in jeopardy. I am by nature restrained. Even an athlete would not like to be publicly played like that, at least at that time. Could be that I have a motive for Eleanora's death. Now, what about the others? My gut is saying that their occurrences, so close in time, do not speak of serial murders. There are motives in these cases; or perhaps only one motive, a motive to cover up.*

Beauregard paid his bill, complimented the owner for his attention to real Italian cuisine, and raced back to the station.

7

The Psychology of Delight

Attorney Norberto Cull decided to lunch at the club, before going to his office. He'd accomplished a great deal with his cell phone and his administrative assistant Sheila. Enough work was done during the time he waited for Beauregard, enabling him to do some digging around for information. He drove his cart over to the pro shop. The pro, Jack Stacy commonly called Jocko, was waiting for him and took his cart. The pro, of course, was looking for any additional news Norbie could supply. He noticed JR, one of today's foursome talking with two detectives; one of them, Ash Lent, was known to him. He wondered who the other one was. He said a 'hi' to Ash and JR and then, "We've never met before, Detective; I'm Norbie Cull."

The tall detective made quite a presentation. Although as tall as the rangy Ash, he had a broader physique. He answered, "I'm Sergeant Bill Border, new to MCU."

Norbie considered what just had been said, thinking, *unnecessary info. I didn't ask if he was a Sergeant, but he needed to share that fact. He also had to let me know that he was MCU. The guy has an ego. Well, this is an opportunity for me.*

"Ash and Bill, won't you join me for lunch on my ticket? There's no conflict as I don't have a client involved in this case, unless you consider my being a witness presents a possibility that I'm the perp, a fact, I doubt sincerely your captain would consider."

Getting a laugh from them both, they agreed with Ash continuing, "Norbie, as a witness it's our job to get as much information from you as possible, even if it means lunching with you as your guest."

They sat at a table in the pub section and ordered the special of the day, Mahi fish tacos with Guinness for Norbie and coffee for the other two who regretfully were on the job.

A golfer, whom Norbie had seen previously at the club, approached Bill, saying, "What are you doing here, Bill?"

Bill's reply included all the personal information he'd given to Norbie adding that he originally was a patrolman in the Holyoke Police Department, transferred to West Side to do undercover, and now was assigned to West Side MCU. Bill introduced his friend as Dr. George Girandeau. George said, "I can't believe Josh is dead and I hear that it may be a murder. Bill, you must be in a funk about it; after all, you two were roomies for two years in that great townhouse in East Longmeadow. What really happened, or can't you tell me? Did the bartender at the martini bar hook you two up? He was always helpful with connections."

Border answered quickly looking decidedly uncomfortable. "Open cases are off limits for gossip, George, you know that."

Norbie invited George to join them. He noticed that Border was uncomfortable with the invite. George was hesitant in accepting until Ash said, "Please join us. You and Bill knew Josh. It would really be helpful if you shared your knowledge. After all, he is dead and we don't know from what. Tell us about him."

George then joined them as their food arrived. He ordered the same but like Norbie ordered with a Guinness, explaining, "I'm a plastic surgeon and I'm out of the office today."

Ash started the quizzing before Norbie could, leaving Norbie with the idea that the two of them may be chasing the same info and could work together. Border said very little, while the Plastic Surgeon enjoyed being the main speaker. He explained that Josh was a patient of his and had a business selling machine parts. "Doesn't sound like his profile, but he made a lot of money in his business. I introduced him to Bill. They'd partied a few times together when Bill and Josh were roomies." He then said, "Bill, you didn't have a lot to do with Josh after you moved out. Did you have a falling-out?"

Instead of answering George, Bill said, "What happened to you and Josh? You were both involved with the same party scene. I met Josh later and he said he'd not seen you in a while."

"Well, Bill, as you know, Josh's idea of partying meant carrying things further than I ever wanted to experience. He met some beautiful people, and I mean beautiful people, like clients of mine, but later; they weren't. After a while, I realized that groupies talk themselves into some pretty strange stuff. Chasing sexual highs can be psychologically dangerous. I stopped then. Josh was ticked off, and I lost him as a patient. He went to another plastic surgeon along with some of his friends. I shouldn't be talking about patients like this, but he's dead now; probably doesn't matter."

Norbie decided to bite the bullet and responded, "Do you mean group sex, sadomasochism sex, drugs, body enhancements that are harmful, or what, George?"

George looked at them, replying, "I think all of them."

Juan and Lilly walked into the bar, breaking up the conversation, with Lilly saying, "Damn traitors, we're out there in the hot sun interviewing everyone and their brothers. Thanks a lot, you guys."

Norbie invited them to join the crew for lunch saying, "You get food while we get dessert."

Norbie truly hoped he could get the information flowing again. To do so, he decided he'd charge ahead with, "Lilly, have you ever seen the victim Josh around? You go to all the gyms for workouts, at least it looks to me that you could be a gym rat?"

"Is that a compliment from the infamous defense attorney, the scourge of West Side MCU? Or instead do you think that I have to work out all the time, Attorney Cull?"

Norberto Cull actually blushed, which on his light coloring was noticeable to all. He shook his head, saying, "Well you do look good. Perhaps I could have phrased that better. I was thinking about Josh Cantor, and he certainly had to have been into gym work. He was very well built. Of all of us, I thought you might have more experience. I'm getting myself in deeper, aren't I? Not a great situation for me. I should know better."

Juan said, "Mr. Cull, that's what Lilly does to us all. It's just meant to keep us on our toes so we don't just assume anything. Lilly has negotiated several gym memberships since I was appointed, and she even goes to my gym at the YMCA. So, Lilly, help the guy out here."

After all that work and discussion, Lilly could say only that she saw him at two of the gyms she frequented, for which she no longer continued with her membership. According to her, "They were just a bit high-brow for me. They all dressed in sports paraphernalia featuring their best attributes, and they didn't know what to do with themselves. He was part of this beautiful people group; they called themselves, 'The Cabal.' I thought their naming themselves was a bit sophomoric, like Sinatra with his 'Rat Pack.' I'd hear each one, when entering by the gym reception desk, ask, 'Is the Cabal here?' I can't take that kind of elitism."

Bill Border looked uncomfortable enough, so Ash said, "What's up,

Bill? Were you ever part of the 'Cabal?'"

Bill said, "Not really, well maybe for a week or two."

Ash said, "Not comfortable with this 'Cabal' business, Bill, are you? At least tell us who you know who was also a member. We'll need to know for the investigation. Your knowing them might put a clamp on who you can interview."

Clearly uncomfortable, Sergeant Bill Border said he would have to rack his memory. "You know it's been several years. I'll try to come up with their names."

George interrupted their conversation. "I'll give you the names of who hung around when I was his friend. You can compare them to the list Bill gives you. Do you have a business card, Norbie? I have to run. I have a non-professional appointment with someone special and I don't want to be late."

Juan said, "Here's my card as well, George. Send the list to me. I need it for the file and Bill will develop his own list without your assistance, okay?"

George was quick in his understanding. saying, "I get it; there are police procedural rules even among police in investigating."

All nodded, with the exception of Bill, who replied, "Nonsense, this formalization is nonsense for such a small department. I can just see the list on your screen, Juan."

To which, Lilly laughingly commented, "No way! Juan takes security seriously. It would take Mason forty-eight hours to get into Juan's computer. What the hell, Juan, you didn't grow up in a barrio. Why so security conscious?"

"Damn, Lilly, of course I grew up in a barrio, as did you. Barrio is a Spanish name for neighborhood or a division of a town or city. You all live in a barrio. I'm security conscious, because my mother is a security and safety nut. She lived her early years in northern Mexico and let's say that suspicion is her middle name. She makes the Italian moms look sloppy in their care of kids."

They all laughed. Lilly said, "I've got to meet this lady, if she makes my Nonna look sloppy in her care of children. My mom's not Italian, my dad is, and his mom, my Nonna, is a tiger."

Juan nodded, saying, "I'll make sure you do, Lilly. I want to be there to see it. Maybe I'll sell tickets to the event."

George left. Ash got up to leave, but turned first to Bill, saying, "Why didn't you tell the Captain that you recognized Josh Cantor? You never said anything until George outed you. What's up with this, Bill? Remember trust is very important. If you hold back info for personal reasons, well, that doesn't play well."

Bill showed his dissatisfaction, but in glancing around, he saw that Juan, Lilly, and Norbie were awaiting the answer. "You do this in front of an attorney. You couldn't wait until we got to the office, Ash."

"Nope, we can't wait."

"Josh was my roommate and a cool roommate, or so I thought. After a few incidents I realized he could not be trusted. I may have been considered a 'player' then, but I didn't go out of my way to birddog another guy's significant other. Didn't matter to Josh. Everyone was fair game to him. I realized that he moved on guys as well as girls. I can't prove that, but he made me uncomfortable a couple of times. First time in my life, I wanted rules, rules of behavior. I'm not a prude, but I was troubled by his ways. That was it."

Bill stood up signaling an end to the conversation. He thanked Norbie and left quickly. Norbie stayed back with the other detectives and initiated a discussion on current sexual behavior. "Lilly and Juan, you two are the youngest detectives at MCU, right?"

Lilly laughed and per usual used the question to reply in a wisecracking manner. "Attorney Cull, why would you ask a lady her age? You should know better."

Before Norbie could reply thinking, *I should know better by now. Lilly's into baiting just for the fun of it,* Juan said, "Cut it, Lilly. The lawyer is desirous of a philosophical discussion on sexual mores. Aren't you, Counselor?"

"Yeah, but the way I stated my question does leave some confusion. I apologize, Lilly. I will be more careful in the future with what I say to you. Twice burned is one unnecessary time and for a lawyer is plainly stupid."

Lilly appeared confused by the apology and responded, "I was only kidding, Norbie. I do it all the time in the unit. Juan tells me that I can't always be a smart aleck and he's right. I learned to use my mouth in middle school when I was the shortest kid in class. Later, when I grew taller, I never stopped with my big mouth."

Norbie laughed and told her she would have been a great lawyer; that being quick on the draw with words could be an asset, but it was clear from Lilly's demeanor that she was embarrassed. Juan continued the conversation saying that both he and Lilly were in their late twenties, and for him, the type of sexual behavior described by Bill and George was not in his experience. He added, "Lilly was in Vice for a couple of years. She can tell you more, right, Lilly?"

"What do you guys think? Just because I was in the Vice Unit, I was in the know about the perps' lives. Most guys we interrupted, like that word interrupted, were sad cases. I did see some dudes who at first glance seemed unlikely candidates for seeking out the ladies' services, but in the end, there was always a personal story. I met some so-called 'sex addicts' who would look like normal businessmen and I met some dangerous men who liked to beat up on the ladies. I have no experience with 'beautiful people' and their sexual groups."

Ash surmised aloud, "Could be the narcissism and lack of empathy that the Captain associates with sociopaths, if accompanied by a deviant sexual need, could ramp up a situation that ended in murder. Just a thought!"

Norbie suggested that an extensive check into Josh's personal history was paramount and that Sergeant Bill Border may be sitting on more information than he was willing to share. He left them with that thought.

Eric Shulman was looking forward to his weekly foursome afternoon round of golf. He'd gone out the other day, the day the police found his neighbor Eleanora dead, maybe murdered. He'd played well that day, a result of his having finally corrected his putting problem. The police involvement with Eleanora's death left him anxious. He hoped this afternoon game would alleviate some of his stress. Pulling into a parking spot he noticed two police cars. He wondered what had happened. Exiting the Club's Pub was one of the detectives he had met at Eleanora's house. Eric remembered when he was interviewed, there were a couple of detectives interviewing them all and this guy was one of them. He noticed a churning in his gut that brought bile rising to his throat. In a moment he decided that it was a result of his anticipation of trouble. When he spotted the police, well, after the other day his first idea was they must be connected to murder or at least to a crime of some kind. He shook his head at his imagination and with some reservation, he walked to the Pro Shop where he stored his Callaway Strata clubs. He hoped to get the gossip about what brought the police to the club today. He figured some overweight guy probably had a heart attack or stroke. It had happened before, actually several times. Jocko greeted him and without any hesitation, said, "You'll have to start on the back nine today. By the time you're through, you'll be able to finish with the first nine."

"Why, Jocko, you spraying or something? Why are the police over there? Don't tell me that one of our illustrious senior members took a dive."

"Eric, be kinder, you're approaching senior class, yourself. What are you fortyish?"

"Right again on both accounts. I've had a bad week. One of my neighbors was maybe murdered. She lived right across the street from me. I see police and I feel antsy."

"This may be a double whammy for you; two murders in a week. One of our golfers, a young guy named Josh Cantor was filling in on a regular foursome. He was searching for his ball in the woods over on the outside of the eighth hole and was found dead. Norbie Cull went looking for him and got a surprise. The police are still over there. Captain Beauregard, you know him because he plays here sometimes with his brother-in-law JR Randall, said that they will rope off that section of the woods. You will still be able to play the eighth hole in a bit, but if you lose your ball in the woods, you can't retrieve it."

Eric asked, "What did this Josh Cantor look like? Is he a tall and really good-looking guy about thirty-five?"

"That's about right. Did you know him, Eric?"

"No, but my ex-wife talked about him. She said he was really smooth, although she thought he was a little too smooth. How did he die?"

"I heard some of the golfers say that he was strangled. Not good for the club to have a murder in the woods. The owners are over there with their marketing consultant attempting to put a spin on it. They have to be careful not to trash Josh, who's a member. It's a big problem. This club has never had a crime problem outside of guests getting into an altercation at a wedding a couple of times. No one saw anyone suspicious around the club this morning. The only odd thing is that Josh was not a substitute golfer in a regular foursome, but that happens every day. Not odd at all, really."

Eric was joined by the other members of his foursome who had already been informed about the murder. Two members of the foursome knew Josh and had played with him. Sal Marino had a great deal to say about Josh. "The guy was a stud. When he walked into a bar, all the ladies gave him the once over. He'd play it cool. Never once did I see him approach a woman. They all came over to talk to him. I guess it's the same as if J Lo came into the bar. She wouldn't have to move over next to any man. The men would crowd her. Same here. He made me feel like a nobody."

Eric said, "With your wallet, Josh couldn't compete. That's what I think."

"Don't agree with that statement, because Josh's business was a cash cow," countered Sal. "Think about it, no one is crowding Jane Esterbrook, who's loaded and is looking for a companion. She has a nice face and shape. All you available guys are looking for 'Candy' on your arm."

Eric looked surprised and said, "First of all, I didn't know Jane was available. She's a nice woman. Secondly, I think that eventually all the women realized that Josh was nothing but a hound dog. He was not interested in relationships from what I heard; therefore, the word would eventually get around to all the women in this club. He, from what I heard, was only interested in cool and gorgeous people and he didn't care what gender they were. I don't know much about that world, but I did hear that. Maybe it was said to slash his rep, but then again maybe it's true. I'm a little older and I'm uncomfortable if a man seems interested in me for other than golf or a drink. It only happened once and it threw me off balance."

Lenny, a third of the foursome replied, "I think that there's a lot of confusion about sex roles today that you and I did not feel or have experience with during our dating period. Eric, now you're out there, you'd better get with it."

"That's the trouble, I'm not out there. I've not gotten over Dorie, you know that. Besides, from what I've read, dating's nothing but a minefield. I'd be afraid to open my mouth because language is the new sexual weapon. For instance, if a guy was looking to get friendly with me, well in the old days I'd just tell him to fuck off and say I was not gay. I'd get killed today if I said that. I wouldn't know how to approach a woman. I've been told that if you run to hold the door open then a response might include a question as to whether I thought she couldn't open the door herself. As to sex, just how and when; I'm a novice, after all these years, I'm a novice. I have a thousand questions. Playing golf and drinking beers seem safer."

Sal was surprised. He said, "Eric, there are many women here at the club who would love to date you. Don't listen to all that liberal nutty stuff on television; that's for college girls. Women are just like us, they're not sure what to say either. If you don't try to meet a woman, you'll be drinking beers and playing golf with us forever."

Lenny laughed and reminded them, "For all of Josh's sex appeal to whatever audience, he's the one who ended up dead. You're smart to be cautious, but listen to Lenny, Eric. You don't want to stay alone forever."

The three men discussed sexuality and their limits as Jocko the pro listened. He'd been a fly on the wall many times as men and women conversed on current and past sexual mores. What, he thought, seemed interesting is these three men were earnestly trying to understand sex as an act between two people who were in a relationship and who cared about each other. These guys, from his perspective, were decidedly middle-class and decent men. He'd heard others, both genders, discuss sexuality with no care for the individual at all, where people were objects used to satisfy. He personally expressed several times that masturbating was probably as interesting as using another person for what was basically only self-gratification. He believed many who were sleeping around liked the feeling of superiority in the manipulation of others. Maybe he thought, *I'm decidedly middle-class myself despite the fact that I was always considered an 'In' guy when I was in college. Being a golf pro has given me lots of opportunity and invites, but I know I'm lucky to have a good marital situation with Mari-Lee. I'm not rocking that boat. I want my kids living in our house with us together. I'm not losing that for a one-nighter.*

8

Background Checks

Beauregard was updated by Sergeant Ashton Lent on the luncheon, its guests, and the information on Josh Cantor, and Sergeant Bill Border's past association with the vic. Beauregard did not pursue the conversation with Ash. Instead, he asked him to work with Juan and Ted on background checks on Josh and Bill. Be discrete and don't involve Lilly. Further, he shared that Lilly's service with Vice and her previous awareness of Josh Cantor may interfere with her distancing herself as she should. The Captain suggested that Mason could help with any computer searches that were beyond their skills and that he would talk to Mason.

Beauregard and Mason discussed the need for secrecy and the Captain was surprised by Mason's reaction. It was honest, but disturbing. "Captain, you think you can keep this QT. You can't; you know that. Bill Border is smart and intuitive. Also, according to your report, he knows that Ash is on to his lying. You know cops, detectives in this case, well they can't leave alone any hint of a focus on them. You better get him out of the office while they're making phone calls. There are no secrets here. Millie and those guys can keep a secret, but the walls have ears here."

Considering this, the Captain called Lilly and Bill to his office and assigned them to a second visit to all the neighbors and families of Eleanora Captreau, Alison Brunder, and Leslie Hosman. They gave him a little static suggesting there may not be a lot more to get, unless they hit their employers. Lilly suggested that Ash should be doing some of this since he interviewed some of the witnesses at Eleanora's death scene. She said, "Juan and I could redo the victim Alison Brunder's background. We had a start on that."

Beauregard spoke slowly, which was universally recognized by all in the know, and indicative of his not being in the mood to negotiate. "I'm not good at explaining my directives, because, detectives, they are directives; but for your information, I often have two teams interview the same witnesses. Can you figure out why I might do that? If you can't, then it's not worth my explaining. Now get out."

Bill and Lilly walked to their vehicle and Bill said, "Even I know better, Lilly, and I've been here less than a month."

"Yeah, I know. I have a big mouth. Juan normally protects me from myself. Let's do a bang-up job on this. He's going to expect me to perform after that dressing down."

The phones and computers in the 'Pit' were busy. The detectives had divvied up the witness lists, the employers, families, and neighborhoods of all three women victims and were scheduling appointments, if after a call, one was needed. Mason had developed a spreadsheet specific to the three murders that when completed would show common threads. Family and friends in common as well as gym memberships, coffee hangouts, clubs, etc. They thought that interviewing any one person or place that each of the three victims had in common was a good starting point for further interviews. Mason was searching for public history which included records checks and monitoring Facebook and other social media sites. They figured they would be busy for days. They still had not received the chemical analysis on drugs used in Eleanora's death. The unit was working details. The Captain loved details. He often said something to the effect that details put together were like words in a sentence. Together they made sense and told a story or pointed in a direction.

Mason turned Leslie Hosman's computer over to Ted, saying, "I've unlocked all the passwords using her home-developed code. Her code was that she interchanged seven letters in the alphabet. Those seven letters resulted in a password using the first in line capitalized. Amateurish but effective for the average Joe. She also wrote on paper with that code. You have it. As you use it, it will become easier. Have a field day, Ted."

Ted was excited. He knew he was the best for detailed work in the unit. Lilly might be the worst, but truly great at picking up on witnesses tells. She sure could spot a liar quicker than any other detective. Although the Captain was good at that, also, and maybe, Ash.

Ted worked for about an hour and then announced to his friends, "This gal Leslie, she's into the S&M lifestyle. Looks like she has had business with several groups in West Side alone. She also mentions some other clubs, but not by name, in Westfield, West Springfield, and Springfield. Do any of you know about this stuff going on around here?"

Ash said, "How does she talk about it? Read it to us. I'm at all the musical events and nobody's ever invited me to one. I can't believe I don't know about them. Maybe you've translated the code wrong."

Ted shook his head and said he had made no mistake. The other detectives crouched behind him viewing the translation of Leslie's diary on Ted's computer. To assist in their viewing, Ted enlarged the type. There were initials for names and cryptic notes next to the initials. Over the course of close to nine months, they could see a pattern for the frequency of the initials used. Several would be seen for a few events, and then one by one dropped with explanations such as 'not up to par,' or 'how did she get here?' or 'good but loaded with guilt,' or 'disappointing in the raw,' or 'too much for 'el' or, 'won't use that group again.' Juan quickly pointed out, the notes all eliminated a name and all occurred on Thursdays. There were several comments in the beginning of a pattern of a new set of initials that seemed to praise a person with, 'probably a keeper' or 'I'd better be careful; he's too good;' this message was also said about a woman. Juan was the first to state, "Group sex at a minimum; any remarks on pain, Ted? That's a big one for S&M. She also says she won't use that group again. Clear to me that they sourced their participants from clubs and many don't last longer than three months."

Mason wondered aloud, "It's got to be like middle school, don't you think? You get into a group that does what you want and then you're dropped like a hot potato. Since I think that these participants are all whacked to be playing these games, what's the chance that one of them will retaliate? Maybe murder could seem justified."

Ash, always realistic, pointed out that there were a lot of initials to chase down. "Where to start? I know that Lilly said she didn't know what the beautiful people were about, but from her work in Vice, she could possibly point to whom would know over there. Maybe the Captain can question Bill. He's been a player, he could have worked this playground at one time."

Juan agreed to call Lilly and see what she had to say, but not to tell her why. He explained that she'd be back here in a flash if it got her off re-interviewing witnesses all day. Ash, despite being one of the most pragmatic detectives, could also wax philosophical when some social issue was brought to his attention. Apparently group sex and S&M were the topics for this day. Further, the topic interested the three other detectives. He asked them, "What's the draw; I like sex with someone who interests me and I don't want an audience. Am I so weird or is this a millennial thing? Maybe it's the opposite reaction to all this free sex with no guilt thing. We've discussed this before, I think. All those yuppies in the big cities like phone sex. The article I read says it's safe and less messy. Maybe, like we have left and right politics, there's a percentage of people who want all the mess possible with many partners and acting out roles. Maybe this is their only entertainment and it's the opposite of sitting in front of a screen for video games or distance phone sex."

Mason laughed and said, "When we were kids there was a manual on how to do phone sex that you could send for. I'll bet I can google for it now."

And Mason googled it. There were at least seven sites that came up with instructions for how to do it effectively. One site said that it was great for spicing your sex life up without cheating. Another said that it was a good way to have sex with your partner while one of you was traveling.

Ash then had Mason google S&M groups. They read several sites and learned several new concepts. Consensuality was a term that meant you gave your partner permission to inflict pain for eroticism. Both partners agree how much pain and what kind of pain are to be used. There has to be a 'safe word' to be used to prevent the one inflicting pain from going too far. One site on the psychology of S&M discussed whether consent can be given if one player has had severe and negative verbal or sexual past experiences. Playing while using drugs and alcohol could also screw up the legitimacy of the consent given.

Consent is not just for the submissive person. The dominant role also brings in the question of consent. Players must think carefully about their limits. Define what is and isn't comfortable.

Ted reacted saying, "My wife Charlotte is always dragging me to various seminars. One time we went to one on human sexuality run by a psychologist who was well-known, but I thought he was a little too focused on all the young women in the audience. To me, he was a creep. The gist of the section on sexual limits discussed S&M and Discipline and Bondage. There are places called dungeons with dungeon masters who control safety. I think that's what they do. What struck me was what they call regular sex. They call it 'Vanilla Sex.' Charlotte thought that was hysterical. I didn't."

Ash asked, "Did they discuss group sex? I think that sex should be between two people. It's not a tennis match with an audience and I sure as hell don't want a threesome or a foursome."

Ted laughed. "Charlotte thinks that we, police, are some of the most conservative folks on the planet, even more so than my former colleagues in engineering. She's open to discussing any issue, but is pretty definite about what she wants or doesn't want to do. I've suffered through a lot of her efforts to bring me into a broader society. I rebelled at all the clairvoyance stuff. I told her I don't want to know about the future. When the future arrives, I'll face it then."

Juan interjected, "So what else do we need to know about this stuff, Ted? I think that sex is embedded in our persona. I want all the associated feelings of good will; I want to be able to rely on my partner. I don't want what we do to be examined by outsiders. I hate the concept of divorce when lawyers and family counselors discover everything about you. I may at one time or another have done stuff I'm ashamed of, but still it's my business."

"Well, Juan, even in the simplest scenario there are rules. I think they call it working within a 'Frame'. As I understand it 'Frame' means a set of rules for the sex. These rules are negotiated between or among the parties. And you never say, 'I've hooked up with someone.' You phrase it as, 'I've scened with someone.'

"Sadomasochism involves a highly unbalanced power relationship. The players use role-playing, bondage, and/or the infliction of pain. The most important psychological concept behind this practice supposedly is knowing that one person has complete control. It gets really kinky after that with all kinds of equipment. In the 80s, the American Psychiatric Association removed S&M as a mental disorder. To me, and as it was explained by the seminar instructor, it means S&M is considered normal and allows the release of sexual and emotional energy that cannot happen in normal sex. It is no longer a pathology. The seminar materials included a list of readings on the subject and several were on a dominitrix's role in 'psychological/sexual release for good mental health.'"

Juan could not let this go, retorting, "Sounds like bullshit to me, Ted. I think psychiatrists can find anything okay. I'm not saying you can't use a little imagination when you're in bed with someone you love, but not everything is okay. I've seen some nuts out there who have no control over themselves in the normal course of a day. This same guy gets hot, and no dungeon monitor, unless he's a combat officer, would be able to stop him. Actually, in fairness to the fairer sex, they're just as nuts."

Ash pointed them to the computer screen. "There's a site here called 'MeetUp.' Let's see if it has any group meetings local."

The detectives focused on the list of a few local groups when they heard the Captain behind them who voiced, "What's so interesting on there? Three detectives aren't needed to view one screen."

Silence reigned for an extended period before Ash stepped up to the plate. He explained what they had found and fumbled a bit with a discussion on sadomasochism, discipline, and bondage. Beauregard did not act as expected. Instead he said, "Voila. There you are. You have found the possible nexus."

The detectives had heard their Captain use that word in the past and it meant that a connection was there. Juan questioned, "Captain, do you think all three murders are connected by this stuff?"

"I don't know, but you are going to find out. The route is not through this 'MeetUp' site. Get Lilly and Vice to help you. All three women are from West Side and all are professionally employed. What does that mean? It means that they have limited time and the desire to keep every effort to fill their desires quiet. Why else would Leslie Hosman write in code and use initials? This is one hell of a start. Investigate everyone in Eleanora and Alison and Leslie's worlds and match initials.

"When did this all start? What date did Leslie start using code?"

Ted answered, "Her date book was new but started in the middle of last year. That alone is abnormal. Her old datebook just lists 'Fun' for one day a week and nothing more. The new date book has a sentence at the top of the first page, 'Journey to the Unknown.'"

Beauregard directed them to use that date as a start date for the investigation into the other victims; maybe it's a window into when and if they had new changes in their lives at that time. Ash thought they all probably didn't meet each other at the exact same time or he decided they could have been more secretive in their actions. He figured that Eleanora may have been a moving force in these endeavors, and asked when did 'el' initials first show up in Leslie's diary.

Ted showed him the date 'el' first appeared was three months after Leslie started her new diary, which was about eight months before. He emphasized, "We have to connect 'el' with Eleanora. I doubt Eleanora kept copious records like Leslie. What did Leslie do for a living?"

"Leslie was a food source intermediary vendor for two area grocery chains and five chain restaurants. Her job would require her to be on the computer and phone, daily. She has a high profile on Facebook, but it's all discrete stuff, which is what is to be expected. Nothing in her computer, with the exception of the two-password protected files, says anything."

Beauregard asked Mason what was on those two files. He was told that he'd unlocked them, but had not gone through them because their immediate interest was directed to the diary. He also announced he had unlocked Alison's computer, but didn't know what Ted and Bill had found. Beauregard was adamant that the detectives use all resources to look for a connection among the three women, instructing them, "Connect these women with Eleanora and with anyone whose initials match those in Leslie's diary. Have you located Alison's parents and just what is the surname?"

Mason responded, "Their surname is Roper and they live about a block over from you, Captain, on Forsythia Drive. Do you know them? I found their itinerary and the flight's due at Logan in two days."

Shaking his head sadly, Beauregard confirmed, answering, "I know them from church. They are good people. Now that you say the name, I think I've met Alison after church a couple of years ago. Her parents introduced her to Mona and me. I should have recognized her. She stood out from the church crowd I can tell you. Janet and Al will be devastated."

"Captain, do you want to do their interview?"

"No, I want Ash to do it. Al is a music professor. Ash will better know how to talk to Al and he has the skills to deal with Janet. Ash, do you have a problem doing this interview?"

Ash did not have a problem. He said that he'd met Al Roper

several times, but they were not buddies and had never played together. Apparently, Al had educated a few of Ash's buddies on music theory. He stressed that each one had high regards for Al's intelligence and dedication to his students. There were a few seconds of silence before further discussion was continued.

Beauregard reiterated, "Get Lilly to connect with Vice now. Juan, you go help Bill interview, while Lilly's gone."

Ted suggested to the Captain, "Captain, Juan is needed here. There's a lot to do and we need everyone. I know that right now Bill can't be involved while we're setting up what we're dealing with here, but can't you leave him out there to go it alone? Tell him to use his recorder if the subject allows it."

Beauregard acquiesced.

9

Border's Limits

Bill Border was ticked off that Lilly was selected to talk with Vice and brain drain. He knew he'd rather do anything more interesting than second interviewing neighbors. The interviews in the neighborhood had not been productive, and he didn't think the day was going to be rewarding at all.

Mason told him, the Captain thought that he, Border, could conduct these interviews with a recorder. Bill mused, *suspicion is my middle name and I know that it is not the norm to have a detective do solo interviews. I'm certain they don't want me at the office. All that sneaky stuff with George giving names to Mason and Juan, but I was to be excluded. Do they all think that I'm that stupid? They figure I'm connected to this freak show and maybe the murders. I wouldn't murder anyone and certainly not women. It's all because I condo-mated with Josh. They don't understand that I left that co-tenancy with some money on the table because I learned he was such a whack job. If they only knew what I saw the night I returned from a trip a day early. The memory still haunts my nightmares. Never understood why I didn't see it coming, there was lots of evidence. Dumb, I can really be dumb.*

Bill remembered his cavalier treatment of women and his competitiveness in chasing the better than average looking ladies.

He knew he wasn't interested in settling down when he was in his twenties. Now he would like a good relationship, but, at this point in time, his reputation for being a heartless ladies man preceded him. He was not taken seriously as a potential love interest by any of the nice ladies he now met. And he often thought to himself, he deserved this. He did wonder if the visions he saw that evening in his condo had damaged him enough so that it showed in his demeanor.

One of the reasons he left the Holyoke Police Department was because he was constantly being harassed by the other detectives and even street cops about his sexual prowess. His reputation was based on his dating activity during his first two years as a police officer. He could never counter their opinions. Border believed it was a joke to be admired for something that was other peoples' public relations fantasy for him. He did think at one time that he was cool, a really cool dude. Shameful was his memory of his 'love them and leave them' attitude. He wasn't totally a thug. He remembered some rules he had: one of which was to tell each woman early on that he had no intention to marry within the next ten years; the second rule was to never play around with a woman who was involved with a guy. Little did he know that some of them were involved with another woman. He knew he would have been more fortunate if he'd met a special person when he was younger, but his parents divorced when he was in college and he thought it had a serious effect on him; maybe he stopped believing in trust when they both remarried within a year. He just knew some playing around was going on before they divorced, although neither parent ever admitted to infidelity.

Border drove to the next neighbor of Alison Brunder to be interviewed. When the owner, Jessica Taylor answered, he was shocked. He knew her. In fact, he had dated her in college. He had not recognized the name, but the face brought back some memories.

She gave him a big smile and joked, "No, Bill, I'm not available tonight. I have to wash my hair." And she laughed.

She looked good to him, despite her wise remark. It'd been at least thirteen or so years since he last saw her. "Jessica, I'm not here for social reasons, but you've negated any possibility for that from the start. I'm a sergeant with West Side MCU and I'd like to question you about your neighbor, Alison Brunder who lives on number 92. Will you help me?"

"Come on in, Bill. I will try, but there is not a lot I can tell you that I know personally, but there are lots of rumors about her. After all she is, or shall I say, was, an exceptionally 'got it all together' beauty, leaving the whole neighborhood talking. I'll make some coffee, or tea, if you prefer."

"Coffee would be great."

Jessica and Bill talked about their college days and their professional lives. He was surprised when she told him her choice of professions. She confirmed his questioning explaining she was a neurologist. He asked, "When did that happen? I thought you were taking a general program in Arts and Sciences. Isn't that what you told me?"

"I might have. It always sounded pretentious to me to say I was going to be a doctor. How did I know then that I could make the grade? Certainly, at that time, I did not know neurology would speak to me. I'm a one step at a time person, Bill, I've always been slow going. I call it the turtle approach. If I told you I was interested in medicine when I was a sophomore, you'd never had called me for a date. As it was we went out twice before I recognized your modus operandi was to call the night before and assume I'd be available. It got old quickly for me."

"I get it; it triggered your great response about being too busy with washing your hair. I may have been dumb then, but I got the clue and never called again."

With a smirk, Jessica remarked, "There you go again. It was always about you and your feelings. I guess you are the same, Bill, although this time you're a detective. I heard you were with the Holyoke Police Department. My information sources have let me down, because I didn't hear that you made a switch to West Side Police. Why the switch?"

Smarting from Jess's remarks, Bill turned on his professional demeanor asserting, "Don't want it to be all about me Jess, but thanks for having an interest in my career."

Jess looked embarrassed, but Bill continued. "Let's talk more about you. What have you been up to? Are you married? If so, to whom and do you have kids?"

"No, and no are your answers. I work a lot and have a great practice. I came close to the altar, but he chose to move to L.A. He's a director in the movies and has done well. We talk, but he's not for me. I'm happy I didn't go through with it. I don't like his lifestyle."

"Jess, this coffee is delicious," commented Bill and stated, "And this is a great house you have. It feels so welcoming. Most of these houses are overdone. They're all kind of similar in size, but many have no curb appeal, because the landscape plans don't enhance the homes. And I bet none are set up like this, with the interior having so much light. It's comfortable."

She laughed and replied, "Don't get too comfortable. I think your partner is about to ring my bell."

Bill turned to look out the window and saw the Captain walking up the walk. He thought, *what's with this. I didn't think these interviews were so important he'd join me; unless something else has happened.* He stood and joined Jess as she headed toward the door. Welcoming the visitor, Bill introduced her to his boss. After Beauregard settled in with a fresh cup of coffee and an enormous coconut and chocolate chip cookie, he remarked, "Nice living room, Jess. I don't know what Sergeant Border has asked yet, but perhaps you could give me a short summary before I start with some questions."

Jess spoke, while noticing Bill's face reddening, stating, "Bill and I knew each other in college, Captain, and we were just reviewing our histories since then. You may start with the questioning since we haven't gotten very far."

Despite Bill's discomfort, Beauregard and Jess talked for over an hour. The Captain questioned Jess about Alison's parents, but more about whether she knew the history and story of Alison's marriage and divorce.

Jess relayed a few stories of her interactions with Alison at the gym, local grocery store, and at Alison's parents' home. She knew Janet Roper from the hospital; Janet was a nurse there. They were friendly. Janet lived through Alison's divorce from Bart Brunder. She seriously suffered, because according to Janet, her son-in-law, Bart, wasn't a bad husband. He was just a man who liked to stay home whereas, Alison liked club venues. Janet pointed out that as a couple, they were enviable. Bart was the awesome stud type all young women would go for. Jess shared that Janet detailed her daughter's lack of interest in having children which was contrary to what she told Bart before they married.

Janet thought the problem started when Alison partied with a woman friend. She did not know her name, because Alison wouldn't tell her. A friend of Janet's had seen them at a bar one night. The friend inferred that she and the other beauty were accepting drinks from various men, which she commented was inappropriate for a married woman. Janet spoke of a tete-a-tete she had with Alison over the gossip she heard and her disappointment when Alison lashed into what she called her mother's meddling, Janet knew there was a problem. Alison had never raised her voice to her before.

She tried talking to Bart. His response was, "I've tried to talk Alison into getting couple's counseling. She's tough. She told me if I want to live a boring life, it was my choice, but she was going after what she wanted while she was still young enough to enjoy herself."

Janet thought Bart was confused but tried to stay the course. In the end she stopped coming home on some nights and he couldn't take it. He filed for divorce and she did not contest and the marriage was 'fini' after only two years.

Jess heard other stories from the neighbors. Alison kept the marital home. The neighbors all liked Bart and hated to see him leave. She wasn't sure how much of the gossip was true. One neighbor said that he heard she was into stuff Bart didn't want to talk about.

The Captain said his goodbyes mentioning he had an appointment, telling Bill to finish the interview.

Bill had his own way of finishing the interview, thinking, *why not. At twenty I was stupid, but now I see the light.*

"I'd like to have dinner with you, Jess. Please don't say you have to wash your hair. At least give me a good excuse that will help me save face."

She laughed. "Your ego is in good shape. Yes, dinner would be great, but I'm not available until, at the earliest, next Wednesday."

"I like hump day. What about The Federal Restaurant in Agawam? Would that be all right?"

With the broadest smile a woman ever gave him, she said yes.

Bill left Jess's house thinking, *she's real. She's smart and despite knowing what a jerk I used to be, she's willing to see me. I better straighten my life story with the Captain. His showing up was to let me know that he's watching me. How do I tell him? His life is so white bread. How do I tell him?*

Beauregard headed toward Holyoke to see his high school friend

Luis Vargas. On the way he stopped at Nick's Nest for two hot dogs. He would never tell Mona. She'd lecture him about nitrates and fat and who knows what else is in a hot dog. He knew that Nick's dogs were the best. He did not buy fries or an ice cream, which from his perspective, made it all okay. He said out loud but to himself, "okay. I'm showing some discipline. I could have also eaten a sundae."

Vargas greeted him, "Okay, you have trouble already with Border. Is that why you're here? Maybe those murders have you down? 'Murder on the eighth hole' sounds like a movie title, Rudy. How do you get these cases in your quiet sleepy city?"

"Luis, can you get someone in here who knew Border when he first came on the force? I'd like to talk about his social habits when he was new on the force then."

Luis said yes and he called a detective who was now in crime prevention who partnered with Border when he was a young cop. His name was Jimmy Vente and he was in the station. He could not leave his office, because his seniority required him there until the rest of the detectives returned, but invited the two, saying, "Come over here. There's nothing going on in the unit right now that's causing trouble; all the trouble is with the detectives out there. We can talk."

Jimmy Vente had nothing negative to say about Border's job performance. In fact, he reported that Bill was the best partner ever, although the experience was short. He explained Bill decided to go over to West Side after just a kind of short service in Holyoke. "I couldn't understand it. He was a go through guy. I thought at the time he might have wanted fewer daily headaches. Later, I heard, I mean way later, he was undercover at the direction of the drug task force. Right from the get-go, Bill could be trusted to cover for me; he'd have been great at undercover. I never felt as safe with any other partner I ever had afterwards."

As to Bill's social life, he said that Bill loved the ladies, but not the ladies on the street. He loved high class and educated women. Beauregard asked about 'the badge bunnies' rumor. Jimmy explained that it was all fabricated because Bill would show up at every event with luscious arm candy. The cops created a myth from just that.

Even later, it was true when Bill was in a cop bar that the ladies hovered over him, but to his knowledge, Bill didn't go home with any of them. His view was that Bill just liked the ladies, but never deliberately went out of his way to keep any of them on the string. He never heard of him being abusive. In fact, for all his bravado, Bill was restrained whenever he made an arrest. He said, "Bill was a great cop; but I only knew him well then. I have seen him out since. He's fun."

Vente thought other cops may have been jealous. He heard Bill topped the Sergeant's exam at West Side and said he was not surprised since from the beginning, he was top scorer in the Academy.

Luis expounded, "I don't know how he got connected to get in your MCU so easily. Do you know, Rudy?"

"Nope, I haven't a clue. Can't get into the top brass' mindset, as you know. Maybe his rabbi plays golf with my chief or my mayor. I can tell you that no one and I mean no one asked for my opinion. He has fitted in relatively well. I just want to know more about him. You have both helped me. Thanks, I've got to run."

Rudy was driving back to the station, when Border called. He asked if Rudy could meet him for coffee someplace outside of the station, saying, "I need to speak with you, Captain. My acquaintance with Josh Cantor has to be explained. It could have effects on the case. I need to assure you of my separation from this situation and I want to tell you alone. I trust you with the information."

The Captain suggested Charlie's Diner on Union Street in West Springfield, not far from West Side.

At the diner, they settled. The tension built until Bill Border initiated what sounded to Beauregard as a painful confession. "Captain, I ran with fast crowds when I was young from the time I was in high school until a few years ago. Each group was the 'in' group at the time, or at least I thought we were a cut above. I was a great student but didn't want to be a nerd. I know better now. When I look back, Captain, I realize that I was cruising to be a victim. I know that sounds stupid to you, but think about it, if you're one of the 'in' crowd, what does it mean socially? It means that you need a group to feel good about yourself. It means that you stunt your individual growth in order to fit in. It means you suppress your opinions if the crowd doesn't share them. From my perspective now, the losses outweigh the benefits. I was perfect for undercover. I was good at it. Remember a person doesn't grow emotionally in undercover because you're not working at being yourself."

Beauregard quietly faced his companion. He was very interested in the conversation. Further, Bill could see he had an audience in the Captain. He just hoped the Captain would not think this was a con job. He thought, *this is the one time in my life I'm saying exactly what I mean. I know most cops I know think I'm glib and a wise guy. The police culture celebrates wise-ass retorts to balance out injustices and evils we see and work with daily.*

Border continued his story. "I met Josh Cantor at a party. Every chick and stud at the party crowded him. He was the man to know. He was successful and what my mother would call, 'an Adonis.' He immediately brought me into his circle. I was flattered. He introduced me to 'his ladies.' He'd go to about three of the, what I call, martini type bars where women grouped to meet guys. His selection included only upper-class bars. It seemed exciting at the time and he was knowledgeable and fun to be with. Everyone liked him or was jealous of him; one or the other. You couldn't ignore him. He owned a company that sold some type of machine parts for the aerospace industry. He'd bought the company from the original owner and grew it. He was an astute businessman and now pretty much had a team that managed it for him. He was golden in everything he did.

"Josh got this great lease in an oversized condo nestled in a paradise of wooded pines. What a crib to bring a girlfriend. Although the rent was high, half was fine. I jumped on it. There were always people visiting. I remember that I'd have to walk the grounds to get some quiet to think, but when you're young, you believe this is what you should do. I lasted short of two years. Then it ended. I'd gone on a trip and because the weather was bad, I returned early.

"My living room which was connected to the dining room was almost fifty feet long with two wooden beams lining the ceiling for the whole length. I had loved the look of the beams that matched the header mantle on the fireplace; I can't look at wooden beams any longer. Josh had decorated the living room with several small upholstered chaise lounges and two couches. It did seem feminine to me when I first moved in, but the materials were masculine, mainly paisley and plaid."

Josh stopped for a minute and downed his coffee. Beauregard did not urge him to finish. He waited.

"Captain, there were threesomes and foursomes on the couches and lounges, and bodies swinging from some contraptions attached to the beamed ceilings. Two of the bodies were women and two men. They were partially dressed in black leather with straps everywhere but their genitals, rear, and breasts were exposed. A gorgeous woman in a mask was whipping them and the hanging people were begging for more. The sight of them encouraged the people on the furniture to continue in a frenzy. The threesomes and foursomes were sexually mixed. Josh was one of the men hanging from the ceiling. No one even noticed me. I was at the door. I thought I was in sex hell. I walked out the door with my luggage. I moved out the next day and never told Josh what I saw. He may have seen me, but I didn't care. I realized, then, that I had limits. I think humans are more than sexual exploitation for the high of the moment.

"I couldn't understand how I had not known about this. I believed then, and now, that these orgies happened regularly. Several times during the almost two years I lived there, Josh would ask me not to come home for a couple of days. He would explain he was seeing a special someone and needed nothing to interfere with the romancing. What a fool I was. I later scrutinized everything said to me at the various bars at which we partied and understood I had been deaf and blind to the innuendos presented all around me.

"Imagine, Captain, how foolish I felt. I have always been top of my class. I wanted to be with the sophisticated crowd. There's nothing sophisticated about lack of respect for our bodies and for each other. In my dreams I constantly see some dramatization of Dante's Inferno showing the second circle of Hell depicting the 'Sodomites.' When I was young and saw the drawing, I was horrified and thought at that time, that Dante was insane. But Dante wasn't insane. What he saw is real today and maybe worse. I'm telling you all this, because I have to. You're my boss. I know I have to come clean, but I have had nothing to do with Josh or that crowd since the 'Episode.' I don't want this out, Captain. Please don't let it out."

Beauregard sat quiet. Sergeant Bill Border sat in a defeated position. Finally, the Captain cautioned Bill, "What happened to you, then, was then, Bill. What you've just said is for my ears only. However, others know. Josh knew. He let you hang with costs from the condo. He knew. The whole time he was playing you, waiting for when you would be most vulnerable before pulling you into the action. This I don't know factually, but, Bill, I know this, for sure. As to the investigation, stay away from anything on Josh. Give a report on facts. Give no gossip. As to that evening when you walked in, you decide what needs to be said. I hope none of this comes back to bite you in the ass.

"On the other hand, Sergeant, I think you avoided a train-wreck by walking that night. Your avoidance shows me your intrinsic morality and good sense. We all do stupid things. There are times when an angel is on your shoulder and you listen. There are other times when you don't listen. You did good in listening, Sergeant; now back to your next interview."

Sergeant Bill Border was deep in thought as he drove away. *The Captain did not give me shit for being stupid. He congratulated me for leaving. He said nothing about my being stupid and narcissistic. I felt like I was going to confession. I'm not even Catholic, but boy, I feel forgiven. I guess this is an example of what they call a 'police Rabbi.' I've got a Rabbi now. The thing is I don't have the connections for getting a Rabbi. I have no connections; he just offered it up.*

Border noticed the next and last name on the neighbor list on the Brunder murder and headed there. He pulled up as a very classy bronze colored Infiniti sedan pulled into the driveway. Getting out of it was a man he thought looked familiar. Checking the name list, he put two and two together and recalled his memory of Charlie Logan. His knowledge just didn't compute. The Charlie Logan he knew was a bartender at the Oxford Martini Bar. In the day, it was a hot spot and was one of the locations favored by Josh and his friends. He started to introduce himself showing his badge, but was stopped by, "God damn it, Josh told me you became a detective. Thank God I don't hang in bars any longer. I wouldn't want you on my bad side. How the heck are you, Bill? You're looking good."

"I guess not as good as you, Charlie. Nice car and nice house, you're doing well?"

"I was in graduate school when I was at the Oxford. I used to tell the women in class that I attended Oxford. Wasn't a lie, just wasn't the truth. You didn't know I was a student?"

"No, Charlie, I didn't. What'd you study?"

"Now don't laugh, Bill, I'm a physician's assistant."

"Charlie, I have to know, what area?"

"Plastic surgery, I'm a PA in plastic surgery and it pays well. I work for Dr. George Girandeau. You may know him. He used to run around with Josh's friends, but later turned his back on him. I'm close with George, but he won't tell me what happened. You're here about Josh, aren't you? Was he really murdered?"

"Charlie, unfortunately that is just why I am here. I do have some questions for you, okay?"

"Sure, Bill, question away."

"Did you ever hear any of Josh's friend talk about their sexual exploits?"

"You're kidding, right? That's about all they talked about besides wine and craft beer, and belonging to the most important groups from the hi-falutin to sports to drama to music to political and social. Every country club was covered by at least one member. They were what I read about in books, Bill, vacuous, pretentious and complete asses. I was always surprised you hung around with them and when you moved in with Josh; well that was a bigger surprise."

Bill said, "Don't you remember, Charlie, you told me Josh was looking for a roomie?"

"I did? I don't remember connecting you two, Bill. Sounds like me passing on info and gossip. Got bigger tips by being a connection guy."

Bill appeared to be uncomfortable with this conversation, but pushed on, inquiring, "Did any in the group talk about asphyxiation to get a better sexual high?"

Charlie responded, "They talked about how long you could press the sweet spots on the neck before there would be damage. That's not all they talked about; they loved to talk about various instruments for delivering pain, just not too much pain. I remember listening carefully to these conversations. Remember, I was in grad school learning all about the body. The first time pressing for a high was discussed in the bar, well the next day I told my classmates in the program. We asked our prof, and we spent the next two hours discussing it. His view was that it was a very dangerous behavior. As a doctor, he never showed us he was shocked, but firmly believed that purposely decreasing oxygen to get a feeling of giddiness and lightheartedness to intensify a sexual high smacked of sexual addiction. He called it, Asphyxiophilia. Any of those 'philias' meant some type of addiction. Many people practice auto-asphyxiation while masturbating alone. They rig all kinds of contraptions. Some result in deaths, but you'll never hear about them. No one talks about it."

"Did Josh like this? Had you heard when you listened to the conversations on this?"

"Bill, it's not like I could stop mixing drinks and listen to their conversations word for word. I'd go in and out, as I walked the bar filling orders. When there was a big crowd, I heard more because there were other bartenders to lighten my workload. But, I think he was plugged into it. He never stopped the talk and he never left while they talked about asphyxia.

"You, on the other hand, were never in the loop while I saw you with them. Did you ever notice Josh and some of the others go over to the dance floor or other end of that long bar and then return just when you started wondering where two or three were going? That's when they would set a date for their, what I call, 'Tryst Forays.' Always wondered what was really happening at those forays, but not enough to try and get invited. Face it, Bill, they were a bunch of weirdos. You're lucky you got away. A few of the guys and girls who were invited to the forays, after a few months were uninvited. They'd come into the bar and were ignored. One gal who'd been thrown to the curb, was drunk and jumped on the bar and stripped, yelling, 'Look at me; I'm good enough. I'll do anything.' I had to call the police. She wouldn't stop until they dragged her out. I got a lot of shit from the owner who had to explain to the police that the lady was drunk when she got here; we did not give her a drink."

"Where were the 'Tryst Forays' held, Charlie?"

Charlie was quiet for a few seconds, finally contending they were at Josh's house, "When you lived with him. You mean, you didn't know? I heard one gorgeous nut say that Josh planned to introduce you to the game."

Bill Border used every restraint his body could allow to hold himself steady as he replied, "Are you nuts, Charlie? It would have meant my job. I don't like that stuff. Besides Josh's condo, where else?"

"There was another guy whose house they used. He lived in Connecticut and they talked about another group that was 'further along' in pursuit of the ecstasy of concentration on self-fulfillment by escape from reality to temporarily lose one's normal identity. They explained and insisted both sadistic or masochistic behavior reduces stress. A group member tried to convince me, and he was quite proud of his participation. Told me that the rest of us satisfied with ordinary sex were living in a small sexual space when so much more was available.

"Bill, I left the job as bartender, but I do know there still are a scattering of S&M and bondage and discipline clubs all over the valley. Mostly, the upper-middle class is involved and occasionally, it costs money to belong. One woman was saving to get into a club. Another woman said that if you had to pay to get into a club, then it was not the highest experience on the ladder and just wasn't worth it. They talked like that; you know, 'in the know.'"

"Do you remember the names of any who may be willing to talk about particular experiences and clubs?"

"No, Bill, first names are all I ever knew. I was a bartender. That's all I have for you, Bill. One regular insisted that there were studies that said that practitioners of BDSM were mentally healthier than were those having normal sex."

"Charlie, can you remember the date the woman was arrested in the bar; at least if your memory includes the month and year."

After a couple of minutes, Charlie remembered the date. Bill walked away happy thinking, *I'll get the arrest record from the bar and chase her down. Wait 'til I tell the others; they'll know just as I know. Josh was looking for action in the woods. He wanted to be titillated by partial asphyxia in a public setting.*

10

All Around Us

Petra Aylewood-Locke was rocking an almost sleeping baby Carlotta. Petra did not stop. She had frequently told Jim, Carlotta was like a cat; if you moved slightly, she'd wake. Petra used times like this to muse on this new life, *never thought I'd be this content sitting. Carlotta plays games, I think, by pretending she's asleep to make me move and then completely wakes up when I do. It's a test. The universe gave me Carlotta to test me. Where does my cynicism come from? I was a Boston beat cop and then a detective. I'm Bolt, who moves fast. What's happened? I could sit here for hours with this little witness from God who tells me nothing but manipulates my actions. Listen, Carlotta, I'm on to you. Your father may be a sucker, but not me. Do you understand me? Carlotta's moving, giving me that gas pain smile, and is finally settling in for a deep sleep. And for just this minute, I'm so content.*

A ringing cell disturbed the peace, and Petra moved the baby to the bassinette before answering. Jim was checking on them. Carlotta did not wake. All was well with the world, until Jim said, "Petra, didn't you go to college with Leslie Hosman?"

"Yes, I did. Why are you asking, Jim, did you run into her?

"Apparently, when we took a few days vacay in Dennis, we never checked into West Side for news and didn't know about two women who were found murdered. One was Leslie."

Petra stuttered, "I knew her pretty well for a short time, but then went to Boston. She was stunning and bright. Almost a combination inviting disaster, but she was always nice to me. She did live on the edge, Jim. She was indiscriminate about who she slept with. In fact, she'd often say that most guys were useless, that they had no imagination when it came to sex. I'd just come from a bad marriage where the only imagining I was doing was checking for evidence on a cheating husband. I am so sorry. I believed that she would have the best of lives. How was she killed?"

"She was attacked a few nights ago outside her home by a guy with a syringe. The attack was aborted by someone outside her condo. She was strangled inside the hall of her condo the next day. They think, according to the news, that she knew her attacker."

"Oh, Jim, that does make sense if she maintained her history with men. I'm so sad."

A short time later, Petra spoke with her mother. She then called Jim, announcing, "I'm going back to work at the three-month mark, Jim. I promise I'll be the best mother, but to do that, I need to work. My mother is looking forward to staying with the baby. Please say you agree."

Jim laughed. "I've told you before, Petra. We're a family including yours and mine. My mom will help. The two of them will compete for babysitting time. Yes, go back, but you have a couple of months now. Sit back and enjoy them."

"Do you think I'm a bad mother for wanting to go back to work and leave Carlotta?"

"Nope, if you don't go back to work soon, you'll be investigating your neighbors for stealing peonies. You're a detective, Petra.

You'll always be a detective. I love my detective."

Beauregard's face was a contorted stress mask. He clicked a new station from the news to opera. He needed opera. He hated going to the opera, because the seats were uncomfortable, except when he went to an opera broadcast at the cinema. There, he could lounge back and close his eyes to enjoy the music. Today, he needed the sound. He'd told Ash to interview the Ropers, but then changed his mind. He felt some guilt in that he might be avoiding speaking with them. It was their loss and he was avoiding them. He felt shame, and now, he was headed to Janet and Al Roper's home. They'd been informed last evening. The Ropers agreed to meet only with him today. They insisted that Rudy and only Rudy would they see. Beauregard rang the bell on the standard 1950s half-brick faced colonial with attached two car garage and a three-season porch/room on the right of the home. He could see the Ropers took good care of their property. A haggard looking Janet answered the door. Rudy thought he'd never seen Janet wearing her heart on her sleeve. She'd always been in control. He said, "Janet, I'll come back if there's a better time. I have many questions for you and Al and it's important that they are answered sooner than later, but it doesn't mean today; I'll come back tomorrow."

Janet reached out and hugged him almost knocking Beauregard off the threshold to the step below. Watching him attempting to steady himself, Janet grabbed his arm to assist, saying, "Rudy, I've felt off-balance from the minute I got the news. How you just felt for a second, I feel all the time."

Janet took his hand and practically dragged him into the kitchen, while calling for Al. Rudy was surprised by her strength, thinking, *it's the need to have something to do, say, or control; otherwise the grief would kill.*

Al Roper welcomed him offering coffee. They sat at the enormous antique pine circular table with a large wooden lazy-susan in the middle hiding pastries, sugar, and cream. Light streamed in from the oversized kitchen windows allowing every crevice on his hosts' faces to be visible. Beauregard waited, getting comfortable with the silence, marveling at the strength these two exhibited. Al ended the silence. "Rudy, do you know who would do this to Alison? She was a workaholic; where would she meet a murderer?"

Rudy responded, "Tell me about Alison. Tell me about her ex-husband and her current social life. Was she in a relationship?"

Janet spoke in anger. "Rudy, why do you cops always think the husband did it? You're off-base on this one. Bart wouldn't hurt a hair on Alison's head. Sure, he was upset when he realized that no matter how good he was to her, it would never be enough. He gave her the damn house hoping she'd eventually come to her senses. Alison was the perfect daughter. She was everything I ever wanted with one exception. Alison wanted what she wanted and would let no one get in her way. Marriage doesn't work that way. Alison was fortunate. She was educated and almost brilliant; her brilliance prevented her colleagues from criticizing her controlling behavior. I don't know how she was able to keep a responsible job involving so many people. She was impossible to get along with in the long run. We loved her and her visits always upset us. She loved us, I think, but she never tried to change, not ever."

Al did not try to stop Janet, but his responses varied. "Rudy, Alison was missing the guilt factor. If I caught her when she was a child doing something, she was never abashed or ashamed. She was just furious she was caught. I've been reading about personalities in an attempt to understand her because she'd been pulling away from us even more lately. She couldn't hide the fact that she didn't want us at her house. Alison seemed narcissistic even in comparison to this current culture and was definitely indifferent to others' needs; we are included in the word, 'others.' People didn't notice at first, just as it took us years to truly comprehend her lack of interest in others' feelings. Everyone I ever introduced Alison to raved about her beauty and brains. She was getting worse. If that other woman hadn't been murdered, I would have thought Alison was killed by someone she worked with or dated."

Beauregard spent another hour with the Ropers, but they had no knowledge of who was in her life. They insisted that someone working with her every day may know more, but also said that Alison was a great secret keeper.

Beauregard did ask if Alison knew Eleanora Captreau or Josh Cantor. The couple did not recognize the names. Al said Alison worked hard to keep her personal life to herself. He ended by describing his sister-in-law's view of Alison. She often saw Alison out with a woman and at other times with a man. If the Captain had a picture of the other woman, he would ask her if she recognized her. Beauregard promised to send pictures with a uniform later in the day. He gave the Ropers his card and escaped.

Bill Border was sweet-talking the records officer and from the looks of it, she was enjoying the attention. Border had spent a period of time in Records when he was first on the force in Holyoke. He personally believed that it was a death knell for inspiration. He also knew that some cops loved it. Perhaps they were OCD types who loved order. Well, police records rooms, if there wasn't tight security, could be quite disorderly. Jeannie, the officer in charge, was flirting with him but still made him go through the paperwork including the need for the file. Border did not want to disclose his reason for searching for the file. Connecting it with an open murder case would bring too much notoriety. The press was famous for discovering who accessed which files for which cases. Instead, he wrote, "multiple assaults in West Side bars." Even this comment may initiate a story on the subject. He'd let Chief Coyne argue it away or maybe the Mayor would be contacted. She delivered the arrest report for one, 'Connie Davenport' and fortunately there was an address in a decent neighborhood that had owner occupied homes. There would be a better chance that Ms. Davenport may even still be living there.

Less than a quarter hour later found Sergeant Border speaking with a woman standing outside the address listed on the arrest report. She had introduced herself as Maggie and she was a friend of Connie Davenport. She'd purchased the home when Connie married. Connie and her new husband moved to a bigger home in a new development not far from there. He headed over, and realized that Connie had hit pay dirt. This home was on Sunnyside Road, the infamous street where a young girl murdered her friends. Petra had told him a few houses went up for sale once the culprit was found. The selling prices were reduced from the effects of the murders and the houses were sold in a week.

Two cars in the driveway gave Bill hope that Connie would be home. As he approached the front door, a woman exited a side entrance visible from the street view and yelled, "Come this way. No one uses the front door. I think it's only for decoration; besides the ring doorbell has to be charged." He headed toward the stunning but very pregnant woman and asked if she were Connie Davenport. With a brilliant smile, she shared, "No, it's now Connie Smith. Simple name to spell but awfully common."

Bill identified himself and saw Connie tense up immediately, asking, "Is this from my arrest in that stupid episode at the Oxford bar? Is this about Josh? I cringe just thinking about it. I was so stupid and, well, I was really sick then. You know, mentally unwell, and Josh took advantage of my weaknesses."

With some coaxing Connie shared a rather sad story. She explained when she was younger she had some problems with letting go. She'd do a research paper and had trouble handing it in, because there may be an opportunity to make it better. Later, too much later, according to her, she sought therapy. Her counselor explained some of her problems related to a combination of good traits that together could get in the way of a productive life. She reported that she still lived with the problem of having difficulty in letting go, but she was now aware that the problem existed. She vigilantly disciplined herself to view what she was doing within a framework of a bigger reality. It was most helpful. Her husband was a researcher as was she, and he truly understood her problems. He could let go, but knew many in the field who could not.

Bill prodded her with questions. "What traits are you talking about? Do they explain your loss of control at the Oxford? Had you had run-ins with the law in addition to that evening?"

"You don't understand, Sergeant Border, I have a doctoral degree in medical research. First, I was trained as an RN and then went back to do research. Nursing was very stressful for me. All the day-to-day suffering I found on the floor, I could not bear being witness. My inability to let go of problems, even problems of others, had forced me inward. I've been a student, hyper-focused on my work for most of my life. I didn't understand the rules of dating. I'd had a few boyfriends before Josh, but then I met him. There in front of me, asking for my cell number, was the epitome of desirable men. Not only was he drop-dead handsome, but he was bright. He could keep up with me. He praised me, hovered over me, gave me gifts, and promised a future. And then it was over. I couldn't figure it out. Our sex life was so exciting; he taught me to let go and I did with him. I thought I was pleasing him. Later he introduced me to groups who were into casual sex with each other. I told him I was uncomfortable. He called these little sex parties, which is what they were, forays. I'm ashamed to tell you more."

"Connie, Josh is dead. You must tell the story. Your arrest report and its veracity are supported by many people. Looking at you, it's difficult to believe that you are the woman who was dancing naked on the bar."

Connie started crying leaving Bill feeling particularly stressed, thinking, *she's got to be eight months pregnant, and I have to make her cry. She hasn't even said that she wants no one to know. That's normally the first request witnesses have. This is a lady, who acted out, probably only once in her life, but the action was so public and embarrassing.*

Sergeant Bill Border took Connie's hand in his, surprising them both. She calmed down and remarked, "I knew I would never be able to put this stupidity of mine behind me completely. It's just that I've been so happy and with the baby coming, well, life is now wonderful."

"Connie, it's not your actions that have brought me here to question you. You know it's the actions of Josh Cantor. He has been murdered. Whatever he did to you is important, because I'm pretty certain that you were not his only victim. Other victims may not have been able to walk away like you. Clearly hard and group sex was central in Josh's life and that's why your experience is important to lead us to his murderer. Help me. Help find his murderer. I can tell just by your walking away and feeling so betrayed that you have a conscience."

"Josh brought me to two of these forays, before I gave him hell. I told him that I loved being with him and sex with him. I asked him why I was not enough for him if he loved me. He suggested that I was selfish and narrow in my thinking. I was so inexperienced in life and lovers. I almost bought it.

"Sergeant, my father wouldn't let me enter beauty contests. I was invited several times by professionals. He didn't believe in focusing on the body. I was well into high school when I first realized I was attractive. Later, with all my studying, I just never focused on myself. I have good friends who would choose my clothes. All my fashion sense comes from them, not from my parents. My mom was a hippie social worker. Dad is all about work, duty, and family. I think Josh paid so much attention to my beauty, I bought his interest as love. He shopped with me and showed me how to better display my, what he called, my 'resources,' and taught me to walk differently. We went to the gym together. I've never gone back to that gym since. I can't face all those people. I'm certain they all know what I did.

"It was at the gym I met many who were at the sex parties. The group at the gym used to call themselves the 'Cabal.' I suppose it is what they were. They were a group with a goal. I just didn't know then what their goal was, and don't for a minute believe, they weren't all united in that goal. They were."

Bill pursued the direction of the conversation. "What do you mean, united in what goal?"

"At the time I didn't understand the meaning of the 'Cabal.' Looking back, I believe they recruited victims at the gym. I was recruited at the gym. I joined that gym because one of my colleagues gave me a lecture about keeping my body strong to save the brain. I'd been working long hours for an extended period of time and was exhausted. She told me to find a gym and I did; I didn't know this gym was an opportunity for them to find victims. It all makes sense now. They could see the body as we worked out. I was just meat for their predatory sex whims. I was nothing to them. They pretended friendship. I believed them and allowed them into my life. For sure, my life experiences had not prepared me for this, and … and Detective, I was dying for attention."

"Connie, please continue with the story. You need not worry, I do not judge you. Honestly, no one is prepared to deal with a narcissistic sociopath who, intrinsic in its name, is incapable of empathy. You feel guilt. Josh didn't have the capacity to feel guilt."

"That may be true, Detective, but I am supposed to be intelligent and I fell for it all. Perhaps I am also a narcissist who needs attention. Let's get on with this horror show retelling. Josh was supportive in the aftermath of the first sex party. He was lovey-dovey. After another month's worth of attention showered on me, I was ripe for another try. Remember, this is how I see it now. It is not how I saw it then. Then, I was an adoring lover of what I thought was a perfect man."

"Connie, go on and if you are able to remember any of the other players, it would be of great importance in our investigation."

"Remember them! I've tried so hard to forget them. Josh took me to dinner in Northampton and gave me a ring. He called it a pre-engagement ring. His taste is impeccable and the ring choice reflected his exquisite taste. What a set-up! He was willing to spend money on a ring to get me to be a player in all that shit; spanking, other disciplines for the masochist, and bondage, and that woman who loved to be in charge directing the inmates of this asylum in sexual deviation. After dinner that evening we went to a nightclub with loud music. I drank too much. Josh suggested we go to a friend's house. It was not the same house we went to before. When we arrived, they were waiting for me. There were about twelve people there; eight of them I had seen at the gym. I was introduced to a stunning woman who embraced me. She told me that she'd heard so much about me, about my intelligence and my work. Drinks were served and there was a tray of fruits and tiny pastries.

"These men and women were not interested in eating. Their appetites were elsewhere. I know now that something was in my champagne. I don't know what drug. I was not completely drugged because I'm able to remember some of what happened. My own sexual desires worked against my moral compass. Apparently, I am somewhat of a masochist and that beautiful woman who embraced me started saying things like, 'You need to be punished' and she undid my dress and I let her. They moved in a frame from behind a screen in this enormous living room and she hung me in it. One by one, I was told by each of them that I was lucky to be here and that my body would finally give me joy as they told me that I was genuinely naïve and had never reached a heavenly climax. Different ones would ask me questions about how would I like to be adored.

"Josh would come over, every once in a while, between their touches and say, 'Soon, baby, we'll be together.'"

"Who and how did they touch you, Connie?"

"Every one of them touched me, men and women. Everyone looked at me adoringly. Every one of them told me I was exceptionally perfect. My brain knew that you don't use exceptionally with the word perfect. I'm a literalist. I would normally react to that use of language. Instead I sucked it in and felt so sexually stimulated. I wanted more. I'm ashamed to admit, I wanted more."

Connie cried putting her head down. Her pregnancy prevented her moving too low. And then she laughed. "I have new life in this body. It feels like an absolution for that night. I don't believe my actions at the Oxford Bar are what I'm most ashamed of; no, it's my actions of enjoying that evening. I've read about abducted women who felt guilt over enjoying sex as captives. My shrink has explained that it is often a survival mechanism. I still feel guilt. Actually, other than my shrink, you are the only person, other than my husband, that I have told. It is hurting less than I would have thought. I almost think that I'm talking about another woman's experience now. Do you think it's an indication of dissociative behavior?"

"I'm not a psychiatrist, Connie, but I do know that suppressing trauma and even keeping secrets are not healthy. My theory is that good people feel shame; bad people don't. Maybe I'm wrong. Shame tells us, in my mind, not to do something again, not to go back there. Shame gives a pretty powerful message, but we should learn from it, not let it interfere with our lives."

"I don't want to go through the rest of that night, Sergeant Border. I'm willing to help you, but the rest of that experience is too sexual and too horrible to share. I would be able to recognize some of the attendees of that foray if you have photos. That I'm willing to do. I can't go further. It is way too hurtful for me and the baby I'm carrying may feel that pain."

Border talked with Connie about some specifics concerning the locations of the two houses which she could not confirm other than they were in West Side, but assured him that she would recognize them if she saw their exteriors. She was willing to drive about town and look at some of the high-end developments to find the houses. She also agreed to make herself available to look at photos, and told him the name of the gym where she felt she had been recruited. It was the 'Health Wellness Fitness Center.' Just as Bill was almost out the door, Connie stated in a confessional manner, "I went to the Oxford that night to get Josh back. No one, but no one spoke to me. They had been at the sex party, but each face I recognized pretended they had never seen me. I started in telling them as a group that they had no right to touch me when I was under the influence. Josh grabbed me telling me he rejected me because I didn't have what it takes, that I didn't make the cut. Since I was already drinking and was on some pills, I went crazy. I felt exposed and they were laughing at me. I now realize that I am simply not important. I'm just a minor player in their fantasy games. I was torn apart, but they went on with their lives."

"They may have, but Josh is the one who is dead; who was murdered," Bill said and he left Connie's home.

Attorney Norberto Cull was dissatisfied with the little he knew about his dead golf partner, Josh Cantor. JR Randall, another member of the foursome, didn't want to know diddlysquat about Josh Cantor's death, telling Norbie he was no longer interested in police work. His past experience in almost losing his wife and son had turned him off. He shared with Norbie, "We were victims once. I'm not getting close to the information source because, Norbie, it's like when a moth dies, because it flies too close to the flame."

Norbie did not feel as JR felt when he attempted to coax him into sharing his thoughts as a witness. He considered now his role as an attorney almost necessitated his desire to know what was going down and yes, it included listening to gossip. Turning to his colleague next to him, Private Detective Jim Locke who was working on another case for him, Norbie asked, "Look, we're through with your report on this case. Do you have time for lunch? I have an interest which calls for your psychological knowledge. There is no client involved. I can't bill it, Jim. Are you game?"

"Free lunch, anytime for you. I'm sure it's going to be interesting. We'll go in the same car?"

"Naw, we'll walk over to Mom & Rico's. Rico has that side room. Normally it's scarcely occupied. Most come in for take-out."

"Ah, a soppresatta grinder and some of Rosemary's cookies and maybe a slice of macaroni pie with the only thing missing is coffee."

"We could hit La Fiorentina's for an espresso and gelato after, if you so desire. Jim, I have to ask, how do you remain so slim and eat the way you do?"

"Easy now with a baby, Norbie, don't you remember all the effort in taking care of a new baby?"

"You think that's difficult, just wait until she's two years, and you have to chase her all around all day. That is work, Jim. Now is the easy part."

They settled in at the restaurant where Jim changed his mind and indulged in Rosemary's buffet. His plate was full, while Norbie enjoyed an Italian cold cut on a water roll. Norbie told Jim about his experience on the golf course. Jim had read about the death, but thought cause of death was uncertain. Norbie explained the choking in the woods and the discussions with Dr. Girandeau and Sergeant Bill Border. Jim responded to this, "Norbie, what did this Josh's strangled neck look like? Were you able to get a close look? Doesn't really matter, I suppose, because the ME will figure it out. Was the weapon left behind?"

"No, but I'm assuming it's a cord or rope and enough strength to break Josh's neck. I did see some marks below the ears darker than the rest and the ME said there was petechiae on the eyes which is expected in strangulation."

Jim was quiet for a moment, but commented, "I'm thinking. You were playing golf and he went to get his lost ball and was strangled within, let's say fifteen minutes, right? And he was antsy the whole time he was playing and was screwing up his game, right?"

Norbie hated Jim's constantly reviewing every detail before he could decide on a direction or conclusion, but that trait made him a great detective and a great psychologist; both fields in which he was trained. Being unable to control himself, Norbie resumed questioning, "Why are you holding back, Jim?"

"Marks on the side of the neck by the ears are near the carotid arteries. Pressing on them on both sides increases pleasure. Addicted masturbators use this process to heighten sensation. If done for a bit of time without losing consciousness, a semi-hallucinogenic state called hypoxia is induced. Add this to orgasm and it's the drug of choice for some. It is called autoerotic asphyxiation. Believe it or not the practice originally addressed erectile dysfunction. It is particularly dangerous when it's used regularly as sport and is called Hypoxyphilia."

"Jim, he did not strangle himself. No weapon was found. If his killer planned it, then he took chances. How could he know that Jim's ball would be lost in the woods at the eighth hole? How could he know that Josh would not put up a fight? If Josh did, we would all have heard it. It's reckless for the killer to take such a chance. Why then? Was time so important?"

"Cripes, Norbie, you're beginning to sound like Beauregard. I don't know the answers to those specific questions. I do know a lot about sexual practices from my training and from my practice. First of all, Josh was not in this alone if he was role playing or carrying out a sexual fantasy. What do you know about him? Is he gay, straight, bi? Is he into some paraphilia activity such as masochism, sadism, fetishes, discipline, bondage, etc.? There are too many to list here, Norbie. He could have had a planned meet with a friend who is into this type of behavior; perhaps participates with Josh on a regular basis in erotic scenes. Maybe the friend had arranged a meet at that site where they both knew it was secluded. Maybe Josh killed himself by accident and the friend was covering it up and making it look like murder or maybe the friend planned to murder him or perhaps it was an accident. Lots of possibilities exist. The location is the most confusing part. If it was planned, then risk taking for the sensation was important. You need to know more about this Josh's lifestyle."

Norbie shook his head and commented, "Why do people do this? If I were to follow your logic, Jim, Josh wanted to be near other people yet secreted from their view. The risk and the deliberate actions taken whether by him or another was for a sexual high. Why did he need this? Do men do this who tend to be impotent, hoping it will help them climax? Is that it?"

"It is currently thought, if I believe the literature, that sadism and masochism, singularly or together gives the practitioner a therapeutic release or escape from life; meaning it gives a lessening of the weight of responsibility and or guilt the person may be feeling as a weight. If you look at the essence of the S&M person, there is a strong need to control which may give feelings of safety. There is the whole power and authority motivation as well. Why, when, and how the emotional traits of a person connect to sexuality is not completely understood yet. Look at that television show, "Billions." It's now in the public domain for all of us to view when we have a serial where the protagonist practices masochism for all to see.

"Early sexual development coinciding with awareness of some event can affect the character of later sexuality. There is the possibility, and it is generally understood, that masochistic or sadistic desires are felt at different ages; some when a child is quite young. Many professionals in the field believe that we all have one or both of these desires hard wired or learned.

"Norbie, sexual practices are personal, even S&M or bondage or discipline as long as they are consensual and do not overwhelm the life of the person. It is when these behaviors overwhelm a life, or when there is an undercurrent of mental illness also involved, or addiction, well then, the activities can lead to sexual addiction, assaults, and even murder or suicide."

Norbie was not satisfied with this conversation and interjected,

"Jim, what is normal vs abnormal? Pursuing a heightened state in a risky setting to further excite himself sounds to me like addiction. If Josh didn't commit suicide by accident, how do we explain the killer's motivation? Would the risk be worth it? Did he kill Josh by accident by pulling the rope too tight? Did he do it on purpose for another reason? He wouldn't just kill on a regular basis; he'd get caught and his masochistic subject to work his sadistic pleasures on would now be unavailable for the future.

"I've had enough of this. You and I had better talk to Beauregard and soon. He needs to know this."

And Norbie made the call to the Captain and set up the meet.

11

Forays

Lilly, finishing her report on her visit to Vice, was interrupted by Juan. He said, "Did Vice try to bring their sexiest detective back into street work, Lilly?"

Lilly laughed and told Juan that she'd never want to be there again, especially after what she had discovered about local home-grown S&M groups. Lilly described how she dreaded what her reception would be, but she needn't have worried. She was greeted like a conquering hero. Her former colleagues were interested in MCU's group of accidental/ murder deaths. The guys, less the currently only woman in the unit who was not on duty, couldn't get enough info. Lilly explained to Juan the stars must have been aligned for her. "When I asked for their help, telling them, 'You guys may be up on some stuff we have no background in. Would you help,' well, they couldn't do enough. Mostly they were interested in our line of inquiry. When I mentioned death by erotic strangulation and questions about thirty-somethings in West Mass who also may be interested in S&M and other stuff, Captain Chilicot had the most to say, but the others who had been involved in several investigations were also quite vocal."

Juan asked, "How were you welcomed by your boyfriend Danny

Abdoul? I know he really tried to help you on the 'Spider' case."

Lilly assessed the look on Juan's face before answering, "Since when have you been interested in my love life, Juan?"

Surprised by her remark, Juan appeared flustered before answering, "I'm sorry if I was too personal, Lilly. I know you would have mentioned him if he gave you info."

"It's okay, Juan. Danny and I had two dinner dates. He is still a wolf, so it ended.

"According to Captain Chilicot, there are at least four homes in West Side, whose parties have resulted in calls from neighbors about noise and naked people screaming. Two calls resulted from 911 calls for ambulances. In one case the EMTs had to revive a woman who had choked herself. He said he couldn't confirm the veracity of the story given, but the victim, when revived insisted the story told was true. He believed somebody else was also involved. The other victim had piercings in her breasts, vulva, and rectum which she insisted she did herself. In two other cases nosey neighbors took plate numbers of cars. He gave me all the listings and the addresses of the four homes the neighbors had reported. Guess what, Juan? Josh Cantor, Eleanora Captreau, and Dr. Girandeau were three of the cars reported and the almost-strangled party guest was Alison Brunder. Vice tried to investigate. Not one known guest had anything to say; actually, that's not quite true. They all had the same script, 'The incident must have happened after I left the party. In fact, it's the reason I left so soon; the party was getting too wild.'"

Lilly told Juan the hosts in all the parties lived in expensive and lovely homes. They were well-known in the community. Two party hosts were professionals and sent a lot of heat. Chilicot was before the Chief and the Mayor explaining why he was bothering important citizens on a little noise when kids were having drunken orgy parties every other weekend where there was a real danger of drunken driving and rape. One Vice detective told Lilly off the cuff, 'There's a lot going on we don't see on the job.' One retired West Mass cop works security in the next city hospital emergency room and he's seen some upstanding citizens there with suspicious injuries that were not from domestic abuse."

Juan challenged Lilly, "We have to inform Captain Beauregard before we investigate. I know that, but what say you and I drive by the four host party houses and get the lay of the land and also check locations on all the homes of the car plates listed?"

Loving action, Lilly agreed, saying, "Out in the field looks good to me. Sign out for us, make nice with Mason for leaving him to cover."

"Where the heck are Ash and Bill?"

"Juan, you're going to have to keep up with the sign-out sheet. They're out in the field supposedly interviewing Eleanora's relatives and friends, and Ted is out today."

"Some sign-out sheet when I can't read their destination and how come it's not logged in the computer? I can read type."

Lilly sighed. "It will be documented later, but things change. Computer history is permanent. Get it."

"The Captain allows this, Lilly?"

Lilly's response was, "One never knows how much the Captain knows, but if signing-out practices get in his way, he'll make changes. We have a 'no ask, no tell' feature here, just like the military used to have for gays. Expect change in the future, Juan, always expect change and you won't be surprised by it."

When they turned into Josh Cantor's street, they realized that the address was one street over from Eleanora Captreau's home. Lilly wondered, "Juan, do you think they knew each other? We need to know; both into maybe the aggressive sex life and living a street away."

Josh's home was one of the smaller ones on the street, but was still more of a show piece than any other home. Lilly gave her thoughts to Juan, insisting that a guy like Josh with his history of being stunning when he walked into a room, would insist that his digs would also be astounding. Juan agreed, and they made plans. Instead of driving to the other houses, they would interview all the neighbors.

Three hours later, the two detectives had cut over to the Little George's restaurant in West Springfield for coffee and ham sandwiches. They had many notes. Every neighbor knew Josh. He was considered the glamorous bachelor, who was known to be outside in his yard only to renew his tan. There were a number of people who did work at his house including one guy who put up and took down Josh's Christmas decorations which were numerous. Several women did not like him and were reticent about explaining their feelings. One lady of the house said, "Josh was always sizing me up and not in a good way. My husband thought he was cool, but I know if I'd given him the entre, he'd be in my bed. Please understand he was not enchanted by my charms, he just liked to one up; in this case it would be one-upping my husband. I couldn't stand to have him around."

Lilly believed the woman because as she explained to Juan, she is a looker but not a tease. Juan in all the interviews attempted to connect Josh to Eleanora. Only one man named Myron Coulter could make a connection. He lived in a home whose rear yard faced the rear yard of a home opposite Eleanora's. Both detectives remembered the interview of that homeowner on the day Eleanora's body was discovered. Myron had detailed that Josh had cut through his yard about a month ago on a Wednesday night. He watched him cut through his backup neighbor and go to Elenora's house. He recalled the incident for a couple of reasons: primarily because it was ten o'clock in the evening and secondly based on the stories his neighbor had told him about Eleanora's parties on some Wednesday nights. He didn't like Eleanora. He thought she was a cold, cold lady who wasn't interested in any of her neighbors. Josh was a little boy in attitude, who wanted one hundred percent of your attention and was always waiting for praise. All-in-all the detectives weren't certain the three hours spent were worth it.

Sergeant Ted Torrington had returned to the MCU office, the 'Pit,' and found only Mason Smith covering. Ted wanted to finish details on two of Leslie Hosman's work mates' interviews, but Mason needed help with calls. An hour later, Ted was consolidating his two interviews.

Leslie worked from an office in a quasi-commercial and industrial space. The office allowed for five separate and partially glassed in separated spaces. He thought it was well done and handsomely appointed. He was expected, for he had called in advance. The group tried for a group interview and appeared to be nervous. Ted said no to the group interviews and tackled the interviews, one person at a time, allowing him to hear for himself the party line they had agreed to give before he arrived. They needed, as many interviewees think they need, a point of agreement on Leslie. He concluded they were nervous and knew more about Leslie than they were comfortable discussing with the police. He wondered if any had been players in the sex games. Later he could be certain.

Abbey Fontaine was the first who, in private, was willing to discuss Leslie's life on a personal level. Ted was relentless in his questioning; enough so that Abbey cried. She said, "Leslie is this petite well-dressed doll who looks as if the angels set her on earth. Not true! She had this lovely contralto voice which she used with vendors to ensure her success. Detective, she was very successful. She also had a mean streak.

She ran this little office as if she were an empress. We were all very afraid of her, particularly me. She would call me her little mouse. I hated her. She made me feel so small and I'm five foot ten inches tall. She was always tired on Thursdays, but lately she was exhausted. Despite her exhaustion, she was really unusually agreeable on Thursdays and Fridays. She'd get into her old ways on Mondays again. She also looked like hell on Thursdays which is a big day for us. It's the day emergency orders are booked and problems on previous orders surface. Sometimes I'd feel sorry for her, but not for long. Frankly, I thought she was a closet drinker but Trinka saw her around and told me that she may be many things, but not a drinker.

"Two of the guys we sell to said Leslie was involved with a group whose tastes were more advanced. When any of us attempted to get more out of them on the subject, one explained he couldn't afford to bring on Leslie's wrath, that Leslie had his boss in her pocket."

Ted got the guy's boss's name, but could not pry out the names of the two salesmen. Ted's next interview was with Warren Thomas, who, once his office door was closed, had plenty to say about Leslie. His conversation was nerve wracking as he would stop one-time frame and start another without warning. It required Ted to pull him back, saying over and over, "When was that?"

The gist of his story was that Leslie was a member of a sexually adventuresome group and there was gossip intimating she was aggressive in pursuing a good time. When asked what constituted a good time, Warren explained he himself was into group sex and role playing. That was how he got his job here. He'd boffed the boss, and when she got tired of him and his group, she hired him to shut him up about her. Warren was spiteful, saying, "I'm great at telephone sales and support, but she upped my salary to a number big enough for me to need to stay employed by her. I couldn't look at her without thinking of our connection, but our group wasn't enough for her. She liked to hurt you, anyway you wanted it. She couldn't get me to accept physical pain, but inflicting psychological pain on me was also a turn on for her. My little group had limits. She told me once, 'You people are so bourgeoise.'

"She liked watching me want her. It was a drug for her. She looked so tiny and sexy. It was nothing but a come-on to get you addicted enough so she could hurt you. She was a bitch and I don't blame someone for killing her. Strange that she'd be strangled; that's not her favorite pursuit. She liked whips and needles or so I heard. She must have done a number on someone. Generally, she looked for people who like pain. I have my limits there and nobody else in my group had serious sadomasochistic inclinations. We're normally excited about watching each other, switching partners, and having every orifice filled."

Ted worked at keeping his composure, aware that maybe Warren could see the distress he felt just listening. He thought, *I can't believe that people like Warren, in a good but normal job, think watching himself and others meet their sexual needs in a public setting is normal. What we don't know about other people's lives. And Warren thinks his behavior is normal. He has problems with what appears to be this next step toward sexual degradation, the issue of receiving and giving pain for pleasure. Is the final step on this sex measurement tape, murder? To me, it is all degradation, but Charlotte thinks I'm a prude. I'm not. I just don't understand this lack of control and it certainly must lead to regret; maybe suicide or even murder. One has to respect one's own body and mind and soul to live a rewarding life; I know that much.*

Ted asked Warren if anyone in his group moved over to a new group, maybe Leslie's group, in the last year. He was told no, no one really was turned on by Leslie to the extent he was. He did say, "My ability to live with her control has brought me to a shrink. I think

I lean toward being a masochist and I'm in the process of getting help. My counselor is going through my life with a fine-toothed comb looking for what he calls psychological lice. There are issues there."

Ted felt compelled to investigate Leslie's history. He returned to her condo which was now taped with police tape, indicating to passers-by it was a crime scene and not a suicide. He called the Captain and summed up his two interviews. He asked him to join him on a review of the scene. Beauregard, at first wondered why he was needed, but then realized Ted would want to speak with the parents and knew that Beauregard knew them personally. He agreed and arrived at Leslie's condo in ten minutes. Ted was most interested in Leslie's picture explaining he did not see her in the same league as either Eleanora or Alison. He pointed at three pictures that showed a beautiful woman but she was petite. Her attributes were modest is how he described her to the Captain, who in return, said, "Don't just look at the physical, Ted. She may not be as showy, but that Warren guy's description is of a powerful sadistic personality and a manipulator. I do agree with one thought of yours; her condo is not loaded with pictures of herself. Eleanora's and Alison's homes had many photos displaying their faces and bodies; this one does not. I'm not a specialist in the minds of this group of sex activists, for want of a better name, but it appears there are pathological underpinnings in the minds of some of them. I had my wife Mona pull some studies off Google on S&M and the other stuff. At least three of them suggest if you combine a deviant mental disorder, my words, with S&M and other philias and sexual addiction, the result will be pathological. The goal of S&M, according to two studies, is not climax, it is catharsis.

"Look at this home. Look at these furnishings, Ted. They are cold. None of the furnishings tell us about Leslie's personality. She has no throw pillows on her couches or her bed. Her kitchen is immaculate, almost not lived in. The stainless fixtures have not one fingermark. Her clothes in her closet have little color. Do you see red, blue, green, yellow, or purple? I know we're in New England, but shades of navy, black, grey, and a few white blouses. She has two formal dresses; that's all. All her clothes are pants, shirts, jerseys, and jackets. If Leslie is part of this beautiful people, she is in charge and she is as Warren says, a sadist."

Beauregard and Ted determined the sterile environment must hold something more of Leslie's true personality. Ted, who'd worked construction to put himself through college, began looking for hidden panels behind several bookcases, while Beauregard investigated behind the clothes in the three main closets. When he had no luck, he checked the utility room and in desperation checked the built-in pantry which was loaded with canned food, pasta, and spices; all were in perfect order. Frustration alone pushed Beauregard to look more closely before he realized the pantry was not a pantry cabinet, but a closet built to resemble and blend in with the kitchen cabinets. He thought it was odd. Mona had rehabbed their kitchen and a large pantry cabinet had been added along with the new cabinetry. This pantry was permanent. He moved some of the larger cans and boxes aside and knocked on the wall. His knock gave a hollow sound.

Beauregard and Ted moved all the food onto the kitchen counters. They banged all around and when the right side was hit, two pieces of thin panel stripping that looked like molding sprung open allowing their fingers to pull open a panel door, the height and width of the inside of the pantry. An eight by ten closet was revealed. On shelving with labels, they found what they thought were accessories for sexual fantasies. One shelf held rolled up pictures. When Beauregard unrolled the first, it was a poster of Leslie almost naked but dressed in a black leather outfit that covered her arms and legs and waist but nothing else. Ted said, "I guess it's provocative, if you like mean looking bitches."

Beauregard agreed this Leslie did not look like the three pictures they had found in the condo. Every poster had Leslie in some form of dress that did not cover her well and one with a whip and a twisted smile on her face. She was, after all, a narcissist, they thought. Beauregard questioned, "If she needs to get at this stuff, does she have to move all the food every time?"

They looked carefully around and noticed a small square in the floor. Ted pressed it with the toe of his shoe and it closed the alcove. He pressed again and the door opened. They had their answer. The food items did not have to be removed for access. Ted queried his boss, "You know her parents, Captain. Did they question her personality? I don't think even loving parents could deny the controlling aspects of Leslie's nature."

Beauregard called the Porgorski's and scheduled an interview.

Both husband and wife met the detectives at the open front door of the traditional style saltbox black-stained home with a three-car garage in the rear. Ted noticed the garage had the same salt-box architectural design which in its simplicity was more stately looking than the neighboring homes. Simplicity was the name of the game in the internal décor. The décor however was welcoming. Old-fashioned braided rugs, a lit hearth, and several small upholstered couches accompanying the other plain wood chairs accounted for the warmth. The Captain led the conversation with the Porgorski's kindly but directly to the personality trait of Leslie's desire for control and secrecy. Hal Porgorski did not let the Captain continue. Instead he reacted. "Don't beat around the bush, Captain. Leslie's dead. What makes you think these traits are important in her death? You wouldn't be asking about them if they weren't important."

Bea Porgorski stopped crying and chided her husband, "Whatever caused her death, Hal, we want to know. Just answer the Captain's questions without making a federal case."

Hal and Bea explained in what Beauregard thought was a forthright, no bullshit, and no pretending nicey-nice manner. He realized how very difficult talking about Leslie was for them but they did not evade questions. The Porgorski's had three children, two girls and a boy. The other children worked in Boston and lived in suburbs outside the city. Each had two children. Leslie never seemed interested in marriage. In high school, she had several boys she dated. None kept her interest for long. She never brought any man home during her college years and thereafter. It was during her time in college when she developed her current dress style. Since she went to Tufts, they thought it was a bit of city drab style clothing. She cut her long hair in a short bob. Bea protested but was told it fit her small stature better, and when she thought better of it, Bea realized the style was really becoming. Hal explained that from the time Leslie was little, she would not hug unless she felt like it. She absolutely hated when her siblings, who were both older, would try to direct or mother her. Hal concluded that Leslie was her own girl from the day she was born.

Ted asked Bea whether Leslie had close girl friends who could give current information on her activities and friends as of late. Bea looked directly in his eyes confessing, "I doubt it, Detective. No one got close to Leslie unless she had a business reason. She was cutthroat in business, but her diminutive size and cute looks fooled most people enough so they didn't notice. I'm certain some, in looking back on their interactions, would have figured her out a bit, but then again maybe they wouldn't. She would have dinner with us once a week and always at a restaurant. She would pay. I wanted to cook for her. I'm a great cook, but she said that eating at home was suffocating to her. We were both hurt, but she was in charge. You may wonder why, but believe me if dining out was the only way we could be with our daughter, then dining out was okay with us. Strangely enough, we could pick any day of the week for dinner with the exception of Wednesday. Leslie elaborated on her tough schedules on Thursdays. We thought it was a weak excuse, given we always were home by ten in the evening."

Hal Porgorski assured the detectives when asked about her room at their house, "Room here! She left us at seventeen and never came home overnight since; didn't stay overnight in summers or during college vacations. She had internships and jobs. Leslie was never an economic burden and she never needed us. Our friends were envious. She had scholarships that paid the full boat at Tufts and she worked during college. The one trait that I can tell you about is simply that Leslie was emotionally unavailable to anybody. I dreamed someday she'd find a man who she would love. Many appear to have wanted her, but she gave every signal that she didn't care a hoot about any of them."

It took a few minutes before the detectives were comfortable leaving the bereaved couple. Outside, Rudy waxed philosophically; at least that's how Ted interpreted his words. "Alison, Leslie, and Eleanora all are physically glamorous, controlling, narcissistic, and indifferent to others' feelings. Alison was taken in an ambulance from one of these West Side forays at a 'big house' almost strangled. That's evidence enough of sexual addiction, when you almost meet your Maker for a sexual high. Why she was the 'strangleree vs strangler'? I don't know the answer, since her behavior sounds more sadistic vs masochistic. Then, again, you've explained that the strangulation is more about a therapeutic release or escape from life and not about suffering per se.

"You've found a possible connection between Eleanora and Josh. He lived two streets from her and was maybe seen going into her home on a late Wednesday night. We have seen no connection between Alison, Leslie, and Eleanora. From the investigation to date, we have knowledge that group sex is not enough for a segment of folks who require some aspect of bearing pain or inflicting pain and who know enough to keep their mouths shut. I can't really understand their needs and further don't want to, but the two things I know is that somebody will talk if we find out who attended these forays and that somebody was ticked off about being ejected from the games or from being maybe less prized by the other game players. There are more than one somebody who has been pushed out of the inner prized circle."

12

Weapons and Surprise Witness

The final report from the ME was in, and the detectives examined it, the delectable details of cause of death. Beauregard thought they all looked like vultures and told them so. Lilly protested, "It's taken too long to get the final reports. You know that, Captain. They held the three ladies' reports until they checked them against each other. Do you think it's on purpose, considering the results? Look at this one for Eleanora."

"Don't go there, Lilly. The medical examiner's office is way backed up. I'm not looking to criticize them. If they get a hunch from their preliminary exams, who am I to second guess them. Lilly, the deaths are close enough in time, getting the final all together is not abnormal. You can't find conspiracy everywhere."

"Yeah, I can, Captain. Look at what's going on in the world politically. I doubt just about everything I hear and see. It makes me better at this job."

Hearing the snickering, Juan replied, "Lilly, get off the point and get back to Eleanora's report."

Moving his head in a yes nod in agreement with Juan, Ash thought, *there's something there between those two. I'm sure. Not surprising and they do look great together. They're great partners. I hope they don't move too fast in that direction. Don't want to lose a detective in the unit.*

Lilly did read, "Confirmed injection of large not therapeutic dose of clostridium botulinum bacteria in the left neck artery which led to massive muscle, nerve, and circulatory damage which stopped the heart. Says that she had asthma which exacerbated the situation, but the dosage was maybe too high to be accidental or inadvertent. Was she murdered?"

The reports for Alison and Leslie were explicit stating death by strangulation. Unknown was the drug used in the attempted assaults the night before their murders. There was no evidence of the drug or the syringes. The attacker left nothing behind. The perp was not taking any chances. The detectives agreed the Perp wanted to kill them, but did the perp want to kill Eleanora. This was the question at hand. Ash expressed his certainty. "Three exceptionally gorgeous women dying within such a short time frame and each appearing to have some connection to active fringe sex groups, and all living in West Side; I don't have to be a detective to conclude that murder has been committed by the same perp or perps. And in my estimation, there is only one murderer here."

There was general agreement. Juan explored another idea. "Josh Cantor is connected to Eleanora's parties on at least one Wednesday night in the last three months. He was an attendee to the sex forays and he's dead. Seems reasonable to me to explore the possibility that they are all connected. We don't have the ME's report on him yet, but the preliminary report says strangulation and we've observed marks near the carotids. Screams sexual gratification and those screams indicate connection to the other murders. Captain, as you would normally say, 'I don't like coincidences.' We have coincidences here: death was in West Side, lives in West Side, attends sexual forays, and had connection to Eleanora. Can we assume they are all connected?"

Bill Border stopped them from assuming with, "Need more than that. Two weapons were used, drugs for the assault on the ladies and for the death of Elenora, and strangulation for the ladies and Josh. There must be two motives or some reason not to use the botulinum toxin A on Josh. It would have been just as easy to use to kill him. Maybe the perp was trying to steer us away from the ladies' murders or the reverse. Maybe the perp had two distinct reasons for the murders. Maybe there are two perps. Maybe there is no connection. We have to look for connections.

"I'm telling you, two of the ladies saw something. Are you forgetting two weapons were used on Alison and Leslie. Syringes and strangling, and strangling was used on Josh. Maybe Josh loved to be choked to climax in a risky setting and is the reason why he wasn't injected. We know that injecting the ladies turned out to be too difficult. The perp could conclude Josh would be too big a guy to inject, although injection is a lot easier to administer than choking a well-built victim like Josh."

Juan butted in, "Look, I agree with you, Bill. I do. There is just more here than weapons; there's motive for the weapons used and the murder setting and for the murders themselves. Why murder these women if they were part of your group, assuming the perp is in the group and assuming Josh is in the group with the women?

"Why murder within the group? It's taking a big risk for discovery. Now maybe you want to think the perp is not with it, is insane. Not true, in my mind, just not true. What do we have to work with? Wednesday night group for the last three months is the primary bit of evidence we have to work with in addition to the weapons choices. The evidence for who is within the group on those Wednesdays exists in Leslie's diary with initials -- and that is a big, maybe. We need to chase initials. We also have not interviewed Josh Cantor's family yet. What is in his background that made him such an asshole? One of you bring a picture of Josh to the Ropers'. The sister-in-law mentioned may be able to identify him as the guy seen with Alison Brunder."

Captain Beauregard embraced his detectives' statements with, "Nice summaries, detectives. Juan is on target. A major consideration is whether the murder victim, two, or three or all four were at the last Wednesday night or not. If they were, Eleanora's nosey neighbor should know. If not, then Eleanora's killer, if he or she has been part of the group, killed the others because they were potential witnesses. Killing three people to cover up the first murder is a big assumption, but certainly worth our efforts in pursuing. We have four murders we suspect are embedded in each other. Still each murder must be given independent and complete investigation. Two of you will work with Mason analyzing commonalities in what we currently know and what we will learn. Bill, you have some knowledge of one of the victims and a witness; seems reasonable for you to work with Mason. Ted, you're a specialist at details. You work with Mason also. Now let's all take some time to listen to Bill about his knowledge of Josh Cantor's family life and friends."

Bill appeared stunned that the Captain would put him under the magnifying glass in front of the other detectives. Juan took pity on him. "That's a good idea, Bill. You're the only one able to keep us from going in the wrong direction. You know all the subtleties about this guy, although from what I heard, Josh was one of the Captain's sociopaths."

Apparently digesting Juan's positivity, Bill gave some information. He asked Mason what he had discovered about Josh's family. The answer was, 'Nil.'

"I'm not surprised, Mason. He never discussed family in the almost two years we shared the condo, and no family member ever came to see him. I think he had a Mid-western accent. It sometimes came out when he was talking. He had a degree on the wall from his study at Western New England College not yet called the university; his degree was earned before the change in the institution's name. The only other thing I can help with is a list of friends' names I remember. It's been a few years. I've described them and what I remember about them in the list. I really shouldn't say friends. No one stayed friends with Josh for long. He'd infringe on everyone until he'd decide whether they had anything left to offer, then off with their heads. I now believe he wanted me as a roommate because I was a cop. We were younger then, before he had connections and made a lot of money. I did not check their initials against Leslie's list. If there is a match, I'm willing to go with another detective to interview the match. As far as his habits, I can say that Josh did no physical work. His physique was developed solely at the gym. He surely found another plastic surgeon after George."

Mason already had an answer to Bill's question about contacting Josh's graduate program for further information. He'd followed through. Josh Cantor's undergraduate degree in business was from the University of Iowa. "His high school was listed and I started searching. Things got interesting. He graduated from the Woodward Academy in Woodward, Iowa. According to its web page, and I'm summarizing it; it is a school focusing on males or females between the ages 12 and 18, who have committed a public offense that is an aggravated misdemeanor or above but not a forcible felony, had a prior adjudication of delinquency, have behavior, conduct, opposition, and/or antisocial disorders, not a diagnosis of schizoid disorders, pervasive developmental disorders, unmanaged depression and/or active psychotic disorder, impulsive and anger control and aggression problems, lack self-discipline, have a low degree of empathy for others, may be delinquent, CINA or private admission.

"No court order was necessary. I called the school and all they would give me is the address of his guardian who was not a parent. Tried locating the guardian and she had died. Called her attorney who was listed as her best friend in her obituary. He said Josh was the apple of his client's eye. She left him her estate. She believed in him despite his acting out. He wouldn't go into it further except to say Josh's parents died in a homicide/suicide pact as referenced with a letter. Neighbors thought both adults were problematic and felt very sorry for the boy who had to witness all kinds of acting out by both the mother and father."

Bill protested, "Josh told me he bought his business from his dad. If the parents died when he was in early high school, he lied."

Captain Beauregard humped, snarling, "Not surprised myself, Bill; are you really surprised? He's in a rehabilitation high school. Parents killing each other causes his acting out. From our witness who danced on the bar, we know he had no empathy for her suffering. Looks like a prime candidate for naming him a sociopath. The thing I've learned about sociopaths is that in the end, they can be conned by someone like themselves. Josh had deep sexual needs and was certainly narcissistic. His life here was a lie. How the hell did he get to West Side from Iowa? Mason, can you get his employment history which may explain his change in geography."

The Captain was giving other directions when Millie came in to the 'Pit' insisting on help from one of the detectives. "There is a woman in my office. The desk sergeant sent her up. He knows her and asked me to speak with her, since none of you answered his call. She looks normal, but she won't give me her name. I've tried every diversion to walk her out of the office. She says they're going to kill her and she wants to talk to a homicide detective not a beat cop. She is not drunk and she has no trouble speaking, but she is immovable. I've been with her for forty-five minutes, you have to help me, Captain."

Lilly jumped up responding, "I'll go, Captain. I've lots of experience with the walking wounded. If she's on a high, I'll know it."

An annoyed Millie corrected Lilly, "Sergeant, I've been around long enough to know if someone is on drugs. That's not the problem. It may be a mental health problem. She is remarkably consistent in her language and has not enlarged upon her request. She says she is frightened for her life."

Captain Beauregard decided he would speak with the visitor and left with Millie. The other detectives conferenced for a few minutes waiting for his return, but received a text from the Captain shortly saying he would meet with them again in the next A.M.

It took the Captain ten minutes of conversation before the unhappy visitor gave her name, Maura Devine. She asked that Millie leave the office. Beauregard attempted to bring her to a conference room, but she insisted she would not allow one-way mirrors and taping of her words. She stressed she knew what the police do in these situations; she saw their sneakiness on television. And she cried, moaned actually. Beauregard waited patiently and attempted not to show his discomfort while he checked her over. The woman, he realized, was well-appointed, as his wife Mona would assess her appearance. He thought he knew what his wife meant by the term well-appointed. She wore a business suit, all tailored with a stark cream-colored shirt, sensible but handsome shoes, little make-up and her hair in a topknot with stranglers of long curls hanging by her face. He guessed she may be around forty years old and he liked her looks. Further, Beauregard believed she was trying to be truthful, and he felt no vibes telling him she was nuts. He continued to wait and slowly she calmed down.

"Captain Beauregard, do I have your name right?"

"You do, Ms. Devine."

"Please call me Maura. They killed Leslie. They don't know I know everything about Leslie. I'm hoping no one knows about me, but I can't be certain. If the killer knows about me then I'm next. I'm certain. I'm so frightened. I have no friends I can talk to about this. I can't talk to the Porgorski's. They don't know about me, or Leslie and me, although we know each other."

Beauregard questioned, "How do you know the Porgorski's, Maura?"

"I grew up in a home two doors away from theirs. They are like second parents to me."

"Maura, why can't you talk to them if you have such a close relationship?"

"Captain, Leslie and I have been a couple for over twenty years. We're gay; at least I am. Leslie's anything. Gender means nothing to her when it comes to sex. Inflicting pain drives her."

Beauregard encouraged her to continue despite noticing she was tearing up again.

"We were friends in high school. When we went to college, she to Tufts and me to Boston College, the relationship grew. We've been together ever since; well not together, but together. Leslie is available for sex and friendship and, yes, love, only on her terms. She had such a strong personality and I so loved her, but I was not enough for her. I was for the first fifteen years, or so I thought. I discovered to the contrary, later; she would go out with men occasionally and even sleep with them during our years in college. When I attacked her for her infidelity, do you know what her answer was and would be, every single time?"

Rudy nodded no. She continued, "No one, but no one, owns me; not even you, Maura. I can give only so much. I need more than what you can give me sexually. I'm experimenting, don't you see? I have a need and nobody is going to stop me. I love you too, but you cry when I hurt you. Leave me be and take what I'm willing to share with you. It's all you'll ever get from me."

"Maura, why did you stay with her all these years knowing she told you she would never change?"

"Because, Captain, I loved her. She's all I've ever known in a lover or all I've ever wanted to know. Sounds incredible to you. I'm actually older than Leslie by a year. I went to Boston first for college. I never touched her in high school despite my wanting to. I didn't want to screw her up if she wasn't gay, and to this day, I don't think she is gay. She would not want to be put into any category. She wanted to be Leslie. I should never have worried about that. Leslie has always had her own agenda on life which she carefully explained was to get all her sexual needs met any way she could. Leslie gave me what she called love, but she could never love anyone. I loved her. I've spent twenty years loving her. Foolish of me, but I so miss her."

"Why do you think someone is going to kill you now that Leslie's dead, Maura?"

Maura's hand shook as she wiped tears from what Beauregard thought were her incredibly true sky-blue eyes. "Captain, I was there that night; the night Eleanora Captreau died. The murderer may have seen me. My car was nearby. He killed that Josh guy who was there that night and he killed Alison Brunder. I met Alison one night when Leslie and I were having dinner at the Casino in Springfield. I knew her. I didn't know Eleanora. Leslie told me about her. She said they were on the same wave length but Eleanora had all the gifts. She wouldn't explain."

"Maura, you're telling me you were at the sex party the night Elenora died?"

"Of course not, I'd never go to one of those parties. I'm a publicist for multiple clients. My reputation is important. They expect me to be respectable. If it got around that I went to sex parties, I'd lose some of their work. I represent churches, schools, temples, and all kinds of non-profits. No one knows I'm gay. It may not be the issue it used to be, I mean being gay, but being discrete has never lost me a client. Why do you think I asked for you, Captain? The Porgorski's respected you for your discretion when the Sunnyside Road murders happened. They knew some of the people who lived there. They knew the story."

Beauregard thought, *I can't fault her or the Porgorski's, but few know the real story and the stress it created in all of us.*

Instead he said, "Maura, what happened that night? Where were you and what did you see? How did you know that Leslie would be at Eleanora's house?"

"I'm embarrassed to tell you. I know better, but you must understand, Captain, I was obsessed with Leslie. The last few months have been the worst. Maybe it was longer than a few months, but about then I noticed her lack of interest in me or her family. Leslie always wanted to know about my clients and their problems. She was great at handling business problems and really understood how to deal with difficult people. I relied on her expertise. I mean when you deal with religious organizations, half of them have church members doing executive jobs who have no education or training in the field. Leslie helped me deal with them."

"Maura, how did you know where Eleanora lived and that a party was there? Did Leslie leave evidence around for you to see; maybe she did to make you jealous?"

"No, Leslie wasn't worried about making me jealous. I was her conquest, the little bug she toyed with. I followed Leslie, Captain. I followed her every Wednesday night for eight weeks."

Beauregard hoped he did not show his feelings as he thought, *Christmas; it's Christmas today!*

"Maura, were all the Wednesday nights at Eleanora's house?"

"No. Only several nights were at Eleanora's and different people went there. There was a smaller group of men and women, all beautiful."

The Captain asked, "Do you remember the addresses of the parties on the other six nights?"

"Of course, but I can tell you the participants were different at each place and only three other houses had parties on the other nights. Wait, I'll check my cell calendar. I've got them listed."

And she did. It was not surprising to Beauregard when Josh's and Alison's houses were listed. To his surprise, the third house listed was Dr. George Girandeau's. Beauregard had read Ash's report disclosing Girandeau's statement he had opted out of Josh's parties a long time ago -- never mentioning he had his own parties. Beauregard questioned Maura, "What about auto plate numbers, and did attendees come alone or two or three at a time?"

"Captain, I did get some plate numbers but not all; I'm sorry. Those who attended were mostly singly but one or two couples came each time except at Eleanora's. They all came singly, I think. You see, no one parked cars at Eleanora's parties. They walked to her house. And yes, I got some plate numbers at Dr. Girandeau's home because he has this big circular drive with bright lighting. It was easy. At Alison's and Josh's, I was unable to capture plate numbers. I have what numbers I got, right here."

The Captain took the numbers and asked, "Tell me step-by-step, Maura, what you did on the night of Eleanora's death?"

"Captain, I work in New York City two to seven days a month connecting with my office there. The rest of the time I work from home. It's not an unusual practice. Western Massachusetts is an ideal setting for everyday life. It sure beats the Big Apple for convenience and general lifestyle. There is, however, the problem of feeling split from my neighbors. My schedule is unpredictable. I might work a Tuesday in New York City one week and not work a Tuesday for several weeks, but several of the larger non-profits I represent as well as some ad agencies require me to connect with them personally for group meetings, and those conferences are all located in New York City. It is difficult to plan my schedule and more onerous to arrange Wednesdays in West Mass for eight consecutive weeks, but I was losing Leslie and I thought she was losing herself in her addiction. My focus was no different than if she were a druggie. I would have tried to protect her in that situation too."

Beauregard chafed at her rambling. Leslie noticed his irritability saying, "Captain, I can feel your agitation, but you must understand my situation. I had to know what the big change was, even though I knew she had found someone who shared her need to inflict pain. I imagined it was someone who could take pain, and all her friends were beautiful, far more beautiful than I am. I was insanely jealous and bereft. I was crazy."

"I won't comment, Maura. You must know you are a handsome woman. Continue with your story, please."

"Eleanora's house is set in a gardener's delight with trees and bushes everywhere. There are few cars parked on the street at night, and I had checked with my friends on community police about their schedule."

"Maura, are you telling me community police told you what times they drive through that area?"

"I know them. They know me. They were happy to tell me when I said I was concerned for a friend of mine who was visiting that area alone at night. A community police car would hit the neighborhood around nine o'clock and then around one in the morning. I knew the parties always started after ten at night. The home across the street from Eleanora's house has a row of shrubs that line the driveway all the way to the street. I parked on the lawn edge behind the shrubs at ten and waited.

"No cars came. I was concerned. I was hyper-alert on the first night. I was in the dark, for the street had no lights with the exception of house lights and low-level street lights located pretty far apart. None were near her house or the place where I was parked across the street. I almost missed the first guy; he practically slithered in. He was so lithe in his movements. The next two were together, one following the other, and were a man and a woman, but I don't think they were together as a couple. I think their timing brought them together, and I don't know why I concluded their singleness. It still seems right to me. Finally, not a group, but close together seven others walked into the house. I could be wrong on the number. I tried counting carefully. It means ten came to her party. On the second party I watched, the week before Eleanora died, I counted only four people attending the party. There may have been others who came before I arrived across the street. I wouldn't have seen or counted them.

"I left at one in the morning to avoid the police car and noticed a parking circle at the very end of the street with four cars parked. I think Eleanora instructed her friends to park there. I know that because Leslie's car was parked there. I returned later at about one forty-five in the morning and there were only three cars left that night; one was Leslie's. I waited until four in the morning and saw Leslie leaving with two cars left behind.

"On the second night I went there the second night I went there, Leslie's car was gone when I returned to the house after avoiding the community policing car. The time was one-thirty that night."

Beauregard questioned Maura on the parties at the other

homes. Similar stories were relayed. However, in those cases the cars were parked outside the homes and all the guests left at around one in the morning. Maura said Leslie was a guest at those parties. Having received evidence and lines of inquiry beyond his dreams, Beauregard had just one more question. He would ask it, and his job would be to reassure Maura would not be the next victim. Whatever Maura knew, he was convinced she would share the info. He was also quite certain Leslie never shared any information about her life with Maura. Perhaps Leslie's employee who'd been at parties with Leslie knew about Maura. If he did that could be a leak. "Maura, do you know any of Leslie's employees; maybe you attended a Christmas party for them."

"Are you kidding? Leslie would never see me socially with a group. We'd go to dinner or a play or concert together. Leslie couldn't stand public touching because she didn't want the world to – you know – to think she was with me. I was her Teddy Bear. I now see she never saw me as a lover, but as a comfort."

"A question just occurred to me, Maura. Why do you think you have knowledge making you a target of the killer?"

"You have her diary, her computer, and her date book, Captain. You must know that all those initials are a code. The murderer's initials are in there. I just know they are, but I don't have them to analyze, you have them. If the killer knows about the initials, he'll think I know who he is. He'll kill anyone to keep his secret."

Reassuring Maura took about fifteen minutes. Finally, she bought into his reassurance when he reminded Maura that Leslie wouldn't tell the left hand what the right hand was doing. He questioned whether she shared any of these details. When he got a resounding no, he told her she was safe. He gave her his cell phone instructing Maura to call him, day or night, if she had safety concerns. Maura left the station.

13

Dr. Girandeau and Others

Beauregard connected with Sergeant Ash Lent to meet at Dr. Girandeau's home. Ash made the appointment. The doctor insisted they not come to his office. Ash reminded the Captain that the doctor had sent a list of names as requested. Ash had not vetted the names. In fact, he was doing just that when the Captain arrived. While in the car, they scanned the names. Ten names were given; a few were known to them both and were also well known in the city. All the names had local addresses. It took the detectives ten minutes before they exited their vehicle, prompting an apparently impatient doctor to open his front door and walk towards them announcing, "Are you coming in or not. My neighbors will think it odd that an unmarked but clearly a police car is outside my home. It would be better if you don't mind, to park in my driveway which has more coverage. My neighbors are nosy."

Ash moved the car while Beauregard accompanied the doctor to a side garden area. Lemonade was served in tall, ornate, but plastic glasses. Dr. Girandeau questioned whether they had received all the names he had sent to Ash, and insisted he really did not have any further information beyond the short statements given accompanying the list of names. The self-assured demeanor he presented collapsed when

Ash asked him why he lied about not attending sex parties, saying, "Didn't you say you stopped attending after you realized that Josh was in a league beyond your desires?"

"Detective, Captain, what makes you believe I lied? Do I need an attorney?"

Beauregard could not help thinking, *damn professionals automatically turn to a lawyer. We're looking at him as a witness. What the hell, he believes we're looking at him as a perp.*

"Dr. Girandeau, witnesses have seen you at several sex parties in the last eight weeks. Two of the parties were held at your home. We have license plate numbers of the cars present on those occasions. I sincerely hope the names you have given include all the owners of those cars."

Clearly struggling to control his temper, the doctor suggested he did host two parties, but couldn't understand why the detectives thought they were sex parties. Ash, with a nod from the Captain, replied, "We do not want to arrest you, Doctor, not at this time, but suggest you take a ride to the station with us. You are a material witness in this case and we are concerned for your welfare. Your lawyer can meet us there."

Girandeau shook with overall palsied movements. Beauregard was concerned. He thought the doctor did not look well at all. He also doubted that Girandeau had the determination or the risk-taking trait to do the kills, despite his ability to use a hypodermic needle with ease. Ash watched the Captain for a sign to arrest the doctor. Instead the Captain spoke firmly, saying, "Doctor, stop the nonsense. We have so many witnesses to your two parties. You will not be successful in your lies even with the best attorneys. I don't think you killed anyone. I do think you know the killer. You may not know you know the killer, but you do. Do not think, however, I won't move heaven and earth to find this murderer and if your life becomes public during the process because you are not smart enough to assist us; well, then so be it."

The detectives waited for the Captain's words to sink. The moment of silence extended to several. The detectives showed no discomfort in the silence, while the doctor tensed and sweated profusely. Ash thought the doctor's sweating was unusual for a man in such good shape and wondered if he was on something. Doctor Girandeau broke the silence. "No one I know would kill or could kill; maybe suicide if he or she were using a choking method without a partner. I'll give you the list of those at my parties, and yes, Josh and the other two ladies murdered were party guests, at least at one of my parties. For your information, I was never invited to Eleanora's parties. She said I had not developed enough sexually. She was such a bitch. She wanted all my connections for injections for cosmetic work, but in return, said I wasn't developed enough sexually. She was just a wicked dominatrix, but she was even more than that. She didn't want to help you find nirvana. She wanted you to suffer emotionally, to beg for more after you've hit bottom and then tell you, you're not good enough. She should have been murdered. She's pathological. So were Josh, Alison, and Leslie. Actually, Alison was the most normal, but was enthralled with the next high for meeting her needs. Leslie wanted to be Eleanora, but whatever I say about Eleanora, she was one of a kind. Nobody was as classy. She was like a surgical knife when she cut you out emotionally. She loved watching you squirm. Didn't matter if it was physical or mental pain; she got off. And afterward you wanted to be with her. She had a special kind of attraction and it was addictive. Someone killed her; I didn't expect that."

The detectives soon left the doctor's home after telling him this was not a good time for a vacation.

Rudy was trimming the rhodies and azaleas in the back of his property. He had placed a cart on wheels next to him containing two Poland Springs water bottles and various garden tools. He seriously looked like a man who was enjoying himself immensely. Sometime during his marriage, about the second year as he and Mona were ensconced in this house, he discovered his love of shrubbery and flowers and grass and the silence of the outdoors. He'd never admit it; rather he complained vociferously to his friends. His boys were intelligent enough at an early age to avoid the back-garden area when their dad was working. Rudy knew they figured, why go there and be invited to assist. What they did not understand was he loved the quiet. In fact, it was the only time when quiet was available for him. Even Mona let him be. He truly believed wives were happiest when their husbands were working on or around the house, at least his Mona was.

The boys had set up earphones for his iPhone and he was listening to the Red Sox game. West Side residents were divided on their allegiances. Seventy-five percent loved all Boston teams, while the others were split on some sports, but certainly leaned towards the Yankees for baseball. Rudy loved all Boston teams and his three sons did not deviate from this parental mantle. Trimming away, Rudy's absorption in the beauty of nature surrounding him was interrupted by Mona offering him a tall and frosty lemonade. "Thought you might need added incentive to continue this hard work, Rudy," Mona said with a chuckle.

His husband antenna went up. He thought, *something's on her mind. That I am certain.*

"What's up, Mona? You wouldn't normally interrupt my productivity in the garden."

Not particularly surprised he caught on, she replied, "Rudy, it's not easy being married to a detective and you don't help. I do have something that's been on my mind and it seemed a good time, when you are so relaxed, to ask you. I'm hoping you won't put me off and tell me I'm nuts."

Rudy motioned by taking off his earphones and they moved to one of the three table and chair sets in the yard. Mona continued, "Drink your lemonade while I talk, Rudy. You do look warm from work and if you are sipping you won't be able to interrupt.

"Some of the teachers at the high school are talking about your murder cases. Frankly, they want info from me. They know better, but they don't leave it be. I can tell you this, Rudy, what they are saying belongs in a porn soap opera. You've not said, nor have the papers written, what the teachers have said. I've heard the students giggling over S&M practices as the settings for the murders. I would normally just get my gossip from them and then try to surprise you with my knowing so much, but there is a problem."

"Okay, Mona, spit it out. Don't hold back. I can't imagine why you would have a problem related to these murders."

"One of my teacher friends at school approached me at lunch and quizzed me on the murders and your thoughts on the murders. She said, 'Are they looking at the sex parties held in the area. If not, they should be.' What is amazing about her approaching me is, Rudy, she is almost non-social. The other teachers who've worked with her for years explained she divorced her husband a few years ago, and she's never been the same since. It's seems pretty dramatic to me that the first social one-to-one interaction I've had with her and she talks about sex parties. I wondered if she knew more, but I didn't want her to think I would go to you with her conversation. I asked almost nothing."

"Mona, what is your friend's name?"

Mona appeared upset at the question. She pleaded, "Rudy, you can't talk with her. Please, she spoke in confidence and she was quite nervous. Dorie wanted to help but not be involved. I'm certain she has some knowledge or she never would have spoken to me. She told me her husband was a very decent person and she wanted no scandal. What that means to me is that she thinks she is at risk."

"You know, Mona, I tire of good citizens who want to tell me a little bit, but not the whole story. Their hesitancy prevents good police work. You know how I feel about this issue. I do have a problem. The problem I have is that Ash and I were scheduled to call Dorie Shulman for an interview. Now, with you, I feel I have handcuffs on me. I wish you'd never told me; but be certain, I will figure a way to interview Dorie Shulman."

"You already knew about her potential involvement, Rudy? Why didn't you tell me before I started telling you? I feel somewhat setup."

Smiling, Rudy almost sneered, "You mean more than you setting me up with a glass of lemonade?"

"You know what I mean, Rudy. I am disappointed."

"Stop right there, Mona, I didn't know Dorie was a teacher and could not have known what you were going to say. If I had, I would have avoided the conversation. Have some faith, Babe. I would never compromise you."

West Mass MCU detectives were present en masse at baby Carlotta Locke's Christening, at least for part of the event. The detectives had traded off equal amounts of time amongst themselves to allow each detective to cover the unit for a segment of two shifts, with Juan as always volunteering for the biggest apportionment of hours.

Baby Carlotta was big stuff attracting her admiring detective crowd. Celebration with Petra and Jim was a welcome diversion from the abysmal murders of beautiful people.

The day was pleasant, but a little cool. A borrowed commercial grill, accompanied with the professional expertise of its restaurant owner, who continuously produced fabulous shish-ka-bob to the more than fifty in Carlotta's loving audience, satisfied appetites. Jim and Petra, hosts extraordinaire, shared the gorgeous baby, limited only by both grandmothers pulling their own holding times. Beer and wine flowed, while Petra's dad gave everyone tours of the couples' relatively new home and its manicured grounds, for which he single-handedly was responsible.

Mona and Rudy, joined by two of their boys, were stuffing some cake down, when Petra's mom brought a woman over to meet them. Mona suddenly coughed as if she were choking, when the woman said, "Don't worry, Mona. I knew you were married to the Captain when we had that conversation. You spoke in innocence allowing me to examine my thoughts. Captain, I'm Dorie Shulman, a good friend of Mrs. Aylewood's. She told me I could trust you; I know I can trust your wife. Do you have a few minutes to talk with me, not at the station but here, and alone?"

Rudy made a split-second decision he hoped he wouldn't regret. Leading her to a grape arbor at the end of the yard, he questioned, "What is it that you want to tell me, Mrs. Shulman?"

Dorie appeared confused. "I thought you would want to ask me questions about Eleanora. Don't you need information on her? Eric explained I needed to speak with you about her."

Motioning for Dorie to sit on one of the benches in the shaded arch, Rudy confirmed what Eric had said. "I am pleased Eric spoke with you. He said you and Eleanora were friends, and perhaps you could be helpful. You are on the list for a scheduled interview. I'm surprised you haven't been called yet."

"I figured as much, Captain, which is why I decided to come here today. I am not, nor ever was, Eleanora's friend. Friendship goes two ways, Captain Beauregard, and unfortunately Eleanora was a one-way street when it came to any form of relationship. Just ask Leonora, who tried to be her best friend, but alas was looked upon as a maidservant who didn't meet muster. Nobody could satisfy Eleanora including relatives, employees, and so-called friends. When I look back on my life then, Captain, I am ashamed. It was vacuous, void of any meaning. I didn't have or want children, or so I thought. I didn't appreciate Eric and his loving ways. I thought our lives were boring. We had everything. I wasn't working. I had no goals but the pursuit of belonging to the in-group of beautiful people; it was junior high thinking all over again. I was a spoiled needy brat and ruined my marriage and my life. Eleanora was a magnet for me. I never asked questions. If she said something was important, then I thought it must be important. I did cosmetic injections I didn't need because she found little flaws in my face. If I had a few less cocktails and went to bed early, those flaws would have disappeared on their own.

"Then, she changed my wardrobe. I started wearing revealing clothes. Next, Josh came onto me. Or, so I thought. She planned it. Josh has no allegiance to any one person of either sex. He made me think I was special. I did not sleep with him, but allowed him too close, if you know what I mean, Captain. He was the entrance to being invited to the post cosmetic party. Everyone knew about the after party. Only select individuals were invited, and not until the night of the party. Not every cosmetic party had an after party at the time I was attending the cosmetic events."

Beauregard asked, "Who attended the cosmetic parties, Dorie? Was there a professional running the program? Who bought the Botox and other injectables?"

"Initially, Dr. George was in charge. He trained Josh Cantor to do all the work. Eleanora conducted the process, telling each of us what was best for our faces. She arranged with Dr. George for body work at his office. I never needed body work. Josh said I had a perfect body for a non-working model, as did Elenora. I was so pleased to be put in her category. Then Dr. George just disappeared from the scene and Josh trained Leslie in the craft. She was more proficient. We all trusted her. Her hand was steady. She remarked that I was the best at handling any connected discomfort. I thought it was a compliment; instead it was a lead in for her and Eleanora. It meant I could take pain. I didn't know that then."

"What happened to have you run away from the parties, Dorie?"

Straightening her shoulders, Dorie quietly sighed her answer. "I was finally invited to an after party. When the other guests left, one of them, Alison Brunder told me how fortunate I was to be invited and not to blow it. She said I should go along with any suggestion made. At first, I was treated like a star, applauded by the seven or eight people who were there. They then broke off into little groups with some disappearing into two of Eleanora's bedrooms. Josh was all over me, and I was about ready to remind him I was married when Eleanora came over and said he should leave me to her. I'm telling you, Captain, she was psychic. She saw I was uncomfortable. She gave me a drink of some whiskey called Pappy Van Winkle Bourbon. I told her I mostly drank wine and she assured me I would relax better with the bourbon and that it was very expensive and she would not offer it to just anyone. I think there was something in the bourbon. Maybe I think so because I let her undress me after a few minutes. Josh handled me by touching my body, caressing me, and swooning over me until Eleanora stood over me talking about how bad I was to let Josh touch me, a married woman, and she pinched my breasts and then rubbed the pain away.

Do I have to tell you the rest, Captain?"

"Tell me what is necessary for me to see what extent they went to. Were you raped? How much pain did Eleanora inflict on you?"

"She wouldn't let Josh enter me. She said, 'You're very naughty, Josh. She wasn't ready. You can't have her. I'll deal with you later.' He looked very happy and walked away, but she wasn't through with me. She had the most lustrous and throaty voice that so comforted me as she told me that I was a sinner with a sinner's body and what could I expect but to be punished. I remember thinking that I should run away, but to my shame I enjoyed it and she hurt me, over and over with ropes and a whip until I passed out. When I came to, I was groggy, but saw her choking Josh while two people watched. I knew it was the dregs of hell I was in. I grabbed my clothes and ran home. I could not face my husband. It was early in the morning when I got home. He was asleep.

"That's it, Captain. I left Eric. It was not easy to do. I realized later, when I finally saw a therapist, that I am a masochist. My childhood was troubled, but cleared up later when my mother remarried a fine man. My therapist explained my childhood experiences allowed for my letting the wrong people into my life. According to her, my marriage to Eric was fortuitous. She thinks I should tell Eric all about this. I haven't yet, but I think he's guessed already. My working as a teacher has helped. I needed to be needed; right now, that's all the acceptance I want. Why don't parents talk to their children, Captain?

"My mother has told me some things about my father she should have told me before. She understands my need to be accepted. She said, 'That's okay! The need to be accepted is okay! But...but, there are limits. There should be limits on the kinds of people you associate with. You must know yourself and your limits. You wouldn't be suffering so much from one night's experience, if you weren't a moral person.' Finally, she said I had no right to punish Eric just because I didn't understand myself."

Beauregard sat quietly for a long time. Ending his silence, he said, "Dorie, who else was there on that evening and other evenings? I need a complete list of names. If you don't have last names, first names and descriptions and other related information will do."

Dorie promised Beauregard he'd have them before she left the party. She was about to walk away when the Captain said, "Dorie, just about every person I know has regrets about an event. Many drank too much at an important celebration and acted the fool. They don't get a divorce over it. They know they were foolish. They recover and allow their friends and loved ones to forgive them. Go see Eric. You owe him and you're a good person. You don't want him blaming himself."

Dorie nodded and whispered a thank you as she walked back to the main gathering.

Detectives Tagliano and Flores knocked on the door of Bart Brunder's home. The condo, although understated in a simple design, was large and quite handsome. Bart answered the bell and without allowing them to introduce themselves, he said, "You must be the detectives Al Roper told me to expect. Come on in."

The condo, professionally appointed in cool and contemporary styling, did not show any personal signs of the owner. The detectives settled in at the kitchen table which made Juan quite comfortable, while Lilly thought, *guy's living alone. If a woman lived here she'd know enough to bring us to the living room or at least to the family or great room. I like the looks of Bart Brunder. What's the matter with some women today? This guy is great husband material; I can just tell.*

Bart talked about Alison, while making coffee, without waiting for questions from the detectives. His tale coincided with their previous interviews. Juan in an attempt, at least to Lilly's mind, to throw Bart off a rehearsed rhetoric, asked, "Just what have you done since your divorce from Alison? Did you ever see her around or meet with her? Do you now have another significant person in your life?"

"Not much, Detective. I've not done much with my life other than work. The marriage to Alison took the shine off -- for relationships, I mean. I should have caught the signals before we married. I was enthralled with her. I loved the Ropers; I thought she would be just like them. Wrong, kids are not necessarily duplicates of their parents. Who am I to assume that what I want is what she would want? We had a great sex life. Ha! Or so I thought for a while, but not for her! She wanted something I still can't wrap my head around. I was boring to her. My friends, both women and men, think I'm fun. Not so for Alison; no, I was a bore. The divorce was not vicious after we agreed on terms, and that was done pretty quickly. I recognized I was out of the loop with Alison. Her parents had a harder time."

Lilly questioned Bart about Alison's friends. His response was Alison really had no friends. His friends were her friends. She was a loner, but the life of any party. He said Alison had no compulsion to please. He'd questioned his mother-in-law Janet asking if he himself was the problem. She kindly told him it was just who Alison was and was not a fault of anyone else. Alison took care of Alison's needs and if you could fit into those needs, then she treated you well. He said, "I no longer fit into her needs."

"Alison was a glossy apple with a worm in it; you don't know the apple is rotten until you take a bite. She was all bright and shiny on the outside with rot in the middle. You can see, Detectives, just look around you at this sterile space I occupy. I've not gotten over this marriage. Believe it or not, her death doesn't help. You'd think it would but it doesn't. I still remember the shiny apple and my anticipation of a life with a stellar future. What a laugh on me, because I did not listen to my sixth sense."

Juan asked, "What did your sixth sense tell you that you ignored, Bart?"

"Alison was all about accomplishing the next thing on her list. She would look at others and attempt to best them at golf, wedding planning, fashion, or anything. Planning a wedding created a gorgeous bridezilla out of Alison. I thought at the time it was the stress of tying the knot, and perhaps it was. She probably knew in her heart she was going to kill our relationship or what I thought was our relationship. Even before our marriage, Wednesday nights were not in the playbook for any type of date or appointment. The Justice of the Peace tried to schedule our consultation on a Wednesday night. They were the Justice's free nights; Alison nixed every Wednesday night. I questioned her. Her answer was that hump day was her day to relax and to do what pleased her. I realized then that we never saw each other on a Wednesday night, and never did after the honeymoon. See, I should have known.

"We were to attend a wake for a friend's mother who had died. It was on a Wednesday evening from seven to nine, and Alison insisted we go to the funeral instead on a Thursday requiring both of us to take off a day from work. Alison hated funerals. I should have known then."

Juan asked, "Just when did you know about her activities and what did you know?"

"Probably about six months into the marriage. I received a call on my cell. It may have been someone we knew like a friend or neighbor. I didn't recognize the voice and the number was blocked. I don't often give out my cell. I still don't know who the caller was; he said I should know what Alison was up to. Next thing is he's telling me she's a masochist and loves to be hurt -- better I know now than have kids with her. He hung up."

Juan pushed for more, saying, "What did you do?"

"Nothing for a while. I watched my wife in everything she did. I realized the verboten nights, Wednesdays, needed an explanation. When confronted, Alison became an animal and physically attacked me. She wanted me to hit her. I remembered what the caller told me. I backed away thinking she either wanted me to hit her for evidence of wife abuse so she could divorce me, or she really was a masochist. I did nothing for another nine months. I'm ashamed to say I rigidly used protection in sex. She never questioned me and we never discussed having children."

Lilly wondered, *this guy put up with all these months of this double dealing. Is he nuts? Can't be that nice or stupid, can he? I like him. Like the Captain says, nice people are suckers for narcissistic sociopaths. In this case the sociopath is also a sex deviant who loves pain but gives psychological pain to a husband who loved her. What is love? Seems to me a misguided word to cover our desires for what we think we want. I'd make a lousy wife. I wouldn't take any nonsense from a husband. Well, marriage isn't in my near future, so I don't have to worry myself.*

Juan pushed on. "Bart, after enduring this stress for months what did you do? Did you finally confront her?"

"No, Detective, I've never been a match for Alison in an argument. She didn't obey any rules on logic or fairness. I knew I needed evidence. My marriage was eating me up inside. Janet and Al treated me like a son. They knew there were marital problems but they are good people. People like that can't imagine their beautiful and smart little girl would be into that kind of stuff. They'd have blamed themselves like I did at first. No, I followed her on Wednesday evenings."

Juan asked him to continue. "Detective, it was the same every

Wednesday night for the first month and then she stayed later at these parties when they were moved to Eleanora Captreau's home. At those parties she stayed until three in the morning. It was after Eleanora's third party that I put it all together. On those Thursday mornings, Alison was charming to me and solicitous and well: she acted all lovey-dovey. Whatever was going on at those parties must have been like smoking pot. You know, she got laid back and all. Except Alison mostly didn't do drugs, just an occasional Ambient."

Lilly asked, "When did you figure out they were sex parties, Bart?"

"Not for a bit. Alison didn't come home for two nights. I'd not followed her that night. She called and said she was bunking with a friend. What a joke, and of course, I knew she was lying. She'd never 'bunk' and she had no friends. She wasn't even trying to give me a good lie. From that lie alone, I knew the marriage was over."

Lilly said, "So you knew the parties were sex parties solely from Alison's use of language. I wouldn't know. I would think instead she'd done drugs or was drunk out of her mind. How'd you know?"

"I wasn't finished, Detective. Two days later, I was home, sick with an intestinal bug. I received a call from Noble Hospital doing a follow-up survey on Alison's stay there. Although I carry her insurance, they wouldn't give me information because of patient privacy. Following the hospital call, I came home pretty regularly to capture the mail and after a few weeks I got the insurance payment with a co-pay listed. I won't say how, but through a not quite kosher method, I got her hospital file for that day. It said it all. Even I know what strangulation means when your wife is gone every Wednesday night and grows more distant, and unkind every day. I understood at that moment I could never, nor would want to give Alison what she wanted."

Juan asked, "What did you do with this knowledge? You must have done something."

"Initially I approached the situation as if I was interested in going forward with our marriage and suggested she see a shrink. I think I half believed she'd go along at that time. I was still stupid. Her reaction was interesting. In essence, she explained her determination to live her own life in the way she needed. Notice she said 'needed,' not wanted. I had some hope for a moment, but it was dashed when she laughed at me telling me I was just as naïve and unsophisticated as her parents. She told me to get out; to give her the house and get out. She also wanted half my pension. I may be on the younger side, but my 401k has a lot of money."

"Bart, we know you gave her the house, how much more did she get from you?"

"Not a penny more! I told her I would make her sexual practices known to family and friends, and go for a guardianship, using her hospital stay as evidence. She must have believed me because she actually got in a left hook to my cheek and left a large bruise. In front of her, I took a selfie, and started calling Attorney Norberto Cull. He's her family's lawyer."

"And…," asked Lilly.

"She cried and when tears didn't work, she was more amenable to common sense. We negotiated a settlement on the spot including statements we would both use to calm her family and friends. My family's emotions did not matter to her. To be frank, they never liked her and when I told them, they were relieved I was getting out of a bad situation. That's all I can tell you."

Lilly commented, "Bart, you can't tell me you just went on with your life."

"Detective, does this home look like I've gone on with my life? My house is sterile, it's nothing but a hideout for me to grieve and wallow in my stupidity. I hired an interior decorator when I moved in.

She was stressed by my lack of involvement telling me it is my home and I should want my personality to show through. I told her I no longer have a personality."

14

Lists and Neighbor

Two days later, the detectives figured they were on the hot seat. The Captain scheduled a meeting with an agenda calling for lists. Taken together, there were so many lists. Ted said it was like having a two-day hangover when you just couldn't see how you would ever feel good again. Stress in the room was almost palpable. It was particularly obvious when Ash volunteered to man the daily calls sent through while the others met. Ash, a consummate musician whose long lean body treasured movement, was not comfortable talking to the crazies of the day.

Bill Border's perspective, which he continually shared with the others, spoke of their fears: it'd been close to two months since the golf course murder and they hadn't even honed in on a person of interest. Bill announced, "No new murder is a good thing, right? If there are not additional murders, then it's as the Captain inferred before, murders with a motive. Trouble is we're heading for a cold case if we don't come up with something."

Lieutenant Petra Aylewood-Locke breezed into the room, shouting, "I'm back to work. Watch out. I've learned some new skills taking care of Carlotta. Like you babies, she wants her own way. Well, I'm the tough parent and Jim's the pussy cat. I hate leaving her, but the Captain and the Chief have given me a thirty-hour work week for the next two months. It'll be a piece of cake compared to four walls, house cleaning, and caring for a baby. Tell me, why haven't you solved these murders? You need me, right?"

Lilly laughed, spouting, "And I thought these hyenas were full of themselves. Look at chu! Talk about ego."

Beauregard walked in, welcomed Petra, asked about Carlotta and without taking a short breath started quizzing. "What have you prioritized from your lists? Let's go over all the autopsy and site reports in order of the murders. Juan and I have separately concluded, we are looking for a motive for four murders. What evidence proves we are on the right track? Are we looking for a single murderer, or are there more than one working on a joint plan?"

Petra, always one to jump into the fire first which explains her moniker 'Bolt' said, "At home, I've been pumping Jim on the psychology behind the S & M behaviors, which I hastily called psychopaths. He says psychopathy is not a mental illness; it is defined by criminal statutes and not by the <u>Diagnostic and Statistical Manual of Mental Health Disorders/ DSM-5</u> published by the American Psychiatric Association, or any other classifications of diseases. Got that; I had to memorize the title and I think the psych people just like to confuse us ordinary folks. However, and I'm not certain I'm summarizing his statements perfectly, Jim told me about the differences between Narcissists and Narcissistic Antisocial Personality Disorders (NAPD). Narcissists do everything for attention and to gain admiration. NAPDs are in for gain in status and wealth and whatever fairytale of their lives they've invented. They are very controlling. They use adaptive behaviors to get what they want. Some of those adaptations include changing their personas to meet their needs, controlling their life stories with embellishments and lies, and controlling others to get them to comply with their made-up world. Narcissists trust. NAPDs don't trust. Trust infers losing control and NAPDs won't allow loss of control. Narcissists, although normally more passive and not proactive, can plan revenge if they are severely injured. NAPDs are really superior to narcissists in long-term planning to get even."

Ash responded, "I think I get the gist of what you're saying, Petra. I also think carrying out sexual drives with pain as an accepted norm for further sexual pleasure is, at the very least unhealthy, and in my mind, abnormal. I don't care if you give pain or get pain to feel relieved; it's nuts. I mean if I got a high from stealing, if it made me less stressed like it does for a kleptomaniac, the practice is unhealthy for society and for the klepto. What drives these people to be so obsessed with their own beauty and still let themselves be harmed, or alternatively be so obsessed with others' beauty but then want to harm them, all to 'come off?' Basic to all of this is we have one man and three women who are into this negative play and are murdered. Motives, we each have thoughts. I, for one, think the murderer may be sensitive and may have been excluded from the 'real fun' group that met from eleven at night to three in the morning. Exclusion from a group is a powerful punishment. We know how that works for high schoolers."

Lilly announced, "Jealousy is always a motive. Eleanora is at the top of the food chain when it comes to practicing sadism both psychologically and physically. A rival in sadism could have been jealous of her. Some of the party players may know who was jealous. I'm thinking the other deaths are a cover-up because Leslie, Alison, and Josh were in the know and were at the last party before the actual murder night."

Petra responded, "Or were excluded from the last party."

Bill said, "I like the concept of cover up. It is the only explanation for killing all of them and since Eleanora was the first to die, her death requires our first full attention."

Ted quietly offered, "If you think about it, the four vics were not nice folks even considering their lives outside of their sexual practices. They offended lots of people both within their sex groups and outside. They were almost vicious, making them ripe for murder. Or bigger than their nastiness, they lived beyond cultural rules. Society doesn't like rule breakers. It could be an individual punishing a bunch of sexual sinners."

A thoughtful looking Beauregard sat quietly and let the detectives continue in their discussions of motives, while he looked at the murder boards and checked the lists in front of him. Interrupting after a few minutes he said, "We have possible motives and if we follow them with evidence already existing, we finally may have a direction in what the British call an 'inquiry.'"

Ignoring the detectives' smirking at the conference table, the Captain continued discussing the evidence, including the various interviews. He asked, "We haven't discussed in detail the weapons used. Let's take a look at the autopsy reports."

Juan recalled without searching for the report, "From memory, Captain, the reports on the choking clearly state silk as the thread. I remember the Lab mentioned using some technical name for Raman Spectroscopy and found a few threads. All were silk. All were from what they said must have been very tightly woven since few fibers escaped; they must have been printed material. The fibers collected in each case were multiple in color. The scarfs used, were made of high-quality silk. Our perp or perps used high quality scarfs without a thought of losing them. Maybe he's careless and didn't plan the murders; don't think so. If he's not a serial murderer, he probably won't keep fetishes. I think he'd be smart enough to get rid of the weapons. He certainly planned the murders; he planned using his own high-priced scarfs. I think it's personal, and it may be interpreted as each victim was important to the perp, and he would only use a weapon in keeping with their significance to him. Otherwise, why not just use common hardware rope?"

"And what about the drug used on Eleanora," asked the Captain. "What was it?"

"Says here, Captain, 'clostridium botulinum'," replied Mason. "Want me to read all the Latin and gobbledy-gook; not much more than we've already assumed except the ME has basis for his decision."

Petra pointed out the fact Eleanora was an asthmatic, but the Medical Examiner thought despite that, the dosage may have been great enough to kill her if she were not asthmatic. Petra insisted, "A good defense attorney could maybe use this fact for wiggle room for an accidental death. I'd like us to look at all our interviewees and discover how many knew Eleanora was asthmatic. Was her asthma common knowledge?"

Ted liked Petra's comment and said so. He initiated a discussion on the drug. Who would have access to that much Botox; after all, he heard Botox was only used for around the forehead? Other injectables are used in other areas of the face. He didn't know what was used in the body, saying, "It's not simple. There are so many brand names for various drugs used to erase wrinkles and fill out areas. Who would know about them? Supposedly, the earlier in the evening parties were cosmetic parties. Is that true for all the parties? We've license plates on some of the party-goers and someone should be able to tell us who brought the drugs. Dr. Girandeau, Charlie Logan, and Leslie have all been mentioned. We have to rule them out in Eleanora's murder. Leslie could have killed her, but who supplied the drugs? If Leslie killed her, why was Leslie murdered? It could be she was murdered by the drug supplier, who did not want to be connected to Eleanora's murder, which by the way, could have been accidental and the other three murders are a cover up for the drug purveyor."

Bill thought Ted was making complications whereas he himself was certain the murder indicated someone who didn't pass muster and was ejected from the special group. He insisted that jealousy and loneliness are powerful motivations. Lilly, always the cynic, insisted it was a cover-up of Eleanora's murder or accidental death. It made sense to her, saying, "If you were the drug supplier in Eleanora's murder, you'd get time for it, especially in this environment. Nobody's going to feel sorry for the supplier of cosmetic drugs to the beautiful people."

Beauregard had had enough and insisted they divvy up the re-interview cases and the new interviewing cases, saying, "We haven't interviewed the cousin's husband, nor the neighbor from across the street."

Next, he asked Ash to pull his notes on his second interview with Reggie, the nosey neighbor saying, "Reggie must have known more about who was in and out. I wish I'd been there for the second interview. Ash, did he say anything that would make you second guess him for a stalker?"

Before Ash could reply, Mille entered the conference room and noticing folders all over the table, sighed. "I want to yell at you about this mess of files on the table, but community policing called. There is a suspicious death in Eleanora Captreau's home, despite there still being police tape around the entrance to the home. The body is, as of now, an unidentified man."

"He's Reggie Sutten, the next-door neighbor, the major gossiper, the watcher. I wanted him for the perp. I was certain," stated a defiant and upset Sergeant Bill Border. "He would have been perfect with his bird's eye view and his supposed disapproval of the goings on."

Captain Beauregard shook his head in a 'no' and said, "Too easy, Bill. It's never that easy. I do believe it confirms Ted's thoughts about a cover up. The perp believed Reggie knew something that Reggie didn't know he knew, or else he would have spilled his guts that morning. Reggie was a talker. An alternate idea is possibly Reggie found the perp here, but there are no signs of struggle. Reggie is displayed exactly, as Millie first told us, in Eleanora's position. This room or perhaps even this house is not the killing site. I'll call Mason to get a search warrant for Reggie's house. Have a uniform keep an eye on his house; no entry or exit until we get the warrant."

Bill said, "Guys, Reggie let the perp get close. He knew the perp. Reggie was in top physical shape; maybe Eleanora or one of her friends were playing him for laughs. Could be that person is the perp, and was frightened Reggie would tell all to us."

A uniform approached the Captain. "Captain, there is an old lady outside. She wants to speak to 'the cop in charge,' that's exactly what she said and she won't say what she wants. Want me to get rid of her?"

Beauregard smiled and stated, "Absolutely not! I'll come outside and talk to her there. Old ladies and little kids are sometimes my best friends. Hope that's so this time." Beauregard thought, *three kids helped me find the 'Spider,' solving a drug infestation and several murders, and old ladies see what the rest of us are too frantic running around to take a look at the big picture or small details. Kids and old ladies try my patience but help me in my work.*

Beauregard walked out the front door. A minute later Officer Cadery introduced a spare woman probably in her eighties and appropriately named, Mrs. Sparey, who said, "Call me Millicent, Captain Beauregard. I've read all about you. You caught a mess this time. I've been reading about those ladies and the guy killed on the golf course; they've all been here visiting poor Eleanora. Don't think for a minute, I approve of her goings-on. I don't. She is not her mother's daughter, not by a long shot. She lost her way. I don't understand the genetics here. I know all about their families, both her and her cousin. I never heard any of them doing sex things they shouldn't be doing."

Mrs. Sparey stopped to breathe, giving the Captain an opportunity. "Mrs. Sparey, are you up to taking a short walk while we talk privately?"

Apparently quite happy the police were taking her seriously, Millicent, after telling the Captain she would rather he used her Christian name, followed him. Once settled on their walking path, she pulled out a carafe of something liquid from her oversized purple leather bag, took a slug, and smiled.

Beauregard wondered, *have I made a mistake here. Perhaps she's nuts, but if she knows all the players!*

Doing his best to be patient, he asked her just when did she see all the murder victims. Millicent laughed at him and summarized six months of her being what she called 'a good neighbor.' "Captain, right away, I saw the lack of diversity in the party attendees. That's not normal. No, it is not."

Before she could continue, the Captain asked, "What is it that you used to do, Millicent; it sounds as if you were police or a social worker."

"Close, but no cigar, as they say. I was a psychiatric social worker. First, I was a nurse, but hated it. I like to know what ticks in the brain and watch behaviors. Had a great career, until my doctors told me to slow down. Should never have listened to them, but I did! On the positive side, and I do believe in staying positive, life has been good with all this free time. I am now intently interested in and focused on all around me. At ninety years old, I can't abide negativity; never could. It brings everyone down."

Beauregard thought, *and I can't abide stream of consciousness in telling*

facts. Ninety years old, what kind of a witness would she make in court…
if she lived long enough to testify?

"Millicent, I interrupted you. Please go on with your observations. They may be important to the murders and, in particular, to this case."

"Captain, I know Reggie was murdered! He did not belong in this house and he's been going in and out for a few days now. He'd watch for the community policing car which from my calculation has gone by every thirty-five minutes. Its route is pretty small and they have been diligently covering our area since Eleanora's death; they weren't so conscientious before then."

"I wish, Millicent, you had called the department when you saw him going in the house."

"Captain, I did call the department and I wish I had asked for you, but I didn't think it was more than Reggie's obsession with Eleanora. He probably wanted to touch her things. He wanted her sexually, but couldn't even get in her door. How could he? She would have thought him common and rough; certainly, he was not subtle? His sneaking in there makes a little sense if you lived in his warped world. And Captain, I was surprised no one from the police ever answered my calls."

"Tell me how you knew about the guests attending Eleanora's parties, Millicent. The parties all started late in the evening."

"Captain, my husband's been gone for twenty-two years. He was such a dear and so scheduled. He kept me on a good sleeping routine. Poof! It was gone the minute he left me, to die early. Selfish, don't you think to leave me alone like this?" And Millicent laughed assuring the Captain it was a little joke.

She continued, "I am up most nights and sleep until eleven most days. I've never really liked mornings and just suffered rising early to please Lyle, my husband. Poor dear and such a worrier about me; and he dies and I live.

"I better get back on track… Eleanora's house is the most interesting on the street on Wednesday nights and early Thursday mornings. No one looks at old ladies walking on the street. I even took pictures when I heard what they were up to in there at the later parties. Here, you can see them."

Millicent took a whole bunch of pictures of men and women who attended Eleanora's parties. They were printed on plain white paper from a computer. The images were clear enough, but Rudy asked, "Can I get a thumb drive for these, Millicent? The court would not like these, if I have to submit them this way for evidence."

"Right here, Captain."

The Captain was surprised that a ninety old lady had a thumb drive when he had just become acquainted with the concept less than a few years ago. Feeling chastened he'd profiled Millicent as an old lady, he continued with a question, "Why didn't you speak with us the day Eleanora's body was found, Millicent?"

"Because I was in Boise, Idaho, Captain, visiting my granddaughter who just presented me with my first great grandchild; so happy, I tell you, to have a baby girl named Eloise for the little girl who lived at the NYC Plaza Hotel in the child's book. I used to read that book every night to my granddaughter and now my son blames me for the name. Seems like a perfectly good name to me."

Beauregard agreed Eloise was a good name. He searched for more information about the parties. Millicent saw changes in the parties. For a long time, she saw approximately twelve party-goers on the earlier Wednesday evenings and some would leave by eleven. She estimated less than seven stayed longer for the second party. Sometimes she would see two or three leave at midnight, but the final group would leave by two or three on Thursday mornings. "Captain, after all the partying, Eleanora would leave her home for work early, looking bright-eyed and bushy-tailed. She was an amazing self-centered woman."

"Are any other neighbors in these pictures, Millicent?"

"Dorie, a nice lady, who lived across from Eleanora used to attend these parties, but she divorced her nice husband and moved away. I don't know all the players, but I can point out the repeaters from the last few parties. All the others, not recent, repeaters were dumped. It was Eleanora's habit to cultivate and then weed out the less important, much like a gardener does. I don't know if that fact is important to you, Captain, but Eleanora could be hurtful."

Beauregard questioned her, "Did you see Eleanora being hurtful, Millicent, or are you guessing?"

"I don't guess, Captain, and I don't infer. I say what I have seen and she tried to be hurtful to me, but I don't let people hurt me. I was walking one afternoon when she was having an argument with a good-looking man, and, to be honest, I was slowing my walk to listen. She yelled at me viciously and unnecessarily if you ask me, saying, 'Walk a little faster, Mrs. Sparey, and spare me your nosiness.' Now those were fighting words to say that to a senior citizen. She had no manners and using the word 'spare' with my name was just an added insult.

"Millicent, do you have a photo in here of the man she was arguing with?"

"I most certainly do."

Millicent showed Beauregard a picture of Dr. Girandeau. Beauregard questioned the approximate date of the altercation and was told it was about two weeks before the murder. Millicent also spoke about seeing Eleanora talking with a man in an unmarked police car a week before her death and she was very angry. She thought it must have been a difficult conversation because the driver drove away almost taking Eleanora's mailbox with him. Millicent did not have a picture of him, but thought it was an unmarked police car. Beauregard asked if she could be certain it was an unmarked police car. Her answer was an absolute yes. Additionally, she volunteered she had gotten a good look at the man.

Mrs. Sparey on leaving thanked the Captain for taking her seriously, saying, "I may know more. I see most people who go down this street and certainly saw anyone going in to visit Eleanora. I may not have a picture of the others, but if you are looking at someone and want to know if he'd been in this area, I'll help. And it is a man, Captain. Reggie told me Eleanora was laid out with care. No woman would bother. I'm a woman and generally think that we, when we kill, kill with vengeance."

15

Dating Hazards and A Liar

Jess was waiting for Sergeant Bill Border at the Federal Bar. He noticed when he entered she was entertaining several men. Jess had insisted he meet her there, not even allowing a conversation about his picking her up at her home. He thought, *this way she can walk out and drive herself home if she doesn't like what I say. She's not taking any chances with me; probably doesn't trust me.*

She waved when she saw him. He noticed she'd saved a seat on her left by putting her wrap on the barstool. Before he could sit in his appointed place, Jess introduced him to Dr. Saul Beardon, a colleague, explaining he offered to drop her off after work on his way home. He lived in Agawam, not far from the restaurant. Saul introduced him to the other men at the bar and within a few minutes, Bill realized they all were regulars at the Federal. Feeling conflicted by his previous assumptions on Jess' motives and all the attention directed to Jess, Bill was relatively silent. For Bill.

Finally, the hostess told Jess her table was ready. Bill thought, *I didn't even make reservations. I thought I'd treat this date as a casual encounter, hoping she'd think I was cool. She gets here first. I'm really bad at this stuff. Two of those guys at the bar are single and they gave her tons of attention.*

Seated by the hostess, Jess broke the awkward silence. "It's a nice table, don't you think, Bill. I requested this table because it has a little distance from entry traffic."

He answered, "You must come here often, Jess."

She smiled and told him she didn't, but that her family dinners were often held here when she was the host. She informed Bill she didn't have a lot of time to cook big dinners for her extended family which, as he probably remembered, was quite large. Since Bill had no memory of her family other than her mother whom he met, he just nodded in agreement wondering, *how freakin' inattentive was I? Did she tell me then about siblings or other family members? If she did, I haven't the foggiest memory.*

They chose to share Risotto balls with truffle butter, but their food tastes split after that. Although they both agreed dessert was not warranted after eating the exquisite dinners, he chose Mac and Cheese with Short Ribs, while she moaned for his heart health and chose Atlantic Codfish. Somehow, sharing food with Jess allowed Bill to relax. Dinner lasted about just short of two hours. Bill talked about his work.

Jess stopped him after a couple of minutes saying, "You know I forgot something. I think Alison was seeing a cop, but I don't know from where. At least three times an unmarked car was parked outside her home. I know unmarked cars from my older brother Jasper, who's a lieutenant on the Boston Police force; he never left Boston after college at Northeastern University. My father was gung-ho for his career choice in policing, but my mom has been in mourning ever since. She thinks he's going to be killed while on duty. My dad's older brother was on the force in New York City, and Dad was crazy with respect for my uncle Jasper. My brother was named for Uncle Jasper who only had daughters; five of them."

Bill questioned Jess further, but she said she saw just his car and for certain she saw small blue lights flashing inside. She was confident it was a police car, plus she said it was nondescript and the guy getting out was hot, not a match in her mind.

Bill drove Jess home. She kissed him on the cheek before he could make a move and said, "I enjoyed dinner, Bill. Call me."

After returning from walking her to her door, Bill sat for a moment in his car thinking, *I didn't screw this up. She wants me to call. I'll wait a day. I don't think she's going to let me rush her. She's in charge here. I'd better talk to the Captain tomorrow. This is the second reference to a cop in this investigation. I remember when Josh first approached me to split the costs on the condo in East Longmeadow. He loved my being a cop and several cops came by; at least they looked like cops to me. I was always busy and because I didn't know them, I took no notice of them. Maybe Josh was working them too. He was always interested in those in authority.*

Beauregard came in late the day after Bill's date. He'd had an appointment with his Primary Care doctor made by his wife Mona. He knew she'd set him up for a lecture from the doctor on his sugar levels, but the lady was fooled this time. Beauregard's test showed his A1C number looking good. He knew he'd been more careful, but not that careful. Maybe he could live with some food controls to satisfy Mona and himself.

Bill greeted him and asked for a one-on-one. After reporting on Jess's sighting of a cop at Alison's house the Captain's ears turned red at the possibility of cop involvement. Beauregard said, "Millicent and now Jessica see a cop, one at Eleanora's and one at Alison's. Jessica never saw a face, but Millicent did. The trouble is, Bill, it may not be a West Side officer. Still, ask Millicent if she can look at our photos. If it's one of ours, it makes sense to rule that possibility out."

Beauregard was left alone, and as he often did, at least the members of the MCU thought, he was muddling over his things to do list. If they saw him drumming his fingers on the desk, they would have known this action was an indicator of a decision. It wouldn't take long.

The Captain moved over to the murder room. Ted, Petra, Lilly, Ash, Juan, and Bill greeted him. Mason was crunching something on his spreadsheets in his office. An impromptu meeting began with Beauregard announcing, "We've gotten off on the wrong foot. We're so middle class. We think because edgy and bizarre sex is involved, we can throw out what we know about motives and human nature. Greed, lust, anger, rejection, and jealousy are motives. We understand motives precipitating action. In this case, there are five murders within two and a half months. Have we looked at who benefits if the motive is greed? No, we assumed it couldn't be greed. We think lust and more lust and rejection from more lust as possible motives; could be, but lust is not the only motive possible. Anger, or anger resulting from rejection, looks good to us for Eleanora's murder; not so for the others. They were not the ones in complete control. Although they could have been bad actors creating havoc for a sensitive perp. Jealousy is the only motive I feel encompasses all the murders with the exception of Reggie's death. Reggie looked good physically, but was not in the others' league and he knew it. So, I rule out jealousy as a motive in his death."

Beauregard motioned for Mason to join them. He asked for the legacies the victims left. Mason's answer surprised them. Eleanora left a large estate to the tune of eight million dollars in a trust with the residual left for her cousin Leonora after a specific bequest to her friend Judith Wallace of two million dollars was made. Reggie left three million dollars with his nieces in California as heirs. The value of Josh's estate was an estimate, since much of it was connected to his business. The business was left in trust with two of his managers named as trustees. The remaining amount, three million dollars, was listed as a donation to an Iowa non-profit for helping children who were in foster care after losing both parents. Leslie's home, which was mortgage free, and her 401k were left to her girlfriend Maura. Alison also had a trust. The heirs were her family and her ex-husband. She left an amount estimated at over three million dollars. Mason commented, "Lots of money but no social life with the exception of S&M sexual parties; thankfully, there are no children involved."

Ted stated what the other detectives were thinking. "If money is the motive, we have only four to look at: Cousin Leonora, Judith Wallace, ex-husband Bart, and girlfriend Maura."

Juan stated, "We all believe only a man would have the strength to strangle Josh; are we certain?"

There was no answer, just Petra and Lilly mumbling something to the effect, "Can't be certain; depends on the woman."

The Captain changed the direction of the discussion, saying, "Who had access to the drug killing Eleanora? Josh helped Eleanora with her cosmetic parties. Dr. Girandeau has lied to us about the timing of his attendance at the parties. There's Charlie Logan, the Physician's Assistant in plastic surgery and Alison Brunder's neighbor. He could tell us who could have access, although he works for Girandeau. There's also another mention of an unknown plastic surgeon. Mason, have you summarized the reports' data. Who, outside of the three just mentioned, could have access to this drug? Is it easy to get illegally?"

"Captain, according to the FDA, interstate shipments including importation of unapproved drugs, whether for professional or personal use, is illegal. Doesn't mean it doesn't happen. There is a black-market for Botox. Much of it not really Botox, but other implantable cosmetic solutions but not necessarily what they are supposed to be, and often quite dangerous. Some doctors have purchased these products, because the black-market version has a reduced price and some of them have gotten into big trouble. According to the ME, real Botox sold in the U.S. is made by Allergan and has a hologram on the bottom of the bottle. Who knows whether the hologram has now been copied! I think some real Botox could be bought illegally from the black market or from professionals. Our victims were not looking for low cost product. The ME and I agree the product came from a professional."

Beauregard thought it best to have Juan and Lilly interview Charlie Logan, and Ash and Petra interview Dr. Girandeau. Adding the dancing on the bar woman, Connie Davenport Smith, he directed Bill and Ted to interview her again, reminding them her profession is in medical research making her perhaps knowledgeable about cosmetic enhancements. The Captain decided to have a talk with Bart, Alison's ex-husband, saying, "He might be too good to be true. Better check him out again. After all, he is getting a good amount from her as one of her heirs. Mason, what about life insurance on these folks?"

Mason explained he was still waiting on insurance policies, as the families had no information. In two of the cases, there were bank security boxes, but no key or password. He was getting warrants. In Josh's and Leslie's cases, they kept personal papers at their offices and he was waiting on search warrants.

Beauregard also asked Ted, before Mason could answer, for he could not remember, who mentioned the other plastic surgeon.

"Funny you should ask that question, Captain. Dr. Girandeau said, according to the report of the conversation at the golf course the day Josh was killed, the group went to another plastic surgeon, after Girandeau supposedly left the group. I don't know how truthful he was being. The doctor said he left the group, when we have interviews with Millicent and Maura proving he is a liar."

It took several calls to schedule an interview with Dr. Girandeau. Petra made the first call and could not get by the receptionist; she made a second call and again with no access to the great doctor, until on the third call, Petra carefully explained the doctor could schedule a time for their visit at his office or home or at the station. If he did not, she would get a warrant for his arrest as a witness. The receptionist's attempts to delay the interview annoyed Petra. Finally, she was able to make understood that the doctor would be picked up at his practice by two uniformed police if he was not at the station by four in the afternoon. Petra was miffed at the doctor's subterfuge and lollygagging, thinking, *if you hadn't lied, you wouldn't be in this mess. For sure, he'll show up with an attorney. Let's hope it's not Cull. I hope he doesn't do a runner.*

Petra and Ash after discussing it with the Captain decided to put uniforms on the doctor's office. Meanwhile, Juan and Lilly scheduled an interview with Charlie Logan for the next morning. Logan was unhappy, saying it was his day off, but he'd come to the station.

Connie Smith asked Ted and Bill if they were willing to interview her at her home, stressing her current pregnancy related difficulties. They agreed to a five o'clock meeting when her husband would be at home.

Millie, who occasionally would feel sorry for her detectives, and she always called them her detectives to outsiders, walked in with a tray of Italian grinders and two quarts of gelato, one pistachio and the other cappuccino flavored. All work stopped with the exception of answering in-calling. Millie told them they had an hour to relax, as she would manage the calls. Petra sang the "Praise the Lord" hymn but changed the Lord's name to Millie. Juan reminded her she was being sacrilegious and so the repartee continued.

Petra, sometimes lately, a slow eater, had just taken the last bite of half a grinder, when a message dinged. She grimaced at the news. Dr. Girandeau was traveling in his car but not towards the police station. The uniforms were following him at a distance. He'd left his office, stopped at home for half an hour, and exited the house with a suitcase. Petra directed the car to carefully keep him in their sights until an unmarked car could cover, but to text if the doctor headed toward Bradley Airport. Ash, almost as quickly as Petra, moved to leave, accompanied by the Captain who would join them in a separate car. He directed Mason to get an emergency Material Witness Warrant for Girandeau and to meet him with it. The quickening, which is what Petra called these actions, raised her adrenaline, and with a look at her colleagues, she saw them affected as well.

16

Fruitless; Maybe?

Girandeau did not go in the direction of Bradley Airport; instead he headed towards the City of Westfield. Beauregard called Petra telling her to head over by another route to Barnes Airport in Westfield, while he would follow Girandeau. He made a call to the Police Chief in Westfield and informed him of the situation. The Chief promised to send an MCU detective to the scene, but suggested Beauregard's detectives make the arrest, saying, "Arresting a prominent plastic surgeon without an arrest warrant is chancy, Rudy. It's on you."

Beauregard explained he was getting a warrant which did appease Westfield's Chief. It took a quarter hour to catch up with the uniforms. By then, Girandeau's driving direction confirmed Beauregard's suspicions. The Westfield Police Chief initiated an action which was most helpful; at least, Beauregard thought it was his work. The doctor had headed to the airport via Route 20 which required his traveling through the city's center congested with traffic at the bridge before heading in the direction of the airport. One of Westfield's traffic finest officers created a traffic jam. Impatient motorists, hot under the collar, honked, while the officer in charge smiled holding his hands up as if to say, "Working diligently."

The traffic delay allowed Mason to get to the airport before the doctor with warrant in hand. He quickly scoped the departures, and after watching a group congregating to board in fifteen minutes, guessed that Girandeau might be going to Florida with them.

The detectives waited until the doctor entered the building where a private jet service operated. He was met by an agent. The detectives followed him and noticed he was joining a small group about ready to board with a destination for Miami. Dr. Girandeau didn't notice Beauregard and his detectives until they were fifty feet away. The doctor looked around for an available exit, but four detectives had branched out blocking any exit but the entry door to the tarmac for the plane. Lieutenant Mason Smith was standing with the agent, but the doctor did not recognize him. With sweat dripping from his face, Dr. Girandeau forced a smile and said, "Captain, how can I help you? It's not four o'clock yet. My lawyer will be there at that time to explain my required travel. I'll be home in two days and will be happy to meet with you."

Beauregard thought, *other than the sweat on his face, the Doc is cool under pressure. I don't feel guilty detaining this son-of-a-bitch.*

"Who is your attorney, Doctor Girandeau?" responded Beauregard.

Girandeau stated he left a message at Attorney Norberto Cull's office to present himself at the police station at four this afternoon explaining he would be out of town for a few days. Beauregard asked, "Did you talk to him or anyone in the office or did you just expect him to get the call sometime today or tomorrow, thinking it would cover for your deliberate avoidance of our appointment with you?"

"Captain Beauregard, I'm just a witness; don't make a federal case about it. Now, I have to leave to board my plane."

Westfield MCU Sergeant Sourcy walked in, nodded to Beauregard, and watched while Mason Smith presented the material witness warrant and requested Dr. Girandeau ride with Detectives Aylewood and Lent. The request was quietly stated. The doctor's answer was anything but quiet. He ranted loudly about police abuse and illegalities, his own good standing as a professional, and the necessity for him to board the plane, saying, "This flight is expensive and can't be refunded." He finished with, "My car is outside. I'll drive it to your office."

Beauregard affirmed taking the doctor into custody. Dr. Girandeau fell on the ground screaming, "My pills, my pills, I've forgotten them."

The ensuing chaos included a boarding group entertained by the fiasco, calls for an ambulance and Westfield uniforms to accompany the doctor to the hospital, while the doctor lay on the floor in a fetal position. All-in-all, it was a story to be covered by local press, nicely suppressed by a good public relations reaction from the airport staff. Beauregard told Ash and Petra, "For the life of me, I can't figure out how the doctor would benefit from having this story spread."

Ash quipped, "He's always had control, Captain. He isn't thinking clearly, and he must have something to hide. What's with calling Cull and expecting him to jump. Has Cull represented him in medical malpractice cases? Plastic surgeons are always being sued by patients who don't get results they expect. Some patients have no sense of reality. You can bet we'll hear from Norbie."

Norbie Cull walked into his home to find his wife Sheri with two friends and their daughter Sydney sorting flowers on the enormous dining room table. He figured they were artificial flowers since he could smell no aroma. It did look like a funeral parlor to him, but knowing Sheri, there would be some sensible explanation. "Ladies, what gives with the floral profusion?"

"Norbie, don't you remember me telling you about Mary Ann Dietschler from Agawam and her "Wreaths With a Reason" organization. It supports former military, who rescue women and children from sexual slavery. She's raised over fifty thousand dollars to date and over seven-hundred people have been arrested. Basically, she runs an assembly line with artistic volunteers. They get free or bargain flowers, backings, ribbons and other decorations and make absolutely beautiful door wreaths and centerpieces. We went shopping today; actually, we went fundraising today and got all this for fifteen dollars. We can't believe how successful we were."

"You must have ten cartons here. Do you know what to do with them?"

Sheri's friend Jada laughed, saying, "Norbie, think of us as the supply vendors who are bringing the flowers to the manufacturer. No different than any business. Don't worry, it's my job today to schlep them over to Mary Ann's house. We love division of labor." She laughed, and he knew they were all laughing at him thinking, *at home, I'm a misfit; in court, I'm a hero.*

His daughter Sydney came over, hugged him, telling her mother to stop being mean to Daddy since he's a man and doesn't understand all this volunteer stuff. Norbie tried to argue with Sydney's assertion but she countered with, "Dad, they do all the important parts of business from purchasing to manufacturing to sales and shipping. The difference is these ladies and men volunteer, they don't get paid. You support business. This is business. By the way, Dad, you have a call on the house phone from a weird client who says he's a doctor. If he's a doctor, then I don't want to go to him; he sounds mentally unstable," and she shushed him out of the room. He all but ran to his study.

Norbie had finished an agonizing trial that day and had arrived home early feeling wiped. His greeting by the ladies, his wife, and daughter did not make him feel better. Turning on a mix of soft Native American flutists and Mexican guitarists, he was attempting to relax hoping to recover from the stress of mentally trying to control his client's answers in a vicious cross-examination by the prosecutor. Norbie prided himself on his careful preparation of witnesses. Still he was worried about the witness, but, in the end, the aggressive prosecutor's tactics were unproductive. Sipping on some Pellegrino sparkling water he'd brought in from the kitchen, he started returning calls based on a written summary, Sheila his assistant, sent to him at each end of day. There were only five calls, but one call, similar to the one his daughter had relayed to him minutes before, took two pages of information typed by Sheila; mostly the almost incomprehensible message was a summary of rantings made by Dr. Girandeau. The doctor was a client. Norbie had represented him for complaints made to the state ethical medical boards. The doctor's work was excellent which made Norbie's job easier, but Norbie had informed the doctor not to take irrational patients in the future. Girandeau, however, was not good at taking advice, and further, was an emotional reactor when faced with legal problems. What he garnered from the call, and from a separate call on his cell, was the doctor's arrest as a material witness at Barnes Municipal Airport. He said he was in the hospital under police guard, and wanted to sue Rudy Beauregard for ruining his reputation resulting in his having a heart attack.

Taking a moment to consider the situation, Norbie sighed while reflecting, *there he goes again. George makes every situation worse with his emotional reaction to everything. All he had to do is call me and we would have scheduled a talk at his house or the station. There is a lot more to this. I hope he didn't have a heart attack. Material witness to what? I sincerely hope he's not involved with Josh Cantor's murder. They knew each other. I don't see George as a murderer, but again, I've been late to the perp party a couple of times. What was he doing at Barnes; did this most emotional client of all time think he could fly away and avoid a talk.*

He called George's cell phone reaching his client on the fourth ring. Clearly doped up, George's conversation meandered and was unfocused. He did tell Norbie to call the Captain and see why he would do this to him. Despite his knowledge his client was manipulating him, Norbie called Rudy and requested a conference at the station. Norbie deliberated and while waiting for a 'yes,' from Rudy, was thinking, *I'd be happier knowing just what George is worried about and what he actually did to warrant this kind of interest from the police.*

Settled in Rudy's office with a great cup of coffee in front of him presented by Millie, whom he knew from the past could withhold coffee if she did not approve of who was visiting, Norbie initiated the conversation. "My client, Rudy, is in no condition to have told me anything; in fact, I've not conferenced with him yet. He is on happy pills. No sense in wasting a trip today going to Noble Hospital. I have no idea if his condition has improved from last night or even what it is. If he had a heart attack then I insist we give him time to recover before questioning. I also ask you to proceed with as little publicity as possible. George has been in a good practice for over sixteen years. He is very well thought of by patients and other plastic surgeons."

Beauregard was quiet. Norbie did not break the silence. He knew the game; the first one to talk was worried. Loudly sipping his coffee when he gave in, Rudy said, "Your client lied to us when it was not necessary, and further, he knew we were investigating murder. We had only one interview with him. It took an untimely amount of phone conversations to get the second interview, and what does he do; he runs.

George was to meet with my detectives at four o'clock this afternoon. Lieutenant Aylewood instinctively felt George would disappear; she put uniforms on him.

"Norbie, he'd arranged with a private tour agency to join with a group scheduled to leave for Miami at four-thirty today, leaving a telephone message that his attorney, you, would be at our office at the appointed time. Bullshit, it's all bullshit! Then he fakes a heart attack and draws all kinds of attention to himself, and you want me to worry about his reputation. Your guy has problems of his own making."

"I can see how George may be frightened. You scare people, Rudy, with your quiet but staring eyes. Sometimes you even scare me."

Both men laughed at Norbie's statement, with Norbie adding, "What are you looking for. I'll see my client today. To just what major crime is he supposed to be a material witness and what was his lie? You know he won't talk to you unless I'm there. He would never had. Frightened as he was to run, when caught, he took a threatening strategy rather than talk with you. He is smart enough to know he's out of his element with you. Tell me what you're looking for, and make this easier for both of us."

Beauregard decided to embellish a little bit of what he knew. "Since when do I work to make your work easier, Norbie? However, in the interest of preventing delay, Dr. Girandeau knows the players in the sex parties to which he attended and lied about his current attendance. We have evidence he was at Eleanora's house on the night she was murdered. He lied about that. The drugs used to kill her were consistent with drugs used in his practice, though they were not illegal. We have him arguing with Eleanora not long before her death. Time, place, opportunity, and motive appear to exist for your client. It is not a wonder he is frightened."

Attorney Norberto Cull looked straight at the Captain and said,

"He is not a murderer, Rudy, he is not. I'll have him in here tomorrow, unless there's a medical reason not to."

Sergeant Ted Torrington and his wife Charlotte were attending a fundraiser for Charlotte's brother, Mayor Curt Fitshler. Charlotte supported her brother with donations, and tonight Ted thought the buffet was worth it; it was like a date night for them. Ted normally avoided such events because he would sometimes be attacked by constituents about police matters over which he had no control. Charlotte, of the two, in his view, was a better politician than both himself and the Mayor. He was surprised to hear a constituent go after Fitshler about the murders. The first three murders had not drawn a lot of attention from the press. Ted was certain the Mayor's friends and partners in their parties, all important people, had some public relations repression skills. Reggie's murder at Eleanora's house was enough to blow the lid off the pot so to speak. Ted thought, *Curt won't take the heat alone. I know him. Will he be foolish enough to ask me publicly? It's commonly known I'm his brother-in-law.*

The Mayor beckoned in Ted's direction. He cringed for a second. Before he could get on his feet, he heard some shuffling behind him. Mayor Fitshler invited Sergeant Juan Flores to the dais to update the community. Ted was surprised. He turned and whispered to Charlotte, "Would the Captain put Juan on the hot seat like this, or has your brother set Juan up?"

Charlotte shook her head, saying, "I don't think Juan would do anything without Rudy's okay."

To Ted's relief, Juan read a message from Captain Beauregard apologizing for his absence. The Mayor invited Juan to give a summary of the case to date and to answer constituents' question. Juan diplomatically used the old 'open case" rule which prevented officers from commenting. He carefully detailed the problems in these cases in that the medical examiner had not determined in two cases the exact cause of death. He refused to discuss rumors and asked for discretion and kindness towards the victims' families ending his statements with, "You may rest assured Major Crimes under Captain Beauregard will find the perpetrator of those murdered."

This comment left open the issue of who actually were murdered.

Ted thought, *great, now all the talk will be around who committed suicide or suffered accidental death or who was murdered. Talk about creating confusion. Juan has a future as communications liaison for MCU.*

Ted and Charlotte joined Juan as they left the event and discussed the audience's reaction. Juan did say he thought the lack of action from the audience was the best reaction and he hoped it was what the Captain wanted. Deciding to make a little fun for themselves they agreed to meet at a local pizza shop, when the group was approached by a young woman. She introduced herself as a Justice of the Peace and asked to speak with Detectives Torrington and Flores alone.

Used to the public wanting to talk police talk when there was a cop willing, Charlotte excused herself and headed for the pile of cream puffs and brownies. Earlier she'd avoided them, but thought, *can't struggle too much against my destiny, can I?*

Charlotte watched the sincere acting woman who displayed a great deal of hand action discussing her situation with Ted and Juan. She then recognized the woman was the justice of the peace who'd conducted Charlotte's friend's daughter's wedding two years before. She unsuccessfully searched for her name; still, she kept watching remembering the woman as confident and stable.

Janetta Grenich spoke in a forthright manner, despite the fact her hands were shaking. "Detectives, I officiated at one of your murder victim's wedding. The papers mentioned they were all single. I hope I am not in trouble."

Ted said, "Why would you have a problem? JPs marry people; it's what you do."

"The woman who was one of the partners in the marriage did not have the same name listed in the paper, but I recognized her face. I hoped you'd solve the case without my coming forward. I know it sounds silly to you, but I don't want any notoriety. My husband doesn't approve of my marrying people. He thinks the churches should do the marrying. This is all he needs to prove I should stop all this 'silliness.' Look, I have my records of the marriage."

Glancing at the names, Juan was the first to speak. "Are you certain the woman named here as the bride is one of the victims?"

Janetta answered with a yes and said, "It's her."

"Who? Which one?"

"I'll tell you only if you'll leave my name out of the witness list. Notice, the groom is a Holyoke police officer. I didn't know who to trust at the police station, because I know you take care of your own; I've heard about 'the old blue line'."

Ted said, "Just tell us which victim. You can't keep it from us, Janetta. You would be interfering in a police investigation, and believe it or not, that is a crime. I don't think your being charged with a crime would make your husband happy."

And she wept quietly attempting to hide the tears. Charlotte could see the situation getting serious and was empathetic. She did not intervene, pulling herself back mentally saying, *it's more than an interview, it's an interrogation. Oh, how I couldn't do Ted's job, nor would I want to do it.*

"Leonora Captreau is the photo of my bride 'Lena Satler Collins' and she was the most beautiful bride I ever married. They were so handsome. Her husband, James Collins, was so enthralled with his bride. It looked like a love match. I don't know how she got a license. The license was issued by the town of Ludlow. She would have had to give the clerk identification evidence such as a social security number, license, passport, address, etc. It would all have to sync. We can't marry anyone without seeing a proper license signed off by a city or town clerk. Their license was good."

"Can you describe the groom for us?"

Janetta described the groom and promised to make herself available to identify him as long as she could come to the station. "Please don't call or come to my home. I'll be there for you. I'll call you and come to you."

Ted took her information, asked to see her Justice of the Peace certificate and driver's license, and thanked her. She promised to come to the station the next afternoon. She explained she owned a bicycle shop with her husband, but left daily at two in the afternoon to do errands.

17

The Wedding and Lies

Captain Beauregard was almost as excited as his detectives with the news that the cop who may have been involved was not one of theirs. Although the detectives were relieved, Bill Border was upset. He knew the detective listed on the marriage license, "He's a good guy. He went through a hellish divorce. He must have been boondoggled by this beauty queen to marry. He wouldn't hurt a woman."

Always the cynic, Lilly said, "Probably not the same guy as stated. If it is, he must be into pain to marry Eleanora. Why would she marry a cop? Doesn't make sense. She lied to him. She told no one she was getting married. She did tell her cousin she might. Does the cousin know?"

Later, when Juan and Ash had interviewed Janetta at the station, there was no question in their minds Janetta believed Eleanora was the bride. Their photos of the deceased brought Janetta to tears again.

The detectives checked Eleanora's work schedule on the date of the wedding which was at noon on a weekday. She did not lunch at work that day nor did she lunch with Mildred Ryan. Mildred remembered Eleanora going out on a supposedly big business luncheon one day, but was uncertain of the date. It was less than three months before her death. She was dressed to the nines and not in business wear. Mildred had said Eleanora wore a knockout flowery dress with spike heels; she was a vision.

The Captain directed Mason to investigate the name Lena Satler aka Lena Satler Collins using the social security number given to the clerk. Mason was to find all properties in the surrounding areas owned by that name. He said, "Eleanora was a wealthy woman. She would have know-how about financial and business matters. I think she'd keep her husband in the dark. How she could do that in western Massachusetts, I don't know. Keeping a secret in this section of the state I find impossible. Maybe she kicked over to Enfield, Connecticut or up to Vermont.

"Bill, you bring the husband in. Let him know, he either comes in on his own as a husband of the dead woman, or I call Holyoke's Chief and ask him to assist. He must know she's dead. There's been so much press. Also, I want her cousin in here. She's Eleanora's heir.

"Ted, take a look at Eleanora's financial records. See who her accountant is, question him on real estate taxes paid on various properties."

Petra questioned Beauregard, "Motive, Captain, what are you thinking about motive? Eleanora was an inflictor of pain, not a receiver. Every interviewee who knew her talked about her beauty and their fear of her. Dr. Girandeau should be able to tell us if she had sex with women as well as men. We don't even know if she was sexually active. We heard of her whipping guys, but nothing about intercourse. Was she part of the group sex scene? I don't see that."

Lilly agreed with Petra. She asked when Dr. Girandeau would be coming in for questioning. Lilly also wanted the cousin to open up more about Eleanora's sexual preferences, asking, "She gets the money. There's a motive. What about this Judith Wallace? Captain, you said she appeared afraid of Eleanora. We need to have her in here again. She's a best friend and doesn't know about Eleanora's marriage. She must have seen some changes in her best friend. And this Otto guy, what's Eleanora doing dating, when she just got married? And was it a date? Maybe he handled properties for her. We never asked him about their common real estate deals."

Juan offered, before being asked by the Captain, to bring the best friend, the date, and the cousin in for questioning.

Juan and Lilly had to push to get Otto Waldner in for an interview. They were certain he would bring an attorney with him; but to their surprise he showed up alone. He remained clueless about Eleanora's party activities. Lilly had enough of what she thought was feigned innocence and asked if he ever read the newspapers or watched television. With a great show of surprise, he explained he only listened to business news; every other sphere of news was just opinion in his mind. "Look, Sergeant Tagliano, I learned a long time ago to put my own spin on information and not to listen to others' spin."

Lilly showed a copy of one news story where it suggested there was strong evidence the ladies murdered, as well as the man, were connected by sexual parties attended by all three. Otto laughed. He expressed the view that the public so disapproves of those who are wealthy, they make up fantasies about their everyday behavior. Eleanora from his perspective was a perfect lady. Juan, normally the subtler of the two detectives had enough of this garbage and said, "Mr. Waldner, did you know Eleanora was married?"

Both detectives realized Juan had hit a nerve. Otto Waldner's face turned a vivid red, as he stuttered, "That can't be true! That simply can't be true. She told me she was about ready to settle down. She told me she found me a most interesting man. She was going to go with me for a complete day. She wouldn't have done that if she were married. You are mistaken."

Juan looked at Lilly. The signal between them precipitated their ending the interview with Otto, with Juan saying, "You've been most convincing, Mr. Waldner; perhaps we are wrong in assessing rumors."

Their next interview was with Eleanora's best friend Judith Wallace. Neither detective had met Judith. However, their preliminary background check disclosed an arrest of Judith after an altercation in a bar's parking lot. The charge was dismissed. Judith's greeting was controlled as was her perfect seating of her poised body. Lilly thought, *all my exercising and I can't sit as straight at this lady. Not a hair is where it doesn't belong. I can't help marveling at Judith's broad white shirt collar opened widely over a collarless suit and the display of a large two carat diamond necklace supported by the thinnest of all chains. She's wearing no earrings. She knows a thing or two about drama; just make folks focus on the diamond and her throbbing neck. I think she's nervous; she just looks calm. She also doesn't look like someone who would make enough trouble to be arrested.*

Juan, in Lilly's mind, appeared bewitched by the lady. His questions were all icky get-to-know-you, kinds of questions, as if they were at a social. Impatient, Lilly was about to go for Judith's jugular when Juan quietly asked, "Eleanora left you two million dollars. Were you surprised, or perhaps you already know you won't get the money without a fight?"

Judith reacted immediately. "I don't know why I wouldn't get the money; I was her best friend. In fact, I'm surprised the bulk of the estate is going to Leonora, who Eleanora didn't particularly respect. Is Leonora trying to stop my inheritance? I wouldn't be surprised. She is passive-aggressive with her little girl sweetness masking her bitchy actions. Believe me Eleanora knew all about Leonora."

"Well, Judith, I'm having difficulty with your suggestions. We've not heard a negative about Leonora, other than she didn't participate in Eleanora's parties."

"Ha, you know so little and I'm not telling you anything you don't know already. I'm quite aware of how police detectives work. You prey on our misunderstandings of the rules. I know about your Captain Beauregard. He finds little details and hangs you with them. You're not getting another word from me. I'm calling my attorney. Take my word for it, Leonora is not getting a penny of that two million dollars. I earned every penny of it."

Lilly almost smirked, but held back any evidence of emotion as she watched her partner Juan surprise the lady with, "Judith, it's not Leonora getting your money, it's Eleanora's husband."

Judith choked before she could get her words out. "What husband? She wouldn't. She just couldn't without my knowing it. Who would she marry? Not that dope Otto Waldner, she'd never marry him. She'd play him for a real estate deal but she'd never marry him. You're lying through your teeth."

Juan and Lilly were silent for an extended period when Judith said, "What is his name? Don't tell me he's a police officer from Holyoke?"

"Which police officer, Judith, what is the officer's name?"

Judith didn't answer. Lilly asked why she would lie to the police and the response was she never lied to the police. When Lilly insisted she had lied about her background, reporting her lack of honesty in not telling them she's had a previous arrest for fighting at a bar, Judith angrily replied, "Not another word from me, Detective. You're trying to suck information from me and you're not getting any. If you looked at my record, the charge was dropped. I was set up. I'm calling Attorney Norberto Cull."

Judith called Cull's office, but he was not there. She informed the detectives if they wanted more information, they could call her attorney. His name, Norberto Cull, could be googled.

After Judith left, Lilly informed the Captain. He was grateful to have the interview info before Bill interviewed Sergeant James Collins. The Captain wanted Bill to question Sergeant Collins about all ladies he knew connected in any way to any of the now five crimes. They were interrupted by Millie informing them their third interview for the day was here. She said, "Leonora can barely stand up. I think she's on tranquilizers or something. Please get in here. I'm not at my best dealing with crazy ladies."

And Millie's assessment was on point. Leonora Sontin was unable to stand nor sit properly. Almost sliding from the hard chair, Sergeant Tagliano and the Captain had to help her sit up. They couldn't decide whether she was crying or laughing or both. Beauregard, exasperated, exited to get Leonora a coffee, thinking, *can't question the lady in this state. Lilly will have to babysit her for a bit. No use sending her home for another day; she may not show then or show in the same condition. She never looked like this type when I first interviewed her. Has she learned something?*

Sergeant Border arranged a meet at the station with the Holyoke detective. Fortunately, Holyoke Sergeant Jim Collins' arrival was a quarter hour after the crying lady. He was grateful thinking, *none of us know which players knew whom. If he knew Leonora and saw her in this state, he may not be forthcoming.*

Jim Collins was a virile and striking looking man. His demeanor spoke of straightforwardness and calm. Bill initiated the interview with his own memories from his time at the Holyoke Police Department and he shared his reasons for moving over to West Side. Jim was interested but wondered whether West Side might be too tame for him. He corrected himself as he recalled the many and unusual crimes West Side detectives had solved. Bill noticed Jim was wearing a wedding ring. He asked him how long he'd been married. Jim's face colored slightly. His answer was a quick, "Not long."

Bill thought, *strange answer and he's still wearing a wedding ring.*

"Jim, I have a marriage certificate wherein you are the groom. Did you marry this woman Lena Satler?"

"Why would you have my marriage certificate? Is Lena okay? She's supposed to be in New York City this week. Is she okay? Tell me. Is she okay?"

Bill tried to figure out how to answer thinking, *he doesn't know she's dead? It was in all the papers. Maybe we're on the wrong track. Mason was going to search for a Lena Satler, but hasn't gotten back to me yet.*

In an attempt to calm Jim, Border asked him if he had spoken with his wife yesterday. Jim said he'd had a nightly call last night from Lena which was her practice when she was out of town which was quite often. Sergeant Border said, "Then I think we might have a case of mistaken identity. Do you have a photo of Lena?"

Jim did not. He said Lena was funny about photos. Despite the fact she was a real beauty, she explained she had a phobia about having her picture taken. A frustrated Border took a picture of Eleanora from his murder file and showed it to Collins. He looked at Eleanora and said, "I can understand your error. My wife, if she wasn't an only child, could be this woman's sister, but this lady is not my wife."

"Tell me, Jim, how did you meet your wife and how long did you know her before you married?"

Collins response was, "I'm not answering another question about my wife unless you tell me what's going on here. This woman is not my wife. That should be enough for you."

Collins got up to leave, stopping only when Bill Border said, "I don't think Lena Satler is Lena Satler and I believe you should be interested in her identity."

Jim Collins slowly sat down, saying, "Spit it out, Bill. What do you have?"

"The Officiant at your wedding identified your bride as one of our murder victims; it's the picture of the woman I just showed you. If your wife looks so much like her, I may have another picture to show you. Just wait a few moments. We need your wife's identity to rule her out. If she's in NYC regularly, there's no problem."

Border asked Petra to keep tabs on Jim Collins by bringing him some coffee, and he headed for Mason's office. Sometime later, he brought a photo without identification from Dr. Girandeau's Facebook page of Leonora Sontin. The two detectives had tried to retrieve one from the Registry of Motor Vehicles, but it wasn't the best likeness.

Entering the interview room, he thanked Petra for bringing in the two coffees. Jim Collins appeared relaxed. His demeanor changed abruptly when Border showed him a picture of Leonora. Practically sputtering, he said, "Where did you get Lena's picture? Why are you interested in her? Is she in trouble?"

Attempting to explain Lena's real identity as that of Leonora Sontin, midst frequent interruptions, Bill eventually resolved Jim's many questions and attacks. At this point, Jim insisted he be able to call his wife for an explanation. She did not answer his call. Jim's demeanor demonstrated his conflicting emotions ranging from anger to sorrow. All was silent in the room until Jim Collins said, "It was too fucking wonderful. What was I thinking? Lena insisted I buy a house in Belchertown. She wanted us to start fresh in a place new to us both. We have a great house we're now furnishing. She likes the ambiance of the historic farmhouse we bought. I would have preferred modern, but Lena said she liked the reminder of a past time when there were rules and kindness. She didn't want to be anywhere near Springfield or Holyoke. I'm a detective and I fell for that. She said she had no family, that both her parents were dead. She did say she had a cousin, but her cousin was a bad influence. Is that the cousin, the first picture you showed me?"

Bill answered his question. He asked about Lena/Leonora's schedule since they married; he questioned if she worked locally and what she did for work.

Bill was hesitant, but detailed she was in NYC at least four days every two weeks and every other weekend. She told him her passion was helping young women who had a poor social history overcome their pasts and become employed. Her corporation was funded by an inheritance from her family. She did all the public relations and management work, but the bank who was the trustee for her trust handled all finance, for a charge naturally. Jim said, "Maybe she was afraid I was after her money, her trust. I wasn't. I am absolutely crazy for her. Maybe she can't marry under the trust's terms. There has to be a reason."

Bill Border thought, *so I get to tell him the reason is she's a bigamist and maybe more. I don't remember Leonora having a trust. Our financial review of her husband and her showed a good income from him and maybe several million in stocks and bonds plus their house. Not enough for a second nice house and a business in NYC unless her trust wasn't picked up by us. I think she told the Captain that she didn't work.*

"Bill, I hate to have to tell you, but Lena aka Leonora is already married; has been married for a couple of years."

"What the fuck. That can't be true. She wouldn't do that to me. Why would she do that? Who's the supposed husband? I want a lawyer?"

"Of course, you should have a lawyer. Who do you want to call? Go ahead."

"Norbie Cull. He's the best and a friend."

Bill told him he'd give him some time to speak with his attorney, but that he was needed for more questioning about other people he may have met when he was dating Lena.

"I only dated her for two months before we married. I never met her friends. She said she didn't have time for a lot of socializing with her work schedule; she explained it was why she hadn't married earlier. I believed her."

"One other question, Jim, do you know a Judith Wallace?"

"Why do you ask? What has she to do with this?"

"Jim, I wondered if you had dated her. She may be a friend of both Leonora and the other lady."

"I dated Judith for about six months before I met Lena. She is a handsome woman, but more rigid and uptight. I think she liked me because she researched me on social media and I caught her at it. She was nice, but I didn't feel she trusted me and her questioning me all the time got old fast. Then I met Lena and I never thought of Judith again."

"Did Judith know Lena, Jim?"

"No, I don't think so. I once asked Lena if she knew Judith, and she said she didn't. The reason I asked was because both Judith and Lena mentioned going to Botox parties. I guess I thought there weren't too many of those. I was wrong."

Excusing himself for a half hour to allow Jim to phone his attorney, Bill asked Petra to stall Jim, saying, "I need a few minutes. Bring in a sandwich and coffee. I don't care what you talk about, Petra. Question him about Holyoke's police department; ask about my service there; talk about the birds and the bees. I want to get Leonora in good enough shape to meet with him."

Sergeants Bill Border and Detective Tagliano joined the Captain in Beauregard's office. It was a tight squeeze given the institutional design and limited seating forcing Bill to stand. He asked the Captain for a moment outside and noticed the Captain's happy acceptance of the request. Outside the office, Border replayed his discussion with the Holyoke detective and asked if Beauregard thought Leonora was straight and sober enough to meet with her second husband. Beauregard agreed but wanted a few minutes with her before, saying, "I don't want her to have a heart attack in front of us or be a suicide later. Call Petra's husband in to assess her condition before we let her leave here. I don't know if Norbie will give counsel here. I hope he does, because he is quite good at preventing chaos."

Captain Beauregard walked back in the room and said, "Leonora, your husband is here."

Jerking her slouching shoulders back into a most disciplined pose, Leonora said, "How did Lawrence know I was here? Did you call him? I did not tell him. I don't understand how he could be here when he's in California on a business trip."

Beauregard answered, "Not Lawrence, Lena, but Jim Collins."

Her answer, blank with denial was, "Why are you trying to trip me here. My name is Leonora not this Lena, and who the hell is Jim Collins?"

Despite her denial, Leonora started shaking, got up and walked back and forth around the chairs and practically snarled at the detectives calling them very explicit names. The Captain announced distinctly to the lady, "We're moving you to a conference room where we'll all be more comfortable. You must be hungry. I know you realize this behavior is not acceptable; could be you're hungry. Lunch is here. Sergeant Tagliano will bring you some."

She acquiesced. She did not return to her crying state and appeared to be in control. When settled and after she ate half of a chicken salad sandwich and drank a black coffee, she asked, "Do I need a lawyer?"

Beauregard said, "We are talking to you as a witness in Eleanora's murder. You know that. Do you believe you need a lawyer? If so, call one."

Leonora made the call, in front of them. She asked for Attorney Cull. Trying not to show any display of feelings, the detectives all looked at the ceiling. Bill Border thought, *it's the third one today to call Cull. What's Cull going to do?*

18

Bigamy Explained

Unable to resist, Leonora asked, "Is Jim really here at the station? What have you told him? He is a good man. I needed a good man. I was just waiting before I told Lawrence. If Eleanora were alive, I just couldn't tell anyone what I did; imagine what she would do to me. Do you think Jim could ever forgive me? I have never been so content before; what will I do if he won't understand? We have this wonderful home, the only place I've felt comfortable in without Eleanora making fun of me. She didn't know about Jim. She couldn't have known about him. I kept everyone I knew away from him. Lawrence will be angry but he'll take me back. For him, it would be more convenient to have me come home than to have me leave."

Sergeant Border asked, "Did Judith Wallace know about your marriage to Jim Collins?"

"No, I told no one, but she saw me the day I was getting married and asked me why I was so dressed up. Was I going to a wedding or something? I was a wreck. I thought she knew, but instead she explained she saw Eleanora a couple of days before. She was dressed to the nines. Judith asked her the same question. Eleanora screamed in her face and told Judith to back off."

"What made you think, Leonora, you could hide all this? Why wouldn't you divorce Lawrence and marry Jim? Didn't you think Jim would wait for you?"

Leonora asked him a question, "Didn't you just ever want to escape a situation so badly you would suspend your ordinarily good judgment? I was afraid I'd lose Jim and he is the best man I've ever met. He was not corrupted by Eleanora or any of those sex wackos. My life as Eleanora's cousin has not been easy. You just don't understand how impossible she was. She was a brilliant and beautiful bully who turned the screws at every turn. She wasn't even sexual at all. She was a sadist through and through."

"Why didn't you tell us all this in your interview the day Eleanora's body was found?"

"Detective, think about it. You would believe I killed her. I certainly had reason to kill her. She almost ruined my life. I was her victim. But I had Jim, and I thought maybe I could divorce Lawrence, change my name, and Jim would never know. Fantasy, right? I believed in what I wanted, and I thought I could make it happen."

"Leonora, just how did you get the marriage license? You must have had this Lena's social security number or license."

"Lena was a friend who moved to California after her parents died. She sent me stuff to settle her business when she moved. She had no one. I had her social security number and an old license. She would use my home address for business here. She died a few years ago. It was easy."

"Who, in addition to yourself, had a motive to kill Eleanora?"

Leonora looked at Sergeant Border with disbelief, saying, "Haven't you been listening to a word I say? Everyone eventually learned to hate Eleanora, even those who enjoyed being subjugated. Dr. Girandeau, Judith, her neighbors, and all her sex players. Eleanora was a psychopath who looked normal at first. Her biggest victim was Josh Cantor, who actually believed she would marry him. He loved to be whipped and belittled by her. It would activate his sadistic side. He liked to play both parts. He got all the new meat in there first."

Border asked, "How do you know so much about Eleanora's activities if you never went to these sex parties, Leonora?"

"I know. I know all about them. She seduced every boyfriend I ever had and each one became her groupie later. I'd always know because they'd start inviting me to swingers' parties; the first step before the S&M forays. She ruined every single one of them for me. One guy told me Eleanora told him I was always going to be just a vanilla sex gal and to dump me. I married Lawrence to have a man who wouldn't go for her. What I didn't think about, what I should have known, was that Lawrence and I have nothing in common."

The Captain, who'd been listening as a witness, stepped outside the conference room and directed Mason Smith who was drinking his fifteenth coffee of the day to check with the Massachusetts Bureau of Vital statistics for a marriage with Eleanora Captreau as the bride, saying, "It's been quite a few months and the Bureau should have the clerk's marriages on record by now. You have her particulars, Mason. It's important."

Mason laughed. "All the reports say she was not marriage material, but some fool would fall for her beauty. Maybe, Captain, she found a permanent victim for her insatiable bullying."

At this time the detectives heard Attorney Cull's voice. The Captain excused himself, anticipating Cull's arrival may cause a stir. Cull was explaining to Sergeant Tagliano why he had not yet brought in his client Dr. Girandeau. He reported it would take another day or two before the doctor calmed down enough to be helpful. Avoiding any more discussion, he asked to speak to Captain Beauregard before talking with Jim Collins or Leonora Contin.

"What is going on, Rudy? I just learned, you have three of my past clients in for questioning about the same murders, at least it's what I'm thinking. Quite a predicament you've created for me. Can you tell me anything in general before I speak with them?"

"Which one will you represent, Norbie? You can't represent them all. Isn't Dr. Girandeau already your client?"

"Yes, he's been my client in the past, but he has not yet retained me in this matter. He's ordered me to be retained, but I've not had a chance to speak with him at length without his being heavily sedated. I've represented Leonora and Jim separately on non-criminal matters before. I'll have to make a decision."

"Norbie, I can help you a little. Your client Leonora has made a bigamist marriage to Jim Collins; perhaps she wants to discuss what to do about it. Could be civil. Could be criminal."

"You're kidding me. Leonora a bigamist! Nah! I could never have predicted a marriage between the two of them, never mind a bigamist marriage by Leonora."

"I can't tell you any more, Norbie. Time for you to find two other attorneys. It'll be interesting to see which ones you pick."

Norbie asked if they were through questioning both Jim and Leonora. Rudy said, "Not quite yet. I want to put husband and wife in the same room to see what develops. After I'm through, they can go home unless something unexpected happens."

Norbie said, "No, Rudy, it would be best for both of us if I speak to each of my clients first."

"But you just said you wouldn't represent them all."

Norbie laughed. "Ha, Rudy, I did. I just haven't decided which one."

Norbie was brought into the first interrogation room and found Jim Collins there. He explained to Jim he already had a client in related criminal matters, but could represent him in unrelated civil matters, while jotting down a name and number of another criminal lawyer. He said, "Jim, this attorney is a good attorney. I'll make a call. He'll get here when he can. I'm giving you good advice. Do not talk to the police until your new counsel comes." They talked about his marriage to Leonora. Norbie saw the pain evidenced by Jim's repeatedly insisting Leonora loved him. He thought, *cripes, a tough and hardened detective feeling lost. I'm certain it never occurred to him he could be had. Leonora has always been such a straight shooter in business matters. I never could have predicted she could invent an alternate persona and be so devious.*

Leaving a devastated Jim Collins, Norbie entered the interview room number two and Leonora rushed over to him hugging him and crying, "Norbie, I know I've committed a crime, but I love Jim. You have to understand."

It took longer for Leonora to explain her situation. She did not seem to care about the murders. She was subsumed by her fear that Jim would leave her. Norbie tried several times to break into her constant flourish of words. Finally, he said, "Stop, Leonora!"

And she did. Norbie gave her the name and number of a different criminal attorney and counseled her not to speak further to the police until she was represented. Leonora agreed, but Norbie didn't believe for a minute she could stop talking. She was obsessed with Jim. He told her they would conference later about her marital situation.

Leaving the station, Norbie headed over to the hospital in Westfield intending to get to the bottom of Dr. Girandeau's situation and discovering, hopefully, what was going on. He was now certain that all the murders were connected and thought, *there's no way this is normal serial killing; not serial murder at all. No question there is a psychopath working here. My guess is the killer is someone of importance and hiding in plain sight. Maybe George can give me some insight. Rudy won't, unless he thinks I know something helpful. Other than that, I just have to accept it's an open case. I don't care what Rudy thinks, I won't leave it alone!*

Beauregard and Lilly settled in with Leonora waiting for Jim Collins to be escorted by Sergeant Bill Border. Lilly felt the tension thinking, *how could a woman do this to a man or anyone do this? I'd kill her if I were the guy. She'd better come up with a good story. Nothing so far seems even adequate to me. Look at him. He's angry but he's looking forward to seeing her as if she is the Mona Lisa.*

Leonora, mascara running down her cheeks, rose, and tentatively walked over to Jim. She said, "I have loved you from the first day I met you. I've done a horrible thing lying to you but I had no recourse, or at least thought I had no recourse. Do not worry. I know I made you buy the house in your name. It was only so you wouldn't find me out. I'll pay for any monies you've lost. Just don't turn away from me."

"Why, Lena or I guess it's Leonora? I don't understand. What made you do this?"

Lena, in what the detectives thought was a succinct manner for one in almost a state of collapse, explained what happened. And Jim Collins bought every word of it. He moved forward pulling her in his arms, and said, "This husband of yours, Lena, he'll be awfully hurt when you tell him you want a divorce. I've never wanted to hurt anyone."

Leonora discussed her husband's inability to feel emotion and, in her opinion, would divorce her without any fanfare. She said, "I have an ample trust in my name and I had the foresight to have a pre-nuptial agreement written by my attorney. If I give him some assets, he'll have no problem with a divorce."

Beauregard could not take the sugar being thrown around and left the room. He was also ticked off Mason had not discovered Leonora's trust. His thoughts also reviewed the reports on the interviews with Lawrence Sontin and neighbor Eric Shulman. His recollection was the reports raised no flags on these two men.

Attorney Cull found his client, Dr. George Girandeau socially engaged with two young nurses. Cull thought, *yeah, heart attack. Is he foolish enough to think he can ignore the police? Westfield had no guard outside his room. I'm damn surprised by that. Westfield helped West Side police, who went to a lot of trouble to arrest George, but now they think he'll be compliant?* A Westfield police officer, who must have just returned from the men's room next to George's room, interrupted his thoughts. He asked for identification and let him pass. Cull spent an hour with his client catching up to George's participation in West Side games Norbie wasn't aware existed. Never surprised by what people do, he was unsettled by the so-called beautiful people looking for escape from lives others envied. He told George, "What will make you happy, George? You have everything and you are good at your work. What would it take to make you content? Where were you the night Eleanora Captreau died?"

Midst protests of complete innocence, George spit out some pretty sordid details; mostly he was worried about Charlie Logan, a physician's assistant who worked for him. He thought maybe he was getting drugs through vendors used by George's practice. George's role in the games was as a masochist. Cull was surprised at this revelation given George's inordinate amount of ego. George talked and talked about every person who hated Eleanora including himself. He insisted she looked for ways to reduce him to nothing. He said he was a doctor and she said he was nothing; being a doctor meant nothing. She said he wasn't interesting and she felt no desire to work with him anymore. He crashed at the slightest bit of pain. George almost cried when he explained she threw him out of her late-night parties and looked so pleased with herself the night she did. He said he was devastated and asked Norbie, "Just where did she think I could go? Nothing could equal the joy and release I felt with her."

Norbie questioned George whether he ever sought counseling and was surprised when George explained he didn't want the notoriety among his fellow professionals. Cull replied, "You weren't worried about the parties and your reputation, but you're worried about seeing a psychiatrist. You could have gone to Boston or Connecticut and seen a shrink who wasn't tied into the community."

George spoke quietly. "I don't want to give it up. I'm addicted, Norbie. I don't need a drink, but I need this."

It took some convincing to get the doctor to admit he did not have a heart attack, just an anxiety attack and his doctor was releasing him. Cull insisted he face Captain Beauregard as soon as possible, before the MCU Captain interpreted his reluctance as guilt.

Norbie called Beauregard and arranged for the Captain to meet him with his client at home at five this afternoon. Beauregard agreed to call off the watch on Dr. Girandeau.

Norbie Cull prevented Dr. Girandeau from having what the doctor said was his usual early evening relaxant: two double espresso martinis.

Fortunately, saving him from a debate on the soothing effect of alcohol on the nerves, Captain Beauregard arrived timely along with Sergeant Ash Lent. Attorney Cull set the rules for the questioning. Sergeant Lent would ask a question, and Cull would determine if the doctor should answer the question.

Captain Beauregard did not argue; he would have, in another situation. In this case, he was certain that Cull was allowing access to a client that wouldn't normally be allowed. In his mind, typically, Cull would instruct his client to silence.

The one thing Beauregard concluded from Cull's actions was Cull didn't think his client was involved in murder. And the questioning went on for almost two hours. Finally, the doctor mixed himself a martini, scolding Cull with, "I need this, Norbie. You've let them torture me."

Norbie walked the detectives out to their cars, saying, "I told you. The guy is a narcissist through and through and a masochist, but the doctor couldn't murder anyone. I don't understand how he's a surgeon. He doesn't like to get dirty. He has given you background, Rudy, and there's no more 'there, there,' as they say."

Beauregard thanked Cull for his assistance and attempted to leave when Cull said, "Not so fast, Rudy. I learned enough today to spark my interest in these murders. I may not have a client yet, but I have three at risk. And, I don't think any of the three qualify. I also would ask you to keep Leonora's civil problems out of the news. She is just wealthy enough to entice a nice little article in social media. Jim Collins is clearly still crazy over her. Let's help them get over this by not helping unnecessary reporting when we are uncertain about the facts."

The Captain with a smirk on his face said, "I hate it, Norbie, when you make me like an attorney. Not to worry."

Cull took his leave.

Rudy and Lent left the Girandeau home, headed for the station, and rejoined in the reconciliation scenario. The Captain started seriously questioning the two lovers. He wanted to know details wondering if Eleanora could have discovered the truth and played some games. Leonora was exquisitely successful in hiding everything about the marriage from everyone. Rudy believed if she missed a cue, he couldn't find it. It could not have gone on much longer. She eventually would have met a friend in Belchertown who would call her by name and if Jim were with her, the unravelling of her secret would start.

He thought, *if Leonora's plan was temporarily successful, then I rule the two out. They both insist they were together the night of Eleanora's death. Previously, Leonora told us she was home in bed alone. She then did not have an alibi; now she does. Unless they worked in conjunction with each other to murder Eleanora, but they'd both have to be great actors.*

Rudy again considered the possibility of Eleanora's marriage to someone. He went over the why and who and when and where and the resulting silence. He wondered, *who was in her life to marry? Did she marry Josh? According to reports, he thought they might. Did she marry Otto Waldner and he's lying? He was the last person to see her that night, but seems to have some sort of alibi. Could be he was there until a little later, killed her, and then created the alibi. Maybe it's the guy who lived across the street. He certainly had motive. Nothing feels right.*

Mason returned with a big smile on his face. You won't believe this, Captain."

"Spit it out, Lieutenant. I'm impatient today."

"She married a guy name Josh Cantor, our fourth murder victim."

"It doesn't make sense. She didn't have to marry him. He was under her control from day one. He was her slave."

"Captain, could be, Cull could help here. Ask him if Josh looked as if he was suffering from a great loss when they played golf."

"I may just do that, but Cull never mentioned Josh in a state of loss;

more like he was in a state of anticipation."

Beauregard caught Cull as he was driving to attend his middle son's soccer game. The boy was a wiz on the field. Sheri insisted Cull attend at least half his games. He too also felt he should. He'd picked up Beauregard's call. After saying, hello and getting a hello he said, "What's this, a love affair, Rudy? You can't leave me alone."

"Nope, you and I could never be in love, you're too difficult. Mona's enough of a problem for me and she's got the heart of a saint. You don't. No, I have some information for you and am interested in your take."

"Okay, what gives?"

"Norbie, Josh Cantor married Eleanora Captreau several months ago."

"What the…. She died how many days before I played golf with Josh?"

"Not long, Cull. Did he act like a man in distress from losing a wife?"

"Not for a minute. He was a man looking around for something. I'm telling you he was looking for someone in the woods. You've got a screwed-up situation here, Rudy. I'll think about this. I want to know more. I know a lot of folks and I'm able to ask questions and get answers. What info do you have and what do you need to know?"

"You're kidding, Norbie; you should know better. Since when have I let a defense attorney do my work for me? Ok, maybe you helped me out once or twice, but I did your job on the Sunnyside Road situation. Besides, I don't know what I need to know. If I think of something, I will call you, Norbie. I'm not that proud."

19

Chasing Motivations

Two assaults, one home invasion, and a kid who tried to shoot his parents kept MCU detectives in a frizzy, causing Beauregard to mentally obsess about the murders. He thought, *a lot of good it does me to think about these murders, when the Chief and Mayor insist I attend Council and press meetings to explain the explosion of violent crimes in the city. I've no time and my detectives have no time to meet and explore. Just who hated Eleanora enough to murder her? Granted she was a lousy human being, but they all let her act out her fantasies. Her marriage must be important. She talked about marrying. Judith Wallace questioned her on the day of her marriage and she went crazy. She did not want it public; this marriage. Was she ashamed of her choice? Could she have been forced into a marriage by say a blackmailer? She was wealthy. Perhaps I'm on the wrong avenue of inquiry. Three women murdered and two men, but I don't count Reggie. I truly believe Reggie was murdered to cover up something he knew or because he invaded the beauty queen's space after her death. I think I'll focus on Josh and his friends and enemies. I'll speak with the bartender Charlie first. Lillie and Juan were to re-interview him, but there's been so much action here lately. He may know more than he was ready to share with Sergeant Border. His interview was cancelled when all hell broke loose here. I'll have*

Millie give him a push to get him in here.

Millie, known for her dedication to Beauregard, called Charlie Logan and in her very best Southern drawl said, "Mr. Logan, Captain Beauregard would like y'all to meet him at the station after work today. He is willing to wait for you if you think your work will keep you late."

Mr. Logan resisted, explaining he had an appointment later, but Milli's answer persuaded him otherwise when she said, "He'll just have to meet you at work. This interview must take place today. I'm telling y'all it must be important. He did say there are uniforms available to pick you up."

A severely disgruntled Charlie Logan appeared at the station at five o'clock. Millie escorted him to an interview room and offered him coffee. His answer was in her mind unpleasant causing her to respond, "Now that's no way for a gentleman to act. I was just being polite. I'm told you are a professional. Your behavior does not indicate your status, Mr. Logan. You should be ashamed."

And she walked out without getting Mr. Logan a coffee.

Slightly less disagreeable, Charlie Logan greeted Captain Beauregard with, "It couldn't wait until tomorrow. I've had a very long day and now I have to be interviewed. There is nothing more to say; I said it all to Bill Border. He probably knows more about Josh Cantor than I do."

"Mr. Logan, I am interested in your understanding of all the participants you knew who were part of the advanced level of sexual partying. I want all their names; who was inside the Eleanora group for a while and who was ejected. You would know all that."

Charlie settled back as if the questioning was in a more comfortable area for him. He went through a list of names, but insisted that he was not familiar with what was currently going on. He explained that his bartending days were long over. Of the names he mentioned,

Beauregard had most of them. He was surprised to find men named Otto and Reggie and Lawrence and a woman named Judith mentioned. Charlie didn't seem to know last names. Beauregard asked for descriptions for the four and found they matched his memory.

Beauregard then delved into a discussion of Charlie's work. He'd been the physician's assistant for Dr. Girandeau for a couple of years and had done his internship there before being hired. The Captain asked, "Dr. Girandeau must think highly of you, don't you think, given you are the only PA who's ever lasted longer than a year with him?"

Charlie agreed and explained, "The Doctor is very particular and not every person is able to deal with his OCD; he does try one's patience sometimes."

"Charlie, how did you meet the Doctor?"

Charlie answered, "He used to come into the bar, specifically, I think to keep tabs on the beautiful people. Later, he got into an altercation with Eleanora. Over what, I don't know. He brought me in to deal with her. Lately, however, they had been getting along. She'd let him come back to the cosmetic parties. I'd been doing them for eighteen months and now he's back. I help him, but there's only room for George when George is in the room."

Charlie laughed at his own use of the word, 'room,' saying, "I mean all air is sucked out in any place George occupies."

The Captain questioned Charlie, "Is it true that only some of the folks who were at the cosmetic parties were invited back to the sex parties held later in the evening? That would mean all the people who were at the sex parties came from the cosmetic parties."

"I see you took logic in college, Captain Beauregard; but Eleanora was not logical. Most of those attending the sex parties came from the cosmetic parties, but not all. Some arrived later. An example would be Eleanora's friend Judith. She never wanted to be at the cosmetic parties, but she was at two of the sex parties. I don't know how long she stayed."

"Charlie, I thought you didn't know Judith Wallace; you just listed the names from the bar, yet you know she's Eleanora's friend. And what nights did Judith attend those parties?"

He answered, "I knew her later. About six months ago, when I left the cosmetic parties, she stayed two Wednesdays in a row. You know she has a black belt in karate and bragged about having learned Krav Maga which is a tactical mixed-martial art/combative and self-defense system. It combines boxing, judo, jujitsu, and aikido. Judith said she once dated an Israeli agent and he gave her instructions. The Israeli forces use Krav Maga successfully. She looks like a lady but don't believe it."

Beauregard asked Charlie for names of those who attended the last four cosmetic parties. Charlie had a list on his cell and forwarded it to Beauregard's cell. Scanning the name listing on his phone, the Captain questioned who was the Lawrence who attended the third to last party. Charlie explained Lawrence was Leonora's husband and laughingly said, "So much for the innocent cousin. She sends Lawrence in to learn how it's done, so she won't have to go there."

"So, Charlie, you were at the party with Lawrence? Why do you think he was an agent for Leonora? You really think she knew he was there? Do you know if he stayed for any of the late parties?"

"I don't know, Captain. He was still there when I was packing up my cosmetics; I don't remember if he walked out with me. As far as his acting for Leonora, I think he wouldn't do anything without her, okay! She knew he was there."

"Charlie, you're telling me you never stayed for the late parties?"

"No. They're a bunch of freaks. You think I want to be part of that scene? I work with their world of 'make me beautiful' because it's what I do professionally. I balance it out by working with accident victims who really need cosmetic help. If I were a plastic surgeon, it's all I would be doing."

Beauregard asked whether he was at the cosmetic party on the night Eleanora died. Charlie turned red saying, "You know, Captain, there wasn't a cosmetic party that night. Are you trying to trip me up? Do I need an attorney?"

The Captain, in an attempt to look chastened, apologized. He said, "I meant to ask you why there was not a cosmetic party that last evening."

"Because the lady was crazy acting for weeks before she died. She constantly changed times and dates and rules for everything. She wanted a higher than usual percentage commission off our products. She said she thought they were illegally purchased. She was nuts."

"Charlie, were the products all legally purchased?"

Charlie took a split second longer in answering than Beauregard thought he should. His answer suggested he did not do all the purchasing for product at the office and he could only speak for himself. All product purchased by him was through normal professional channels and when he made this statement he slammed his hand on the table in emphasis. Beauregard calmed Charlie and thanked him for his honesty.

A detectives' conference, the first in a few days, and held in the 'Pit', was most notable for flying opinions on motives. Mason was vocal on Eleanora's marriage, stating, "It was no love match, but it could have worked for both of them like the Parisians say 'Marriage blanc.' It is a marriage of convenience often for social or economic reasons. Josh was her human relations and marketing contact. Eleanora was not someone who would go out and solicit potential sexual partners. He had no shame in that context. Her marrying him, unless we find a pre-nuptial agreement, maybe makes him an heir. Leonora could be left with a fifty percent reduction in her inheritance if this marriage was real. Makes her look good to me. Judith, if there's enough to cover her specific request in the will, and at eight million there looks to be plenty to cover it; well she doesn't lose whether Eleanora married or not."

Lilly and Juan both had reservations. Juan said, "We still don't have matches for the partial footprint in Elenora's backyard, nor the one on the lush carpet. However, right now, I like this Judith for Eleanora's death. She has the strength, the height, and the repressed anger to choke the three victims and now we find she lied about attending the cosmetic parties. This gives her knowledge about injections. She is in Eleanora's will. Why would Eleanora leave her money to Judith, and money is important to Judith? I think she was disappointed Leonora got the bulk of Eleanora's estate. I think she believed she was getting most of it for herself. Money is the motive; her strength allows for method; she's lied about her attendance at the parties; and she's one of the most uptight ladies I've ever met. Given that she is one handsome woman, why would she be so nervous? My bet is Eleanora had a hold on her. Judith went apeshit when she even thought about Eleanora getting married. Did Eleanora go both ways? Come to think about it, we don't even know if Eleanora had sex at all; the only indication of her having sex was from Reggie's statement and he doesn't say it was Eleanora. He just said it was two people by the bridge. We have no DNA on the panties at the Eleanora site, which could mean they were just a prop meant to confuse us. The whole site was a setup."

Ash could not contain himself, saying, "It's all too easy. There are money motives for Leslie's girlfriend Maura, Lawrence who is Leonora's legitimate husband, Leonora, and Alison's ex-husband Bart, in addition to Judith. These shiny upstanding beautiful people, the hoi poloi, all are under my spotlight."

Lilly laughed at Ash's use of 'hoi poloi', a term her grandmother used. She asked him just how old he was. He gave no answer knowing the Captain was frowning. It was time to settle down. No one spoke. There was silence. It surprised them all to the point where not one detective spoke up. There was a lot of fidgeting. Mason and Ted never fidgeted, nor did the Captain.

In exasperation, Juan said, "What's up, Captain? I can't stand the silence. It's not what I'm used to. There's no silence in a Mexican household."

The Captain looked up saying, "I'm sorry, are you all through with your comments? Where do we go next?"

The detectives stumbled over themselves stating their ideas. There were many good ideas, but as Captain Beauregard commented, "None of them are in the same direction. We don't know why Josh was killed. I'd like to think it's because he married Eleanora, but why kill him after Eleanora's murder? It's too late to prevent his estate from going after his portion of her estate; unless the murderer didn't know she was married. Did the murderer have a sexual relationship with any of the group of people we are looking at? Could Josh have been involved with a man?"

Bill Border interrupted the Captain's verbal wandering. He said, "I think Josh was about adrenaline fixes, and his fix was pain. He liked to give it and receive it. His mind was twisted. We know from our interviews several have said he cultivated both men and women. From my experience, even when I didn't know he was fostering me for his antics, he was always charming. He was the classic seducer but not a trifler. He had more than one motive as a Lothario. He needed Eleanora to give him pain, and yet he didn't suffer when she died.

I trust Norbie Cull's analysis of the man. He spent years culling men and women for Eleanora's needs. Confusing because it doesn't easily compute for me that he found someone else."

Two calls came in from robbery about a shooting at a convenience store. The disruption was almost welcomed by the detectives. Juan said his head hurt from all the potential motives. Ash and Bill went on the robbery shooting call, leaving the others to rotate staff for lunches. Juan asked Lilly to join him in an Italian lunch. He said, "You must know a good place for lunch with great Italian food."

Her answer was a surprise. "I'm in the mood for Mexican. What about that place in Chicopee? A new place will help us clear our heads."

Twenty minutes later, they had ordered and were talking generally about the case. Lilly asked, "Juan, do you think this work we do every day makes us suspicious about people?"

With his yes answer, Lilly appeared deflated. He continued with, "Lilly, our work is like that of a social worker. We see things we don't want to see. We look for trouble on a daily basis and find it. Could we lose our way? I think some cops do lose their way. My ideas about life were infused in me by my family life. Looking back, I remember we always talked about right and wrong at the dinner table. Mamita let us know from when we were babies what she wants from us, and Papi would just nod his head in agreement. He'd never disagree with her teaching us. I am always remembering the rules. When I was in high school and college, I always remembered the rules. It's ingrained. I want that kind of family for me whether I marry an American or Mexican woman."

Lilly laughed at him. "And just what would Mamita say if you brought home an American woman, Juan?"

"Why don't we find out. Mamita is having a family dinner tonight.

Come with me."

The waitress brought their orders of beef deluxe burritos with sides of guacamole and chips. They thanked her and started to eat when Juan said, "An answer please; I've invited you to dinner, Lilly, to meet my Mamita."

She looked into his brown eyes and said, "She might not like me. No, I know she won't like me."

He laughed. "I like you; she'll like you. So, it's a yes?"

Nodding yes, Lilly said, "Juan, my mother's not sure she likes me. She's says I'm brash and too quick in making decisions."

"You are, Lilly, but it's you. It's what makes you a great cop. You're a great friend. I think you'd make a great unlikely girlfriend for a shy Mexican detective."

Lilly did not answer; just ate her lunch in gulps.

Attorney Norberto Cull wandered into the Oxford Martini Bar and settled at the quiet end of the long bar. It was a nice vantage point for viewing the goings on and to watch the bartender. He'd finished fully interviewing over the phone his several new potential clients. It was not difficult to get specifics from them without asking. Judith, particularly, who explained she had a civil case in protecting her interests in Eleanora's estate, was verbose. Knowing he'd met her once before, he thought this behavior to be inconsistent. Judith was venomous in her dislike of Charlie, the Physician's Assistant, and Dr. George Girandeau, the plastic surgeon, but she displayed a greater anger for Leonora. Since the martini bar was mentioned several times in her conversation, he thought it may be a good starting point. He did not have a client who he thought needed representation for the murders, but he was very interested in the partying in his town which may involve illegal drugs and behaviors; besides, his wife was gone for the evening with three of his kids. His remaining son was at a gaming contest.

The bartender was older than the reported Charlie Logan. On Norbie's third beer, the bartender, whose name was Emmet, gave the rundown on the lady customers' activities. It was a higher end older meet and date bar. No actual pros worked it, but Emmet assured him there were ladies who were regulars here who often left with different guys. He whispered the bar was the site for those interested in pushing sexual frontiers. Generally, it was not gender pushing, but there were many who were bi-sexual and homosexual who were involved in meeting up with the right groups.

Emmet was a talker. Norbie was a good listener. He ordered an appetizer, dumped one of his beers in the plant next to his bar seat and thought, *Sheri would be furious with my killing a garden plant. Maybe beer is a fertilizer.*

Emmet joined him again and said, "You're a great listener. Have you ever tended bar? Sometimes when the bar isn't busy, I get stuck listening to some guy's marital problems. I can tell you the hours go by slowly on those nights. In a few minutes, this place will be jumping so I won't have time to discuss tonight's game with you."

"What's going on tonight, Emmet? It's only Tuesday; can't be a busy bar night."

"You think not? Charlie will be in tonight. He was bartender here for years while he was in school. Now he's got a great gig going for him."

Norbie expressed interest pretending he had seen Charlie a while back when he tended bar. Emmet described Charlie's history. "Charlie used his bartending position to pick up women. The trouble is it was too easy for him. The young women fell for him. You must remember,

Charlie is one handsome dude and has this little boy way of making them think they fascinate him. I think the pickings were so easy, he got greedy and went for the glamour set. Some real sophisticated beauties, men and women, who used to party in groups. I heard the parties had no sexual boundaries. I'm too old and conservative for that shit, but they did all their hunting in here. I asked Charlie what he meant by hunting. It meant pointing out the cream of the crop who may be open to manipulation."

Norbie asked about who else was involved. Emmet whispered, "The boss doesn't want me to talk about it, because four of them have been murdered. I don't think the police know about this connection. Frankly, I don't think the murders have anything to do with us. The central core has to do with their stupid partying for a sex high. It's just like drugs or alcohol. They were all addicted."

When he questioned about Josh Cantor, Emmet was vocal in his view, saying, "He was more than a player. If you watched him for long enough, you could figure out he used everyone for his personal pleasure. He lied to the newbies, treated some of the frequent party-goers as unimportant; you know, like inconsequential. They might not like it, nobody would, but they never crossed him. Every once in a while, a few really gorgeous ones would come in. One of them was murdered. Her name was Eleanora. Josh kissed her ass. He never once crossed her. Charlie got into it with Josh over cosmetic costs. Josh thought he was charging too much or something. I never got the complete gist of it, but Charlie was the beauty doctor and it paid off for him. I know he isn't a medical doctor, but he gave the party-goers what they wanted."

Norbie was left by himself when Charlie Logan entered the bar. Several women moved over to sit next to him. Norbie thought, *this guy is like a magnet. I don't hear anything about Botox, just questions about the next 'big' party. He's acting like he doesn't know and getting some backtalk.*

Norbie watched as a good-looking man dressed in Eddie Bauer type high end casual gear walked over to Charlie. It interested Norbie because the outfit did not fit in with the sleek euro look worn by other men in the bar. The man looked familiar, but Norbie couldn't recall who or how he had met or seen him. His conversation with Charlie looked almost intimate to Norbie. Within a few minutes, they both left; he noticed they had not settled their bill. Norbie waited for Emmet to walk back to his end of the bar and asked why Charlie didn't have to pay. He was told Charlie had a running tab. He was the only one, other than Eleanora who was now dead, the owner allowed a tab. Norbie asked, "Emmet, who was the guy dressed like he didn't belong here?"

"You mean Lawrence? He belongs; especially since Elenora's gone. She didn't let him into the scene, but he's one of the important ones now."

A light went on, and Norbie asked, "His name, is it Lawrence Sontin?"

"Yeah, that's it. You know him? He seems quiet at first, but he had Charlie in his spell."

20

Who's Most Likely

Captain Beauregard and Attorney Cull lunched at Charlie's Diner in West Springfield. Norbie said he didn't want Beauregard to think he was trying to bribe him with a ham sandwich, but this was a go-to place for hiding from lawyers and beautiful people. Since Norbie called the meeting, Rudy waited for him to disclose the agenda for the lunch. When Norbie reviewed his evening at the Martini Club, Rudy quickly reacted. "What the hell were you doing there, Norbie? You have no reason to be investigating a police case. You don't have a client who's been arrested, or do you think one of your crazies may be arrested?"

"Rudy, think about it. I'm nosy. It's who I am. I'm a defense attorney who was present at a murder and you think I'd leave it alone. No way. I'm not interfering in your case and as far as I know, right now, my nosiness has nothing to do with any potential client. Why are you complaining? I'm giving you my thoughts and a summary. Think of it as my layman's contribution as a good citizen to police work."

His smiling did not relieve Rudy's distress, but Rudy removed his troubled expression and started asking questions. He wanted an analysis of Norbie's opinion on Charlie Logan and he got it. Norbie said, "Logan looks too good, but watching him let me know he's

227

one of your own, Rudy."

"What do you mean one of my own? He's not a cop."

"No, but he's a sociopath for sure and I think your Josh Cantor was a sociopath. It sounds as if your dead Eleanora was one too. You're in a minefield of sociopaths. My theory of sociopaths is two can survive well together, but three or more is way too many. Someone had to go. Since Eleanora and Charlie were the only ones allowed a bar tab at the Oxford, they were leaders. They were considered leaders by all the players including any sociopaths. For sure, Eleanora and Josh were eliminated by another sociopath. I think your job is to see if Charlie is the only other sociopath in the group. I'd bet not. I believe the motive was to eliminate Eleanora and Josh. The other murders are either a cover up or punishment for their not recognizing the power of the murderer. How's that for pseudo-scientific psychoanalysis?"

"What do any of us know about who is a sociopath until they act out? I do agree with you about this group. They are some of the most narcissistic people I have ever met. They don't have a strong understanding of right as opposite from wrong, at least from a sexual perspective. They seem to ignore the feelings of others and find ecstasy in giving or feeling pain or both. Yeah, Norbie we may have a cabal of sociopaths here. Isn't that what they called themselves? In my mind, Cabal just means a group with common interests. This cabal is predatory. They make me afraid for the future or who will be chosen next for their pain fix."

"Rudy, I don't have interviews from the murders. You do. My advice is to look carefully at your interview data and speak with your detectives. I think you'll pick up a power motive in there."

Rudy asked Norbie about all the folks who called him for representation, naming them. Norbie did not want to discuss them saying, "I've represented George, Leonora, and Jim Collins before.

I can't discuss my clients even if I'm not representing them now."

"Norbie, Judith Wallace also called you. Was she your client at one time?"

"I wish I could remember. She called. She said she was a former client, but new potentials often say you've represented them before to get you to call back. I can't remember, but I was a public defender at one time. Could be back then. I don't have those records on my computer. They're in a box in my basement. I did meet her once before at a party that I remember, for she was memorable. I will ask Sheri about her. She remembers everything."

Norbie and Rudy examined their history related to power as a motive. Both agreed that the whole sexual situation tended to confuse analysis. They also discussed Charlie and his access to drugs which both agreed was a hanging thread. Perhaps the old stand-by motive of greed was over reaching here; or maybe yet, combined with power pushed the murderer to act. Then again, jealousy, just plain jealousy, could be involved. They finished their lunches. Norbie promised to keep Rudy abreast of any of his findings. Rudy promised nothing.

Rudy did say, "I'm suspicious of groups, Norbie. Individual evil or acting out on the edge is one thing, but when they group together; I'm afraid. It's like a cult. The members think everything's good. They're having some fun, but mark my words, groups can't be trusted. Leadership and then values change. Trouble. I smell more trouble ahead for us unless these murders are solved.

Attorney Cull left court at four in the afternoon. His temples were throbbing. His client, while crying on the stand and putting him in fear for his defense strategy, redeemed herself by incriminating her boyfriend. Nothing previously stated by her to him, ever included this information. Not for the first time, he wanted to strangle his client thinking, *I don't know why she didn't tell me the truth. I am on her side. She could have avoided thousands of dollars in legal fees. This defense is now foolproof. Not only that but I get street creds from the Assistant District Attorney and the Judge who both think I planned her statement for its dramatic effect. She is off the hook. I didn't plan it.*

Cull called Sheri and planned a dinner date; she was not only willing but he got creds from her for being a thoughtful husband. She said, "You knew I was depressed about my friend Lorie's problems. How very thoughtful. I'll dress up."

Again, Cull was getting credit for something he knew nothing about. He just wanted a quiet dinner during which he would ask Sheri about Judith Wallace. He said aloud, "Cripes, I've turned into a manipulator."

They settled on Cimi's Restaurant and Chop House in Wilbraham. The food was always good and Sheri loved Italian cuisine. Therein lay the problem, everyone they ever knew seemed to be having dinner there. Sheri couldn't understand why a Wednesday night brought the world to Cimi's. The waitress, when asked, told them there was a coupon in one of the local publications. She said people loved it. It was only good for this past Tuesday and today. Finally settled in, and after two wines, Norbie asked Sheri if he had ever met a Judith Wallace before saying, "She called the office and said we know her, but for the life of me, I don't remember her."

Sheri laughed hysterically. Norbie looked confused. She said, "Norbie, how could you forget a woman who looks like Judith Wallace? She sat at our table at the hospital fundraiser. She outbid me on a shopping spree at Nordstrom's. No one, and I mean no one but you, could forget her. I should be pleased. Apparently, I am more attractive than Judith to you, but I can tell you it's a shocker you don't even remember her. Why did she call you? Now that you're paying attention to the glamour lady, I will have to worry."

"Just a civil matter, not anything of consequence, but I didn't recall her at all. She must have been kind of girly-girly and I don't normally listen to conversations of ladies' talk."

"Spoken like a true misogynist; I'm a bit disappointed in you. Judith Wallace is far from a girly-girly type. She would probably not have shown interest in you because she likes to be in situations she can control. She would know just by looking at you, well, Norbie, you can't be controlled. Sometimes I'm successful in manipulating you but not often."

Norbie appeared appalled at her statement and told her so. He continued to elicit comments from Sheri until she wised up and said, "She must be important to a case for you to show that much interest in her. I'll tell you what I've heard. I don't know if anything I say is the truth, but I'll give you the gossip on her. Judith has some money and a career running a medical staffing business. She supposedly was left at the altar by her fiancée a number of years ago. He left her for her college roommate and then the new romance went nowhere. The guy moved away. The ladies say she's smart, quick-witted, but sarcastic. She's dated a few people, but the romances don't seem to go anywhere. Oh, and I remember, Barbara says she's a martial arts expert. if I were you, Dear, I'd do good legal work or you may have to answer for it."

"Sheri, did your friends ever hear whether Judith liked men only or was she bi-sexual?"

"I got no vibes from her, Norbie, but, frankly, I think I'm out of her league. I may look okay, but at heart I like being a wife and a soccer mom and director of the drama club in town."

"Thanks a lot, Sheri, you also like managing your husband. Put that on your list. It's always good to have you in my corner."

Later in the evening Norbie sat in his library and wondered, *Judith Wallace has never married. She's been stood up at the altar, and it was a very public event. No wonder she's sarcastic. A martial arts expert requires knowledge of strength and strategy. She could be a killer. Why would she kill? If her motive to kill Eleanora for two million dollars in inheritance is true, why kill Josh and the other ladies and Reggie. Did she love Eleanora? Is there evidence she was enthralled with her.*

Why would Eleanora leave money to Judith in the first place? I liked my college roommates but they're not in my will. Even if I were single, they wouldn't get anything. I suppose if they were economically suffering I'd help out, but that's all. Eleanora had all these men adoring her; she marries one but has left her money to her cousin and her college roommate. Maybe she felt guilty because she treated them both so badly. Did she even have a speck of morality to feel guilty? I think she was one of Beauregard's sociopaths; according to what I know, sociopaths feel no guilt. I have to wonder why she would feel guilty and leave her money to these women. Why would she marry? Rudy said reports from some interviewees state they never saw her have sex with anyone. Why would she marry? Maybe it was a cover-up. She could have been asexual with a pain infliction need. She could like women sexually. Some puzzle Rudy has in these murders. Well, I do have a connection. I'll go fish in Alison Brunder's background. I know these people. They'll tell me more than they'll tell Rudy.

Norbie called Janet Roper; she and Al had been his clients a few years back. He'd not gone to Alison's funeral which was a morning in the church affair, because he'd been in court. Sheri had attended for both of them.

Janet was now standing in her front door waiting for him to drive up. She walked out to greet him. He hugged her and Janet got weepy saying, "Sheri was so understanding at Alison's funeral. I know you understand victimhood, but you also understand people, Norbie. You want to know everything about Alison; I'll tell you. I simply couldn't tell the police everything knowing it will go in a report to be resurrected at trial someday. I have to do what I can to protect our reputations, Norbie."

Janet had coffee on the kitchen table ready to pour. He waited, ate a piece or hunk or whatever of apple crisp and ice cream and looked totally comfortable thinking, *I hope I don't upset Janet with questions. Right now, I feel I'm with family.*

Before he could tell her his thoughts, Al Roper barged in from the garage through the kitchen door surprising them both. "Did I get here on time? Hi, Norbie, thanks for coming. Janet and I want to tell you everything we didn't tell the police. We want her murderer, but we need some privacy. Alison made choices. They broke our hearts, but they were her choices, not ours. We need to be able to go on after this is all over. Don't think we are not grieving, we are."

"Al and Janet, what do you think? I need to know what's up to help you."

Janet talked for fifteen minutes and explained Alison's differences from her friends, not to compare, but to understand. They had no problem when Alison wanted a divorce, except they believed she didn't want a divorce. She just wanted to keep her husband in cold storage while she did what she wanted on Wednesday nights. Janet explained, while Al squirmed, her view on Alison's social-psycho history. Alison thought only about herself. Any expression of interest in another person, including her parents, was to seize an opportunity to manipulate. She had good social graces, but you'd have to be a fool to be taken in. Bart was taken in.

She continued saying, "When Bart told us about Alison ending up in the hospital as a sexual asphyxiated victim, we were truly afraid. We've never stopped being afraid. We both knew we'd get no information from her, so Al called a former student of his who's on the West Side police force. He asked him to put the fear of God into her. She may have been disagreeable to Bart when he asked her about the incident, but she's always been slightly in fear of authority figures. We didn't tell the police about calling Al's friend. We don't want him in trouble. Besides, he was not successful. In fact, she laced into him and threw him off her property. He said she was really upset when he named people who'd been at the party. Josh Cantor's name enraged her. We would have shared that clue with the police but he's dead."

"The police, according to what I've heard, took her computer. What do you know about that? Do you have a copy of what was on it, like a back-up copy?"

"They're keeping it until there's a trial, but Al took some back-ups for it. They're not everything, but most of her stuff will be on it. She backed up data once a week on a USB disc."

Al pulled the disc from his pocket and gave it to Norbie, saying, "Alison was super organized. You should have no trouble seeing what's on it. Her password was PAINX. Don't say anything, Norbie. I didn't tell the cops about the password because I didn't know it then. I found it in the bottom of a shoe box with a pair of platform silver shoes and a key. I don't know what the key is for, but I think it's important. I'll give it to you. You may have to give it to the police. I know that from all the television shows. I don't want you put in a bad position. Just tell them I found it recently."

Later the next day, Norbie asked Sheila, his paralegal/secretary/

admin assistant and general nuisance about the identity of the key. Looking carefully, she jested, "Okay, brilliant defense attorney, since when can't you read and use a computer?"

Knowing he must have missed something, he said, "Sheila, you are here as my eyes, my nose, my ears, and as a cultural specialist. I don't even know what you mean. It's a funny shape and has a number. That's all I see."

"Since when have you been unable to at least check on google. I feel so sorry for Mona."

"Wait a minute, Sheila, this is a Yale key and has A and six digits. How am I supposed to know where it's from?"

"First of all, Norbie, it's not a house key. Maybe a locker key but a bigger one than usual. Find yourself an older gym with lockers. I think I've seen one of these keys before. Go to a local locksmith and get it identified. Want me to do it?"

He did and said so thinking, *I think Sheila talks to Mona. They both have the same message; do it yourself, Norbie.*

He wondered about the gym business. All the murder victims were gym rats, but which gym was a favorite? He stopped Sheila in her tracks, asking, "What's the most high-class gym in or near West Side, Sheila?"

It took a minute before she replied, "I've actually looked into two. They are considered expensive, one far more-pricey than the other. They have personal trainers available without having to hire them by the hour. Although I heard that 'Health Wellness Fitness' also offers weight and nutrition classes for zilch. It's also way more expensive than the other grand gym. I'd love to go to it, but I live in Springfield way over near Longmeadow. I don't want to drive to West Side three days a week and I surely don't want to pay that monthly fee. You could include it in my perks, Norbie."

"Maybe next year, Sheila. Call them about their locker keys. Could they have old lockers?"

"They're located in the old men's gym but have rehabbed it. It's like being in Los Angeles. It's got a health bar and television social room. If the old lockers were really nice, maybe they kept them. I don't remember seeing the lockers when I toured the facility."

While Sheila made the call, Norbie reflected, *I can't withhold evidence from Rudy, but I should at least look at this computer to see if there is any evidence and then give it to him. They will be able to trace my looking at it. The hell with it, inquiring minds want to know.*

Norbie struggled to load the USB drive. Sheila would normally be the go-to person for computers, but he didn't want her compromised in any way or called as a witness if there was really good stuff on the drive. To Norbie's amazement, the process went quite smoothly. No question about it, Alison was one organized woman. She had notes organized in one file, summaries of her work in another file, a divorce file, a file called 'Suspicions,' accounting files, financial, banks, and tax files, a family file, a correspondence file, and current file. He wasn't sure where to start, but was encouraged by her organization. Sheri had files all over her screen, many duplicates, making it difficult for him to find the latest in an area. His daughter often told him, "It's just like Mom's brain, Dad, she doesn't miss a beat, but you never know when or where she'll attack. She's a Ninja mom, and her computer is set to confuse anyone."

Norbie understood from Alison's organization one thing; she thought her computer was safe from others' access. Until now, that is. She didn't expect to die. He decided to start accessing the current file, then check the bank file for unusual money entries, then the Suspicions file, next notes, and finally the correspondence file. He worked for over two hours, interrupted only by Sheila who informed him the gym had old really nice lockers with keys as she described to them.

Norbie made the call to Rudy. They agreed to meet again the next day.

21

Words and Facts

Lieutenant Mason Smith formed a big smile, thinking, *something's up with those two. I smell romance in the air. Juan must have made some headway with Lilly. I've watched for months. I didn't think he had a chance with her. She's a flippin' smart ass. He'd be so nice, and she'd give a wise remark back. He never retaliated. I was going to tell him nice guys finish last, but lookee, I was wrong. If these two think they're fooling any one; ha.*

Lilly and Juan were reviewing two interview files on Judith Wallace. Lilly had pulled the West Side arrest report on Judith Wallace. It was dated eight years ago. The report said there were several people involved in the skirmish but all of them pointed to Judith as the instigator. The charge was dismissed by the court. Lilly knew the arresting cop and was about to call him for further information. Juan said, "Lilly, this cop, Jack Phelan, is he a straight shooter; I mean can we believe this report?"

"I do believe the report. And like you, the report surprises me. The lady was no lady that night, but look who were two of the accusers."

"Eleanora and Josh. I don't know the other names. They're not in our current search. We can check them out later, if we have no other directions to follow. Eight years is a long time and still Judith was supposedly best friend to Eleanora, and Eleanora leaves her a great deal of money in her will. Lilly, there's a bigger story than this. The club site was the martini club."

"Think about it, Juan, why would there be an altercation with both Josh and Eleanora and others at 'the Club?'"

"Because Judith realized she was being recruited after Josh turned his back on some relationship with her, just like with the other lady. That'd be my guess, Lilly."

"You mean maybe she was dumped again in her mind, and Eleanora was behind it. She loved Josh, and realized he wanted to only play with Eleanora. If it's true, she could have seethed over it. But, Juan, eight years is a long time to seethe. We'll never get her in here for a conversation again without her attorney. This one's the Captain's call."

Juan placed his hand on Lilly's and she did not move away. He said, "Call Jack and get the full story."

The spectator, Mason, had all the confirmation he needed. His smiling reverie was interrupted by Ash Lent, who noticing Juan's hand on Lilly's, laughed, saying, "Love sneaks in. Never know when. Can't look for it, Mason. It just happens. Now why did Cupid hit those two?"

"Easy, Ash; first is proximity. They had a chance without pressure to view each other from a distance and without expectations. Second, they are the right age. Third, they have the same values. Fourth, our Juan had the chutzpah to try. Gonna mess up MCU. One will have to leave eventually."

"Why do you always see the negative, Mason? I see two young lovers with great potential."

"Ash, you're a romantic. I'm a realist. Lovers never, ever have an easy road. But au contraire, these two will be okay."

Ash laughed. "Mason, no one expects you to be so ingrained with French words, romance, and history, when you are the most cynical cop in this unit, probably in the whole West Side force."

"I'm like Popeye, 'I am what I am and that's all that I am'."

Ash shook his head in defeat.

Meanwhile, Lilly told Jack Spector she had her partner Juan on the phone for their conversation. She asked if he remembered the arrest of Judith Wallace at the Oxford Martini Bar eight years before. He groaned and complained about detectives expecting cops to have long memories. She gave him details from the arrest report which triggered his memory. Jack said, "We arrested the lady. The bartender called about her creating a disturbance, which by the time we got there had moved out to the parking lot. She tried to leave and gave us some shit. Two witnesses, not the bartender, said she attacked them. She said she was just trying to protect a victim, a young woman. Trouble was, the supposed young woman was not there.

"We arrested this Wallace lady for creating a disturbance and assault. All the witnesses refused to testify and said they maybe were mistaken. The charge was dismissed. That bar was not a troublesome bar; only had a couple of problems as I remember. It was sort of a pick-up bar for the crowd in their late twenties and early thirties. So, Lilly, you going to tell me what you've got the lady down for now?"

"Just looking at her, for her ability to tell the truth, Jack. What did she say to you, when you arrested her? What was her excuse for causing a disturbance?"

"She was furious with two of the witnesses for taking advantage of the disappearing victim. She said, I quote, 'Two worms who belong underground with Satan, and you believe them over me!' She didn't say much more than that. We arrested her because there was a crowd of upstanding citizens insisting she was a dangerous drunk. She had knocked a really good-looking guy to the ground, but he was in denial. Probably made him look bad. Just a little drunken chaos we normally would never hear about if we hadn't been called."

"Who, Jack, who was the guy she knocked to the ground?"

"I just put him in the list of names present, because he wouldn't admit he was a victim. The other witnesses later all shut-up. The leader was the Eleanora woman. The guy was that Josh; both of them murdered later. I couldn't have seen that coming. Don't think, Lilly, I don't read the papers. You think this Judith is good for this?"

"Don't know, Jack; I have no evidence. By the way, the report doesn't list the name of the bartender."

"No reason to, Lilly. The fight was outside the bar, but the bartender was a regular there, a nice guy named Charlie."

"Jack, thanks for your help."

Lilly had a puzzled look on her face when she clicked off and asked Juan, "What do you make of it now? She may have been angry with Josh, but was it because of the other woman, or was she really protecting the other woman? Why would Eleanora let all this go on and then bring police to the scene? She normally lets Josh do all the dirty work. And is this our bartender Charlie Logan who says he really doesn't know Judith?"

Juan had no difficulty answering, "Eleanora and Judith have history that includes Eleanora always hurting Judith. They were roommates in college. Judith says she wouldn't play those party games, yet a witness says she was at two cosmetic parties. Eleanora snookered Judith's fiancée and then dumped him. She wants to hurt Judith and did so whenever she had a chance. I'm not surprised she did it this time. Maybe she instigated the situation. What I don't understand is why she left millions to Judith in her will. Can't compute that one. And I have problems, Lilly, with the supposed victim; maybe there was no victim at all."

Juan finished writing up the report and left a note on the Captain's desk with the file suggesting it would be best if he'd pick up with a re-interview of both Charlie and Judith specifically mentioning the disappearing victim.

Attorney Cull and Captain Beauregard met for beers and bar food at the Student Prince bar in Springfield also called the Fort. It was a favorite hangout of business folks, cops, tourists, and area residents. The booths supplied needed privacy although both men were treated with hellos. The greetings ranged from, "Oops, you two together from the opposite side of the fence!" to "Rudy, what are you doing outside of West Side; you think you have lots of murders over here too. You looking at Norbie!" with laughs from the bar. Norbie gave Rudy the key from Alison's shoebox, and told him he suspected the key was from the Health Wellness Fitness Center in West Side. He said he was not certain, but explained what his secretary Sheila had found. He also gave Beauregard the USB stick. He was honest about reviewing the files when asked by Rudy, "I suppose you've seen everything on this?"

"Well, Rudy, I did give it a cursory glance."

"A lawyer's cursory is more than cursory, Norbie. What's important in there for me to view?"

Norbie said, "The most salient items were in a list of notes collected in a file labelled 'Suspicious'. Alison had notes on a Lawrence, Josh, and Eleanora. She cited Lawrence as a newbie and husband of Leonora. Leonora got short shrift from her as 'one of Eleonora's family charity cases.' She wrote specifically about Josh and Eleanora and their hold over everyone. She was disappointed in Eleanora. She said she was getting soft and wanted to discontinue the parties; just keep a few for some 'regular exercise in control' was how she phrased it. Eleanora also said, 'It's been ten years in development; I know how to get rid of the wannabees more easily. It's time to hone in on a survivable operation; one that won't draw attention. We've been very lucky to have fun under the radar so far'.

Alison's notes stated, "Josh is the worst one; he has no allegiance to anyone but Eleanora. He hurts everyone; and I believe watching and belittling those who trusted him was his favorite form of sadistic behavior. Of course, he particularly only let Eleanora hurt him. They are a match of evil."

He inferred in several statements relating to Lawrence her thoughts to whether he would be able to meet Eleanora's guidelines to go to the next level. He'd been under scrutiny for a few months. She wrote, "Eleanora just wants to punish Leonora for marrying," citing why marry someone like Lawrence. She says, he has no emotions and it's tough to truly punish a person who feels nothing. She thought he was one of those men who feels no physical pain and wondered why he wanted into the Cabal.

"She's tried to draw Bart into the scene; I know he came to a couple of cosmetic parties. She's wasting her time with Bart. He's straight up. I think she's using Bart to get tighter control over me. She thinks I still have feelings for Bart. I do. I regret hurting him, but he's on his own in this situation. I'm not going to save him from Eleanora. I couldn't save myself."

Norbie finished reviewing his notes stating, "Let's go see what's in the locker, Rudy. She hid it for a reason."

"I can't bring you, Norbie. Maybe one of your want-to-be clients could be implicated. I don't want to cost you a fee."

"For cripes sake, Rudy, I don't have a client. If you find something against any of them, I won't represent that person."

"I hate to say no to you, Norbie, but I can't."

"Well, I'll give you a hint. Did you know, Alison has a three-million-dollar trust? She's pretty young for earning that much. She ran a medical supply firm, a franchise of a national firm. I know how much can be made by such a business and I don't believe for a minute the trust money is funded all from her earnings, given her living and dressing standards. Alison had an additional income source."

The Captain and Sergeant Lent, accompanied by a uniform opened Alison's locker. Inside they found a few personal items and twenty-five thousand dollars in cash along with a notebook listing dates, initials and marks. The marks were a check, a zero, or a dash. There was no title to the notebook and it had not been referred to in her other files. He thought, *maybe it was and we weren't smart enough to notice it. I'll get Ted to review the files. This looks like a bookie's collection book. We'd better look at her finances again. Maybe there's some account we thought was normal. The trouble is we haven't reviewed her finances completely. The money in the locker, was it for collections on blackmail? Why did she leave so much in her locker? It was an even amount. Did she use it for living expenses so the taxing authorities would never see it? You can't pay your electric, gas, cell phone, cable with cash. It could be noted. You could buy fancy clothes and pay for restaurants and bars. It's tough to hide ill-gotten gains today. Maybe she had to bribe someone and was forced to find money to pay the bribes. I'll go through this notebook.*

Beauregard shared his thoughts. Ash added an old phrase his mom told him, "'It's rare if only one vice is involved in a situation.' You know, Captain, the victims and the Perp or Perps are all smart and have what most Americans seek: money, position, and beauty. What are they all jockeying for? They want position within the S&M parties; to be favored by Eleanora, the queen of mean; they want to control. Their vices include in addition to pride maybe: anger, jealousy, **greed, lust, envy, or wrath**. The wrath led to murder. All the others helped build up the need for total control which ended in murder. Our problem is, all who were not murdered, are still control freaks."

The men returned to the station for report writing, documenting the money, and conferencing with the other detectives. Beauregard gave Ted what he called, 'the bookie book' while the rest reviewed, again, the interviews of potential perps.

Sergeant Lent compared initials from a copy of the 'bookie book' to some initials from Leslie Hosman's book. There were seven common sets of initials collected from data from the last five months. He could see some connections. EC, JC, JS, CL, BB, JW, and JS were a few listed about a month before. An hour passed before Ted was ready with a report on the 'bookie book'. "I've matched dates with her checking account. Deposits of cash were reported by the bank, bi-weekly, and not on the specific dates of her entries. Of interest, is the deposits always totaled around twenty to twenty-five thousand dollars. I'm supposing the twenty-five thousand in cash was a summary of payments she received from about ten people based on her current checks offs for initials. I think where there wasn't a check, maybe a payee balked. I don't see transfers out of her bank to others. It looks as if she is into blackmail or is charging for belonging to the 'in group.' I've only gone back two months but did scan eight months of bank accounts data. She also deposited other amounts, rather large amounts, but only on a monthly basis."

Ash showed the sets of initials listed as belonging to Eleanora, Josh, Bart, Dr. Girandeau, Charlie Logan, Bart Brunder, and Judith

Wallace. He said, "I looked at checks to others. Nada, but she does withdraw about forty percent of what she deposits each month. There's only one such withdrawal monthly. I think we should also look at Josh and Leslie's bank records. Could be there are regular deposits and withdrawals from their accounts."

Beauregard suggested including all seven of the initialed folks, saying, "Greed for money is a prime motivator. Are any of our potentials in financial trouble? Judith Wallace was not playing nice about the potential loss of her inheritance. Financial problems there, or maybe just greed."

Millie walked in and quickly whispered something in Beauregard's ear. He immediately rose and left with no explanation. Several attempts were made to ferret info from Millie, but to no avail. Lilly said, "Must be personal."

Captain Beauregard rushed home. His wife asked for his help. He prayed as he drove rather uncarefully as noticed by observers. When he got into the house, the extreme quiet of no music and no lights further roused his fears. He called for Mona. She didn't answer. After checking the main rooms, he entered their bedroom only to find an unmade bed with no one in it. He yelled some more thinking, *Millie said Mona was in trouble and needed him. Why doesn't she answer? She can hear a paper drop. Where could she be? The laundry room was his answer.*

He ran to the other end of the house to the step-down area near the back where Mona had located the laundry production facility when they first moved to this home. On the floor lay Mona writhing in pain. He didn't bother to check details. He called 911 and then got on the floor with her trying to discover her problems. He checked for signs of stroke, but since she couldn't seem to talk, and her face was twisted in pain, he gave up. She was sweating and feverish. She did not acknowledge him, but her groaning reassured him. He had to leave her to open the front door and as he got up she gave him a frightened stare, only to receive a smile from her when he returned to sit on the floor by her side and rock her in his arms.

The EMT folks were all business. They reassured him, but he saw them administer medication and oxygen immediately. He could not get any substantive information from them. After they left, he followed in his car to Baystate Medical in Springfield. He called Mona's doctor who surprisingly answered after a few minutes. His advice to Rudy was to not anticipate too much, that Mona was a healthy and vigorous woman. He could give no information about possible pre-existing medical problems.

A frustrated Beauregard thought, *Mona's my rock; I can't remember when she was ever sick. Her family has good health history. She's only forty-nine years old. She hasn't hit menopause yet. What could it be?*

Rudy waited in the emergency room for an answer. He was certain Mona had a heart attack or a blood clot to her heart or a bleed in her brain, but he remembered that although she was too weak to answer him, her eyes were alert. He was invited inside her cubicle in the emergency room ward and found his wife sitting up. She smiled at him. He was ashamed as tears slipped down his cheeks. Dr. Taliendara joined them for a conversation. He explained, "Your wife had a severe attack of a large kidney stone moving through the ureter. It downed her. We've given her pain medication and it has helped, but we don't know yet if it's passed or if there are other stones. We'll be testing her for a few days. What surprises me is she says she's had no symptoms."

Rudy addressed Mona. "Mona, think about it. You've been complaining about pains in your back for a week. Would that be a symptom, Doctor?"

As Mona insisted they were not bad pains, the doctor assured them both, the pains were symptomatic of kidney stones.

A few hours later, a grateful Beauregard left his wife to return home to assure his kids that Mom would be fine. He thought, *these medical problems are real problems. They cause suffering, but they are not a result of a person doing risky things. This whole group of murders in West Side appear to follow some strange and unnecessary behavior which we would never have discovered if not for the murders. How many groups or cabals are operating with no call to the police? Are any of the prospective perps back operating a new cabal? We've never checked for that possibility. I can't get my head out of my work even when my wife is suffering.*

22

A New Cabal

Detectives Aylewood-Locke and Tagliano were on a mission. The Captain had suggested they check for new Cabal activity with their current list of potentials as members. Both knew the Captain had an inkling and was ready to push it despite his being compromised by his wife's illness. Petra commented, "If it couldn't wait until he came in tomorrow or the next day, you know he had an insight. I never underestimate his insights, plus it just makes sense. These people are addicted and murders won't make a difference or prevent them from exploring possibilities."

Lilly's answer was, "What say, we call community policing and using our potentials' addresses, see if there's been activities on Wednesday nights for the past several weeks. Mostly MO's don't change."

They split the calls to the four sector policing teams on the second shift and waited for calls back. In no time they had three addresses with activity on recent Wednesday evenings. The Community Police said there was an abnormal group of cars, over six, at the homes of Dr. Girandeau, Lawrence Sontin, and Charlie Logan. Girandeau's parties were every Wednesday night, while the other two men alternated nights for their parties. The detectives believed Girandeau was up to his own antics with a less aggressive group, and would never be involved with Charlie Logan. Given that his parties were on the same nights as Logan's and Sontin's, they believed this was confirmation for their view.

Lilly and Petra's problem, as they discussed it, was the question of who was attending each party. They had a few plate numbers from one of the parties at Charlie Logan's house, because a neighbor complained about cars obstructing the street at eleven in the evening. They decided to visit the neighbor who was known to Community Policing as a 'Mrs. Kravitz' type person who lived alone and was named Mrs. Solomon.

As they pulled up to Mrs. Solomon's home, they found her looking out her large picture window. She waved at them. They knew this would be a long morning. Inside, the home was decorated with bookcases filled with beautiful dolls; all kinds of dolls with some that looked like vintage dolls. Lilly had an aunt who collected dolls and knew the value of three of the dolls as over fifteen hundred dollars each. With the collection Ms. Solomon had of over three hundred dolls, Lilly mentally calculated their value at close to a half million dollars. Lily addressed Mrs. Solomon saying, "Your collection of dolls is mind boggling. Would you allow me to hold one of them?"

Petra couldn't believe her partner's statement thinking, *what's wrong with you, Lilly? I spend half of my twenty-four hours holding a real baby who fusses and cries and you want to hold a doll. Maybe that's normal. Looks awfully weird to me.*"

Mrs. Solomon was excited. She said, "Of course, Sergeant Tagliano, I'll let you hold one of my favorites," opened a glass cabinet, and handed her a very old looking doll. Here is 'Bebe Mothereau'; I know you'll be very careful with her. I normally don't allow touching, but you immediately knew their worth and I love it when visitors don't think I'm nuts, but instead notice I have collected a valuable group of beauties. 'Bebe' is from the eighteen hundred's and is French; worth around nine thousand dollars. Isn't she exceptional?"

Lilly handled 'Bebe' with exquisite care, and suggested Mrs. Solomon give her some gloves so the oil on her hands wouldn't transfer to the doll's clothing. Her request resulted in Lilly's endearment to Mrs. Solomon, who said, "I didn't realize police could be so sensitive. You are very special, Detective. How can I help you? You're here about the partying, aren't you?"

After Mrs. Solomon removed the antique doll from Lilly's hands to Lilly's relief, she hosted the detectives to tea and little cakes. She rambled on about Mr. Logan. "I suppose I should expect nothing more from him. He got his start as a bartender, but when he became a professional, well I expected more from him. Instead, he has these parties, only a few so far, but the people attending are inconsiderate. They park anywhere and they stay late on a weeknight. This is a quiet neighborhood."

Petra said, "Mrs. Solomon, are they too noisy? We need a substantive complaint to do anything."

"You can't fool me, Detective. Community Police would normally take care of this neighborhood complaint. Obviously, you have bigger fish to fry. He's in trouble, Mr. Logan, isn't he? I saw him a few months ago having an argument right out in front of his home with a tall man. The man was murdered later on. I recognized his picture; Josh Cantor."

Lilly interrupted, "Why didn't you call the police when you recognized Mr. Cantor and Mr. Logan arguing, or at least when Mr. Cantor was murdered?"

"Detective, I don't want to cast suspicion on Mr. Logan for murder. That would be too much. His behavior is not up to par and has not been for the last six months. He's had a beautiful woman visiting for a while. I don't go along with that."

"What does she look like, can you give a description?"

"Detective Aylewood-Locke, she is a handsome brunette. However beautifully she's dressed, she looks tightly wound; not a woman to be played around with."

Petra complimented Mrs. Solomon, saying, "I just showed you my badge for seconds and you got my hyphenated name and Sergeant Tagliano's name correct. It's unusual. How do you do it so perfectly?"

"Detectives, I worked as an attaché to the American Embassy in Egypt for twenty years. If there's one thing I can do, it is to remember names. Don't think my love of dolls is symbolic of senility; they are a valuable investment."

Lilly continued her conversation discovering Mrs. Solomon's attention to details in body language in her analysis of Josh Cantor. Petra had a photo of Judith Wallace on her phone. Mrs. Solomon identified Judith as the woman who visits Mr. Logan regularly.

When questioned further, Mrs. Solomon thought Judith Wallace had a thing for Mr. Logan. Despite Judith's controlled behavior, she continuously seemed to flirt with him. She also believed Mr. Logan was just being polite as if Judith were a client and not a personal friend. She could not document if Judith stayed over commenting she was not so interested in her neighbors enough to stay up past ten in the evening.

Petra asked if she took plate numbers of the cars at the parties and she smiled, saying, "Isn't that Community Policing's job?"

Both detectives laughed and agreed, but were surprised when Mrs. Solomon went to the antique table in her living room, opened a drawer, and pulled out a typewritten sheet of paper with nine plate numbers on it. All were Massachusetts plates. She smiled and said, "I thought from the one time I was roused from my sleep at two in the morning and saw a car double barreling out of the Logan's driveway, I might need to know who was in my neighborhood. I took the plate numbers that night, several weeks ago. One plate is often there and that is Judith's.

As they were leaving, Mrs. Solomon said, "I don't know what is going on here, but I don't have a good feeling about my neighbor."

Juan was direct. He said, "What say, Queen Lilly, want to go out tonight?"

Just as direct Lilly said, "Skip the Queen business. Yes, I want to go out with you and I don't need any pretense. Where we going?"

Clearly pleased with her reply, he answered, "Well we could go out on the town or we could play undercover cop and go to the Oxford Martini Bar. We should be able to see if there's new action. If you dress up, nobody will know you're a cop and I would love to see you all decked out."

Several hours later, the two detectives, looking decidedly like two lovers, waltzed into the bar. There was a combo playing great background music allowing them to settle into a table with a view of the bar. It didn't take long before there was what Juan called sexual invitational action taking place. Lilly thought it was typical action you'd see at any bar and told him so. In disagreement he pointed at a woman who had her hands all over another woman while the man next to her on the other side was also busy feeling her up. It appeared to be acceptable behavior to the three. A fourth showed up who was a handsome gentleman and he intimately touched the hair of the woman being fondled. Juan said, "Un uh, not normal, not even for a bar in the U.S. and it's not a big city bar. She's being groomed, just like we heard."

He walked up to the bar to ask the bartender if he could send over some snacks while also asking him, "What gives with that group? I've never seen such public play before."

"Stick around, there's a group comes here all the time. The action always revolves around someone being fondled as if he or she is the most important person in the world. It's weird, but I've gotten used to it. They never give any trouble; if they did I'm supposed to call a former bartender who's now a Physician's Assistant. He walks in and everyone behaves."

When Juan returned to the table, he suggested they go to dinner. He drove over to RTE 20 Bar and Grille on Boston Road in Springfield hoping to have a special environment for Lilly, and although the place was new and more casual than their outfits called for, the food was really good. Settling in with two vodka martinis, they discussed what they learned at the Martini Bar. Lilly said, "Charlie's in charge now. What we have to figure out is whether he is collecting blackmail fees and if he murdered in order to control. Do we have alibis for Charlie? What's really between Charlie and Judith? We have no forensic evidence; just evidence people have lied to us. Mrs. Solomon does not like Charlie and she's not too fond of Judith, but it's not enough. How do we get financial information on Charlie? We may be able to get Judith's bank statements. She is after all an heir in Eleanora's death."

After ordering, the two detectives dropped their professionalism. In fact, to onlookers, they were clearly an item. So much so, the hostess felt some reservation before bringing them drinks ordered for them by a guy at the bar. Juan looked to see who Santa Claus was only to be shocked to see Liam, Captain Beauregard's brother, walk over. Everyone liked Liam O'Callahan and particularly loved the idea Rudy Beauregard had finally found his long-lost brother and his family. Liam said, "Looks to me like two lovebirds here. Do the other detectives know? I won't talk about it if you don't want public knowledge."

Lily reacted first. "It's not that obvious is it? We've only dated a little while."

Juan responded, "Don't listen to her, Liam, I brought her home to meet Mamita. She'd better be serious."

Liam sat down and they chatted. Just before their food arrived, Juan asked how Mona was doing? Liam did not know she was in the hospital and complained about Rudy's inability to share problems. He rose and said, "I'm going to jump over there now. I'll get the scoop and wring Rudy's neck."

Juan and Lilly, encouraged by Liam, discussed how they felt about each other. Juan was all sweetie-pie, while Lilly, putting on her tough exterior, said, "You'd better be who you pretend to be; the guy I'm in love with. If not, you can bet, Juan, I'll be your worst enemy in a break-up."

He laughed and said in his best gangster portrayal, "Whatcha gonna do, Babe, smash me car; squeal to my Mamita; tell on me to the Captain?"

"No, Juan, I'll just kill you and leave no evidence just like these crazy sex maniacs we're dealing with now."

Liam found Mona resting in the hospital and pleased to have company. Two of her kids had just left. The oldest wanted to come home from college to check on her, but Mona knew he had exams and put her foot down. They talked and Liam asked how Rudy was doing with the five murders yet unsolved. They discussed some of the public issues Mona knew; both aware Rudy would kill them if private facts leaked out. Mona's nurse arrived to do the usual routine. A happy woman, Amelia said she was fascinated with the murders in West Side. She told Mona she has lived in West Side all her life and was grateful for Captain Beauregard's professionalism; given the history of serial murders the city suffered for such a small city. She carefully explained she should not be surprised since she met so many seriously mentally ill patients every day who do not act out. She then whispered, "I once met the woman, Eleanora, who was murdered. I've never met a more physically attractive woman, but one who was so cold. My brother lives two doors down from her home and said funky things were always going down over there. He'd tell your husband, Mona, if he asked, but he'd never call in. Captain Beauregard should call him. His name is David Church."

Liam told Mona not to worry; he would speak to Rudy about David Church. He left knowing Mona needed some quiet time and headed over to Rudy's home.

He decided to give Rudy some shit about not calling him concerning Mona's condition. It was always his thinking to keep Rudy off center a bit, if not for any other reason than to have a bit of an edge over Rudy's overly logical view of the universe.

Rudy showed his concern for Mona despite the doctor assuring him she would do well with surgery if it were required. He said, "Mona's never been sick other than a cold or flu, and when I found her on the floor, my heart stopped."

"Yeah, Rudy, it's called love which causes fear; get used to it."

Eventually, Liam got to the issue of David Church, saying, "I know the guy and was going to speak with him myself, but realized it would be a waste of time. You have to be the one, but I think we should go together. He'll tell me everything. I've done some investments with the guy; he's very smart and a decent man. Let me call him. He'll see us now."

Rudy, exasperated, said, "Are you crazy, Liam. It's eight o'clock at night, not a time to interview someone."

"Ha, I forgot public servants keep stringent nine to five hours. He'll be too busy to see you in the daytime. Listen to me, if Dave is at home now, he'll see us."

It took another five minutes of debate before Rudy agreed and a half minute phone call before Dave agreed to see them at the Country Club bar in ten minutes.

Dave Church appeared to be a normal and decent enough 'suit' which is what Sergeant Tagliano would have said about him if she were there. He did not mind talking about Eleanora, saying, "She was a spectacular example of art with no substance. A gorgeous face and body, but she could only talk about business, investments, and commercial real estate. I know she was bright, but she had no interest in theatre or the arts or books. She didn't even play golf. Most women in business play golf; she didn't have to. Every business guy I know just wanted to be seen with her. She was kind of a professional arm candy. For all her success, she was not on any charitable boards. She just didn't care about anyone but herself."

Before Rudy could direct the conversation, Liam asked, "Tell us about her visitors and her parties."

"I was never invited to her parties, but my wife told me we were never to accept an invitation. I asked her why and her answer was, 'She is a very mean woman. I don't want her in our lives and Dave, I don't need that kind of competition for your affections.'"

Rudy questioned who attended the parties. Dave said a whole bunch of people from a local gym who were interested in cosmetic enhancements. He said, "I know Charlie Logan who used to be a good-natured bartender with a shady past. Now he's 'the Man' all the women go to for enhancements."

"What do you mean, 'A shady past'?"

"Charlie had been a juvenile delinquent from the wrong side of the tracks, who lucked out when an older partner in my firm took him under his wing. Leon, my partner, was always working with the Big Brothers program and the court diverted Charlie over to him. Charlie did really well under his tutelage. He never got into any more trouble and is quite likable. He is now a Physician's Assistant; so successful, I understand he's leaving Dr. Girandeau's practice to go out on his own."

Liam questioned whether he'd make as much money out on his own as he would with the Doctor. The answer according to Dave was he could make a lot more. Charlie, he insisted, was a delegator and would develop one of those big skincare solutions companies. Maybe he'd even be able to hire a doctor for cover. He said, "My wife says he gets all kinds of products that her skin specialist won't use on a regular basis for patients, but Charlie uses them. She thinks he's a sleaze and wouldn't trust him. You can't listen to her; she's a typical cynical New Englander."

Dave remembered seeing Josh Cantor at Eleanora's house on a regular basis, especially in the month before Eleanora's death. He had no use for Josh. He thought he was a pervert. He knew about Eric's wife leaving him and the rumor was Eleanora was behind the divorce. He also said Reggie, who had died in Eleanora's house, was obsessed with Elenora and probably knew something, saying, "I'll bet that's why he was murdered. Reggie was religious about note taking. Did you find any record in his home about Eleanora? He documented Eleanora's every movement. You should double check. He had all kinds of hiding places for documents."

It took another round of drinks, which Liam was happy to supply, before the three men finished. Liam drove Rudy home, saying, "I don't know if you learned anything, but I'd do another search on Reggie's house if I were you."

"I agree, Liam, and I have a thought; we have two unmatched footprints at Elenora's murder site. We never checked Reggie's home for a match. It's a start in a case with no evidence and too many motives."

Mona faced surgery the next day. The doctor placed a stent in her ureter, and three hours later she was on her way home filled with some drugs. Known for her tolerance for discomfort, she did not complain. Rudy didn't believe for a minute she was without pain. Her sister-in-law Sally shooshed Rudy out of the house and took over Mona's care, citing his inefficiency and hovering as interfering with recovery.

Not knowing how to calm himself, he called for Ash and Ted to meet him at Reggie's home. They were instructed to bring the previous search records and pictures of the two footprints found at Eleanora's death site.

The house had been closed since the previous search. Although Reggie's relatives had been notified, not one had shown for the funeral. Rudy had called Reggie's estate attorney and was told to go ahead and search the home. All expenses for the home were being paid by the estate until a sale occurred. He said he wouldn't think about putting it up for sale until a minimum of six months had passed.

Ted checked the twenty-one pairs of shoes in Reggie's house and found a match for the partial in the backyard, but no match for the one on the plush carpet inside. Ash theorized Reggie went into the yard to investigate what was going on at the water feature but perhaps never went inside. Still, there existed the possibility he saw something inside he kept quiet about.

All three detectives looked through the extraordinarily neat home for evidence. They found nothing. They sat on the oversized couch feeling deflated when Ted turned on the television for news. It was an enormous seventy-inch TV on an extra strength stainless three-dimension holder which allowed movement of the TV. Ted moved the TV towards the direction of the couch when a small notebook fell to the floor. It would never had been seen if he had not moved the television. The notebook had been wedged between two black steel plates loosened when Ted moved the bracket slightly. The notebook cited dates and names of visitors to Eleanora's parties and a reference to an Excel sheet named 'Gotcha.' They knew the computer had been reviewed by Mason, who at the time said there was no password. It had been returned to the home at a later date. Ash quickly located it and turned it over to Ted saying, "I don't do Excel. You better check."

The file 'Gotcha' was typical of Excel files. A matrix was laid using positive and negative whole numbers. Since there were no cents or dollar signs, it could have been related to anything, but given the use of initials matching visitors listed in the other black book and the listed dates, the detectives felt certain there were collections and a few returns of collections. They got Reggie's bank statements from a file and there was a perfect match of the monies listed. The amounts did not match what had been previously found in Alison's bank statements. They would have to look at the statements side by side to see if there was collusion between the two, Alison and Reggie, or if each were operating on their own.

Beauregard remarked, "Lucre, filthy lucre, may be the motive; not lust nor envy; but possibly pride is included here. What are we left with? Money exchanges have been made and must be traced. Are they continuing? Ted, when did Reggie last get a deposit similar to the others? Was it after Eleanora and the others died?"

Ted searched the statement and it showed two deposits, both posted after the others' deaths. He said, "Blackmail, it's one of the oldest motives for murder, Captain. It also explains Reggie's shoe print outside by the water feature the night Eleanora died. He was forever watching her, but was never invited in to participate. He would have been a great victim for Eleanora."

"Maybe, maybe not; Eleanora had him under her thumb already. I don't think she knew he was a blackmailer. If she did, she would have done away with him quite easily. He was afraid of his own shadow; Eleanora was not afraid of anyone. The important issues are that the perp or perps did not know Reggie was a blackmailer before Eleanora's murder. He may not be the only blackmailer or just be a player in the scheme. He would have been killed the same night as Eleanora if the perp knew about him. I believe Reggie saw the murderer. He didn't fess up, because he thought he had the perp under his control. He thought Eleanora was killed for sex or anger or pride."

Ash said, "Reggie's notebook lists all our known potentials as attending Eleanora's parties by date. He differentiates between early and late parties. He has Judith Wallace attending only the early parties. He has noted as attending the last party: Eleanora, Charlie Logan, George Girandeau, Alison Brunder, Josh Cantor, and Leslie Hosman. We have information of later attendees for the new parties at Charlie's house showing Bart Brunder, Lawrence Sontin, and Eric Shulman attending along with a bunch of newbies. Why would Eric and Lawrence join in the forays when our information tells us they were one hundred percent against this display of sex?"

Hazarding a guess, the Captain said, "I don't know, but I can speculate they may be trying to solve the murders. Bart lost his wife and had trouble getting over it. He may want to find the murderer for closure; the same could be said for Eric, but I think from the reports, Eric's wife would go back to him in a minute. Sontin is a question."

23

Blackmail

Mona returned home from the hospital with definite instructions given for her to rest. It would take at least a week before the stent would be removed from the ureter and she was told to make some dietary changes. Rudy could not understand. Mona was the most controlled person he knew when it came to eating a proper diet and he told the doctor so. The answer was, all patients are different and what is commonly thought to be healthy for the general public doesn't work in all cases. Mona was to cut down on her consumption of black tea, chocolate, and protein. She tended to eat a lot of protein and vegetables while Rudy sinned with carbohydrates. The doctor lectured Rudy, who had diligently been questioning him on Mona's adherence to the best diet, on the benefits of moderation and drinking lots of water. Rudy could not do enough to make Mona more comfortable, until she finally said, "Enough's enough, Rudy, go to work."

Just before he left, Mona thanked him for vacuuming the family room. He couldn't figure out how she knew. He had vacuumed, because Mona vacuumed every day, not because he thought it needed to be vacuumed. He asked her how she knew. She laughed saying, "See your one perfect footprint near where you put the vacuum in the closet.

Wouldn't be there if you hadn't just done the job. You're my gem, Rudy. You weren't even going to tell me you did it."

Rudy focused on the footprint in the plush rug near the end of Eleanora's sofa. The perp had deposited her on the wrong end of the couch and then stood at the other end inspecting his work. Not for the first time, he thought, was it a woman. He was certain. A woman would not have left a footprint. A woman would have posed Eleanora facing the television.

One footprint; attendance at forays; sociopaths galore; but absolutely no evidence. Practically no one had alibis with the exception of Otto Waldner, who in Beauregard's mind was so out in left field, he couldn't murder anyone. Beauregard parked at his assigned spot next to the Chief's spot. Looking around in an attempt at avoiding small talk, he rushed inside only to be accosted by his favorite Attorney, Norberto Cull, who was holding court with the Desk Sergeant. Frowning slightly, Beauregard said hello and directed Cull, "You're here to see me? Which client, Norbie?"

"Judith Wallace is not your killer."

"I agree, Norbie, but why do you think she's innocent."

"Rudy, I've just spent an hour with Dr. Girandeau and he insists that Judith is a wack job. He said she could use some injections, but she's deathly afraid of needles. She'll use any type or cream or abrasive but no needles. She doesn't get a flu or pneumonia shot either. I doubt she could inject Eleanora, despite the fact she may have hated her."

"So, Norbie, that's all you have? You came over here to tell me that."

"Nope, wouldn't waste your time. But I have a couple of theories. Do you have time to listen?"

"If an eight hundred dollar an hour attorney has time for me, then I have time for him."

The conversation following required remembering some of the details of the murders. Beauregard knew all the details, but was surprised to hear Norbie familiar with details not reported in the news. It made him wonder, just who was talking to whom. Norbie dissed all reference to his sources saying, "I've heard lots of stuff but some things keep popping up in my head as unanswered. For instance, who sent Josh in as our fourth on the day he died? Josh told me Jay Adams sent him as a replacement. I later asked Jay; he said he didn't know Josh Cantor and couldn't have sent him. I checked with the pro and he didn't, nor did the other two in my group. As I recall, he was just waiting there and joined us. How did he know, or was he just waiting for the first opening? What would he have done if there was no other incomplete foursome going out? Maybe he'd have played as a single; that would also have work if he had scheduled an assignation at the same time.

"So, in my mind and given the other later murders, Josh was set up for this murder by someone he could not resist. He surely was bi-sexual. I'm betting it was a man; it took some strength to choke him. I know in the beginning he was just getting a sexual high, but he would have figured it out soon enough to try to save himself. A man would have the strength to hold on and kill him. He surely wasn't missing his new wife, because I think he had little esteem for women.

"Another thing, Rudy, Emmet, the Martini Bar's barkeep said only Eleanora and Charlie Logan were allowed to keep a bar tab at the Martini Bar. I think it's significant. I think those two had the most juice and when push came to shove, Josh was just a sophisticated player. Emmet said Lawrence Sontin was respected by Charlie Logan; he said he was now an important player."

"Norbie, you've eliminated your potential clients as perps and you're setting me up to look at two possibles; or do you have more suspects?"

"Rudy, I just don't know. I do know there's a plot here; at least two are rearranging the forays and the business side. I think it's two guys and I believe both qualify for your view of them as sociopaths. I am suspicious of Lawrence who is late to this game, because I learned that Eleanora would never let him up his ante to join her late parties. He wanted to join. She would not let him. She was in his way. Now, he's one of the big timers, or at least I think he is. He has motive. Josh brought him into the fold, but now we know Josh would never go against Eleanora, even if Lawrence, for instance, met some of his needs."

"There is also Bart as a possibility, Norbie; or have you excluded him?"

"No, actually, he showed up at the country club to play golf on the day Josh was murdered. Don't police dislike such a coincidence?"

"Yeah, normally we do. We have no evidence. No one has alibis for the times of the murders, not even Josh's murder which occurred in the daytime. We have a footprint for forensics as well as evidence of knowledge of strangulation techniques and the drug used on Eleanora."

Norbie noticed Rudy did not tell him which drug was used. He knew from his connections, but he wouldn't let Rudy know. He asked again about Otto Walder, the guy who took Eleanora on a date, but was assured he was the only one with an alibi. Rudy ended the conversation by saying, "Norbie, I do thank you for this conversation. It is always helpful to view all of the facts. My job is to re-interview, redo backgrounds, and find a reason to search homes for footprints. The trouble is, forensics says it's a common enough shoe print for a size ten to ten and a half shoe; probably leather sole. I'll get to work."

It was Thursday, a good day in Beauregard's mind to make some decisions on the murders and the perps. He'd felt the swelling of details, paltry as they might be, along with his feel for what may have happened. It was time to meet with his detectives. Perhaps there were details they forgot in their interviews. He also wanted to re-interview all three persons of interest.

The group of detectives met with folders of details and their laptops and directed by Petra gave their thoughts on significant info on each person of interest. Ash was the first to say, "Finally we have a direction. I thought it would never happen. You're thinking, Captain, two people want to control this scam for the future. Is it for the money, because Ted's found quite a cash flow here that was not initially obvious?"

The Captain said, "Motive is maybe plural. Not about sex except as a weapon for control. Money and control are the motives, and I'm certain it's a partnership between two sociopaths. Otherwise, there would not be five murders with no one screaming something. Do you realize the press is not after us? They don't particularly care about these victims, and the families are not complaining. I think the families are deeply ashamed of the sex practices of their victims. Perhaps they hope none of it will be made public. I would have expected Reggie's family to have interviewed with the press, but I'm told Reggie was not close to any of them. In fact, they thought he was off-kilter socially."

They went through what was known. Lawrence Sontin's file was the thinnest. He was just a husband of Cousin Leonora. It was Leonora's bigamist marriage discovery shedding light on him as a victim of his wife that first put him under scrutiny. Later, when information about his desire to be brought into Eleanora's foray, his participation became more interesting. The Captain suggested Ash and Juan interview him again.

Additionally, he requested Lilly and Petra do an in-depth interview with Leonora. If she asked them to contact her lawyer, do it that way, but he didn't think she would. The Captain said, "Other than making a bigamist marriage, she's an innocent. The importance in interviewing her again is to discern more about Lawrence. Has she told him anything about her new marriage? Are they getting a divorce? Did he know she was Eleanora's heir? I wouldn't tell him that, but we should know. If so, how much will it cost her and how did he react? That is the story I want from her."

Captain Beauregard asked if Mason had interviewed the Justice of the Peace who married Eleanora and Josh. He had. The JP said, "They were the handsomest couple I have ever met; but they never kissed or even held hands. It was a strange ceremony. She paid the fee. She was in charge. They left in two cars. I figure it was a business relationship. It's all I could see in those two."

The Captain directed Bill and Ted speak again with Charlie Logan, saying, "Go to his house with the expressed intent you're looking at Leanora and her husband. Keep pumping. He won't go silent. He's just narcissistic enough to want to help you entrap one of them; even if he is in collusion with one of them. He will tell you some stories. Charlie was a bartender; true to his history, he'll gossip. We need to know what he knows about these two. Also, guesstimate his shoe size while you're there."

The Captain called for all new interview reports to be on his desk by Monday morning.

24

Finger Pointing

Lilly and Petra settled Leonora in Interview Room number two with a latte. She did not ask for representation. They offered to wait for her lawyer if she wished. Her answer was succinct, "No. I have nothing to hide other than my marriage, about which I've not told Lawrence yet. In fact, if the police don't tell him, I'll never tell him. Detectives, will you have to tell him?"

Petra spoke first. "You know, Leonora, we never know which direction an investigation and prosecution will take. We can't make any promises; although we would never talk to Lawrence about Jim, unless Jim and Lawrence are involved in murder. Then all bets are off."

"Detective, may I call you Petra? Your hyphenated name is long."

Petra told her to go ahead.

"Petra, Jim would never be involved in murder or anything illegal. I always thought Lawrence was a straight shooter. He is almost emotionless. I'm certain it's why I continued to look for attention after I married. Lawrence is almost devoid of expressing anything in a caring manner. Even during sex, it felt as if he was technically doing a good job, but he had no real interest. He would always say the right things, and so I believed he was crazy for me, and I was the one who had a problem loving back. Remember, Eleanora hated him from the first day she met him; she refused to come to my wedding. I thought she felt betrayed by me, but now I think Eleanora and Lawrence had some traits in common."

"Like what, Leonora?"

"He was unfeeling and downright cold always. It wears on a person. I've been absent, pretending I've been in New York when I was really with Jim. Lawrence was not upset. In fact, when I came home a day early because I had an abscessed tooth, he looked frustrated. I remember, it was a Wednesday. He said he had plans for the evening and he couldn't take me to my four-thirty appointment. I was in such pain, and I couldn't understand why he wouldn't cancel. We got into an argument and he told me I was a narcissist always thinking of myself. He said, 'When you're away, you don't care what I do. You come home for one evening and you expect me to change my plans for you.'

"Of course, he was right and he made me feel guilty. I suffered a root canal and lots of drugs and came home and slept it off. When I woke at four in the morning he was just sliding into bed. He claimed he was working in his den. It was so unlike Lawrence, who likes a regular sleep schedule.

"Later on, I heard he was dabbling in forays. Dr. Girandeau said that Lawrence tried to join Eleanora after she ejected the doctor and she told him basically to pound sand. So much for the husband I thought adored me. I feel no guilt about him, but I don't want him to know about Jim and my inheritance from Eleanora."

Lilly asked, "Have you told him you want a divorce?"

"I told him I heard about his going to the sex parties and I could not live with a husband who did. He was rational, but told me I would have to give him the house and a settlement of a hundred thousand dollars or no divorce. I threatened him with public exposure and he laughed at me. When I told him I was serious, he threatened me, saying, 'Baby, take the offer or worry about what may happen to you. Don't turn your back. I wish you had more but you have a great job. Divorce this way or else.'

"I pretended to be afraid. I've already served him for the divorce. Norbie said he'll have a quick hearing set up with the judge; then it's a matter of waiting out the time. He'll leave me alone as long as he thinks he's got the upper hand."

Petra asked, "Didn't you see what he was before you married, Leonora?"

"No, to put it bluntly, he kissed my ass for the first year and then I started noticing he was spending a lot on himself and couldn't take criticism about it. I wasn't focused. I knew, then, my marriage was not a good one."

Lilly asked if he was ever out of the house for long periods. Leonora said he would leave early on Monday mornings and come home late. He was in IT and had to go to the main office in New Haven every Monday. Lilly asked, "Who owns your home?"

"I do. Why do you think he wants me to give it in the divorce, because in the normal course of events, he wouldn't be entitled to it?"

"Would you be agreeable to a search of your home. You mentioned he had worked in his office; does he have his own office?"

"No, Detective, it's my office. He just has a computer station he uses. You believe he's connected in some way, don't you?"

"All possibilities are open in cases like this, Leonora. We're checking anyone connected with the sex parties."

The interview ended shortly thereafter when Leonora authorized a search of her home. They informed her they would connect with the Captain for any legal-related problems.

Petra called the Captain to relay the substance of the interview.

He was grateful for their call and told them he would hold off on the interview with Lawrence until after the search.

Detectives Bill Border and Ted Torrington were met by Charlie Logan at his home. They had explained in their call their interest in Leonora and Lawrence Sontin and his history with them. His attitude was quite different than it had been a short time before. He was more than willing to meet with them after work.

Charlie had coffee ready for them while he mixed a martini for himself saying, "I know enough not to offer a drink to you guys when you're on the job."

The three chatted about the city and local politics until Ted said, "I know you were a bartender for many years and we hope you can cast more light on the relationship between Leonora and Eleanora and Josh. We've interviewed several people in the sex party groups and they inferred some relationships existed. We wondered if you could give us any confirmation."

Charlie sat back and smiled. He was in good cheer and said, "So, finally you're looking at Mrs. Goody-two-shoes. It's about time. If ever there was a scared wanna-be, it was Leonora. She so wanted to be like Eleanora; in fact, in looks she almost was, but she pretended this morality. Ha, anyone could see through it. She wanted all the mystique of Eleanora with none of the risk. She fell in love with Josh. Big mistake that was. Josh was only in love with himself and in pain with Eleanora. No one stood a chance of interfering in that relationship. Leonora thought he was in love with her after two dates. What a joke; shows you how insightful she was with relationships. Eleanora put an end to that dating when she discovered he was grooming Leonora.

Don't know what she said, but Josh ended it quite unkindly."

"Were you there when he ended it?" asked Bill Border.

"Yup! It was like watching the Titanic sink. Sad; she was so dumb. She stayed away from the bar for a while after the breakup."

Bill asked, "Was she a drinker? Maybe with a few brews her judgment was impaired."

"Absolutely not, she was one of those trusting souls, almost simple. But she did not trust Eleanora and made that clear."

"Why have you never told us about Leonora before, Charlie?"

"She didn't seem important, such a non-competitor despite her looks."

"What about your relationship with Judith Wallace, Charlie? You never told us about her; you've explained Josh's relationship with her and Connie Davenport, but not your own. Was she just there for the taking?"

"Judith, you can't think I would be interested in Judith. She is a pillar of stone, no emotions other than anger."

Ted said, "We've been told she visited you regularly. Why?"

Charlie said, "What are you thinking to ask me about her? She's her own problem and has become obsessed with her looks. They all do when they hit their middle thirties. She's even showed up here at my house a few times. She's a bitch and wants individual attention. I had to ask her never to come back to my home. I hear she's back with Dr. Girandeau. I've seen her name on the appointment sheets for him."

"Who else is on those sheets, Charlie?"

"I can't see them normally. It was a one-time thing when I saw Judith's name accidently. What's this all about? I thought you wanted to know about Leonora."

Ted said, "Actually, we're interested in her husband Lawrence. We understand you're a friend of his. It seems strange he would be involved, given Leonora's complete dislike of all the beautiful people."

Charlie sneered at him, saying, "You think Leonora's husband is like her. What a joke. He's a very cool guy who looks like he's the Marlboro Man in Cebala's clothing. His tastes are not plebian. I think he married her for her money and her connection to Eleanora. He wanted in, but Leonora had no clue."

Bill responded, "But he never got in, did he? Eleanora wouldn't let him in. Now he is in the Cabal."

Charlie said, "Who gave you that info? He's just a good guy who wants a little excitement in his life. Can't blame him for having some needs beyond the ordinary. And I don't know if he's in the Cabal or not; I don't know a lot about the Cabal."

Ted opened his notebook and took his time to find a written note. His slow flipping through the notebook brought all the attention in the room to his efforts. Locating the note, he said, "We have a witness who reported parties every other Wednesday, late at night, at your home. Also reported were the license plates of most of those who attended. Lawrence Sontin is one of the attendees reported. Was this a Cabal meeting, Charlie? How well do you know Lawrence?'

Charlie's face ashened and then reddened. He exploded, "Get out of here! You think you're going to set me up. If Lawrence and Leonora have a problem, don't bring my harmless little get-togethers into it. Call my attorney if you want to speak to me again."

Ted asked, "Please give me your attorney's name; I think we may want more information from you about the people you know."

A calmer Charlie said, "I don't have an attorney, but I guess I'll have to get one. Are you really just interested in those two and not me?"

Ted said, "We go by evidence. You were known to have parties and denied being involved. We were told they were sex or Cabal parties or whatever you want to name them. Your denial bothers us."

Charlie stood up and said, "Detectives, I'll walk you to the door."

On Monday morning two uniforms and two detectives waited in a shaded spot for Lawrence Sontin to leave his home. An unmarked car was at the intersection he would enter to detail his progress to the interstate. Once he entered I-91 South they radioed their colleagues and Leonora allowed them to enter. They were to search carefully and replace every object moved. The goal was to look for evidence, but not allow Lawrence to know they had searched. Sergeant Ted Torrington led the team. He was the resident detail man who noticed everything. Two hours later they left with notes from his bank statements and a photo of one of his dress shoes and the dress shoes. Leonora told them he would not miss those shoes. She rarely saw him wear them.

Back at the station they submitted the shoe and photo to forensics and were promised a report shortly. Ted worked quickly on Lawrence's banking statements for the last six months. The statements were telling.

Forensics sent a report. The shoe fit the impression in the rug in Eleanora's condo on the night of her death. The Captain said, "This puts Lawrence in the condo on that night. We had no idea he was even involved with Eleanora before. The big question is, did he kill her? Was he just a member of a plot to kill her? If so, who was also a partner and why did the others, other than Reggie, have to die? And finally, how do we prove any of this?"

Mason answered, "You asked for a complete background check on Lawrence. I have the report right here. He's supposed to be in IT and his position involves sensitivity to privacy issues; normally requiring a stellar background check. He was arrested as a college student for hacking the University's computer system. As a result, he was thrown out of that college and finished his career at a state university; from Ivy League to state university. He was not from money. His mom was a single mom with three sons. Two live near her in upstate New York. They haven't heard from Lawrence in ten years; didn't even know he was married. I have his application and his resume from his current position and it's all lies. He has letters of recommendation from faculty who never heard of him. He has this big job in internet security; looks to me we have a con man here, Captain. I don't know if he's a murderer. I have a contact where he works; she says he had an affair with one of the Vice-Presidents there before he married Leonora. The Vice President left the company because she was pregnant. No problem with that; she was married. However, there were a few rumors because she said the woman was married for twelve years and had no children; this was a surprise."

The Captain asked Lilly who was present to give a call to Leonora and ask her how she met Lawrence. They would eat lunch while waiting for an answer. Lilly said, "Okay, but don't eat all those sandwiches from the Rosemont Italian Deli while I'm gone." They gave no assurances.

Twenty minutes later, an excited Lilly returned and said, "She met him at the Oxford Martini Bar. She saw him there three nights in a row before he tried to buy her a drink. She thought his patience was a good sign of his interest."

Bill said, "There's more here. She's really not the brightest in social interactions, is she?"

Ash insisted, "He asked around about her; probably discovered she was the cousin of the gorgeous and powerful one and thought it was his entre into the group. He didn't know Eleanora wanted nothing to do with Leonora in her sex life. Was Charlie the bartender then or Emmet? I think it's important in discovering who may have been doing some run downs for connections then."

The Captain said, "I'll get info on what Emmet knows first. We don't want to make Charlie any more antsy. I see Charlie and Lawrence as partners. We want them both; for sure I think Charlie will give Lawrence up to save his own skin."

The Captain continued. "I want them both. Josh played a role in this; he had to die. Why? Someone offered him something he couldn't refuse, maybe more pain than Eleanora offered. She married him. Was it to keep him loyal? Was he being wooed by one of the others? I think this is where the money enters. Let's look at the trail. Mason and Ted, what do you have?"

The money trail was filled with some twists, stoppages, and turns. What started as suspected cash payments to Eleanora changed later to a portion paid to Josh. The payors at first were Leslie, Alison, and Dr. Girandeau ; however, Alison and Leslie became payees later. Later, some of the comers, and former comers to the parties, were also payors.

After the murders Bart Brunder, Lawrence Sontin, and a few other sex party attendees were payors. The amounts increased. Shortly before the murders, when Alison and Leslie stopped paying; they still received payments from Josh and Dr. Girandeau. Eleanora and Josh's cash inflows originally came from Alison, Leslie, Dr. Girandeau and a couple of other party-goers; making the detectives suspect Alison was not really the architect of the money scam, although she was involved. Then there was Reggie's involvement in receiving payments from some of the party-goers. Since he never was allowed to attend the parties, or never wanted to attend, the detectives agreed his motive was blackmail. The payments confused the detectives until Ted came up with a flow chart and dates proving Eleanora and Josh received net positive amounts. They concluded Eleanora and Josh let Alison and Leslie start a blackmail scheme and then turned it upside down by taking eighty percent of what was collected from the two blackmailers without most of the blackmailed parties aware of their involvement. Alison and Leslie were still in the black, but Eleanora and Josh were sitting pretty. All the other payors from Dr. Girandeau to the later ones, Bart Brunder, Lawrence Sontin, and Charlie Logan were in the red. Then, about six weeks after the murders, all payments were made to Lawrence Sontin and Charlie Logan; but the payments to Charlie were from Lawrence only. Ted said, "Lawrence never paid dollars to Charlie until after the murders and some of the money paid after the murders was going to Lawrence, Leonora's husband's account."

The Captain summarized, "Bart jumps into the parties after Alison's death to search for her killer. Lawrence became the new blackmailer. He knew about the blackmailing scheme, if it was blackmail and not entry costs to the parties, but we don't ever see him paying other than later to Charlie. He wasn't allowed into the forays before Eleanora died. Makes him a prime candidate for her murder. There is the question of how he knew about the blackmailing scheme. Charlie Logan was a payor under the old scheme. He knew what was going down. This old blackmailing scheme explains why Alison and Leslie had to die. How, just how, are we going to prove this?"

Ash said, "We have never talked with Dr. Girandeau or Bart Brunder about the new blackmail scheme. We can put them under the spotlight; they'll tell you who they paid and are paying."

Petra agreed but said, "What kind of gall does it take to renew a blackmail scheme after murdering five people? Aren't they afraid of discovery? Did they think we would never look at bank records?"

Juan said, "They're sociopaths, they're killers. Part of their narcissism is to think they are smarter than everyone. That arrogance is also their major flaw."

The detectives were all on the same page now. They could understand these motives. Captain Beauregard developed the plan to bring home much needed evidence.

Norbie found himself again at the Oxford Martini Bar conversing with Emmet the bartender. Rudy requested he get a few answers from Emmet without Emmet becoming aware of police involvement. Norbie loved doing this, noting to himself his preoccupation with interrogation, thinking, *just one of the hazards of lawyering. I get to love looking for info. This habit of mine drives Sheri crazy.*

Two hours later Norbie had confirmation of several bits of gossip. First, Emmet was witness to Leonora's first meetings with her husband. Emmet portrayed Lawrence's search for info on her. He told everyone she was just as good looking as Eleanora, which was probably true. Although most felt she didn't have the 'Je ne sais quoi' or that take-charge personality that would allow her to hook others into her dreams. Leonora was a mouse to Lawrence the fox. Emmet thought it was harmless, but later realized Lawrence had big plans for the forays. He said Lawrence absolutely spewed hatred for Eleanora.

A second point of information gained was unexpected. Bart Brunder and Eric Shuman got together regularly at the bar. Emmet said they got friendly with Lawrence. He thought they may now be involved with the parties, which surprised him. He told Norbie they didn't look or act like the typical sex addicted assholes. He liked them both.

Emmet thought Judith Wallace was an irritant for Charlie. He noticed lately that Charlie couldn't stand to see her at the bar.

Leaving the bar, Norbie headed over to Rudy's home. Beauregard was pleased to see him, and more so, because Mona was out for the evening along with his two sons allowing him some business privacy. After analyzing the results of Norbie's evening, the two were certain of one thing: Bart and Eric believed they could find the murderers themselves, not understanding the danger they may be in. Beauregard would have to intervene and now.

Beauregard requested Millie to carefully set up interviews for both Bart and Eric, fifteen minutes apart from each; he thought this would work despite his awareness they would chat with each other before coming to the station. Beauregard was convinced they would connect immediately after Millie called, and would feel safe with what they would consider a fifteen-minute conference. It would not be fifteen minutes, but they did not know that.

Beauregard and Sergeant Torrington interviewed Bart first. This Bart was much more assured than Juan's written summary of his first interview. He was willing to discuss the sex parties from a moral perspective and how the parties had destroyed his marriage and his life. When the Captain posed the question as to why he was now attending some of the sex parties, he turned red and became very quiet. Hesitantly he said, "You planned these interviews with Eric and me, didn't you? You think you can stop us? The murderers cannot go unpunished. I bet you didn't know about the blackmailing scheme, did you?"

The Captain was direct, saying, "Are you being blackmailed? It's important you help us. Your life is in great danger, Bart. They have killed five people; what makes you think they won't kill you and Eric? You think they don't know you're novices in this? They know. You're under their radar. How much have you given up of yourselves in this undercover stuff? Pros have trouble getting back to their ordinary lives after doing time undercover. Dirt sticks, Bart, dirt sticks."

Bart said, "We've been careful. Who do you think are the killers?"

"Who's doing the blackmailing, Bart?"

"Judith Wallace is collecting a fee for our entre to the parties and our education into the seduction aspect. The longer we take to come along the longer we pay a higher premium. We each pay five thousand every two months right now, but get a reduction to half if we bring in a new prospect. We haven't brought in anybody which I admit is making them look at us suspiciously."

"Who's them, Bart?" asked Ted.

"We think, but can't be certain, it's Charlie Logan and Lawrence Sontin. Charlie is the smooth one. Lawrence has no mercy. We started by going to the cosmetic parties. We had to pretend to be interested in correcting wrinkles and Eric pretends he's concerned about his receding hairline. We read up on plastic surgery and sado-masochism. Eric says I fit the masochistic personality and he, the sadist. Neither is true. I think you're right. I think they're on to us. We attended a half hour of two parties and then were escorted out. What we saw was some sick stuff, but not much worse than a porn movie. We think they are testing us and maybe we've flunked. I've been followed the last two weeks, enough to make me nervous. I stay at Eric's house for safety reasons. Lawrence asked me why I was living with Eric and I pretended I had a thing for him, but how did he know I was there?"

The Captain asked, "When were you going to tell us?"

"Captain, we stopped paying the going fee last month but continued to go to the parties. Judith warned us. She said, 'You're out of the parties next week. What did you think would happen if you welched? Even if you can't come to the parties, you will still have to pay if you don't want your life ruined. They have evidence on you both.'

"That's the first time we realized they would go so far as to blackmail us."

Petra knocked on the Interview Room door. The Captain joined her. She said, "You were right. These two guys are nuts. From what Eric has said, I think they're in trouble while Eric thinks he's Special Forces. He's got Bart living with him. Really, Captain, they're both secretly afraid they're the next to die."

The Captain answered, "And maybe they are scheduled to be next."

Beauregard issued orders next: uniforms were to pick Judith Wallace up immediately. If she would not come easily, then she was to be arrested on a blackmailing charge. He said, "Just let her make her obligatory allowable lawyer call; nothing more."

Ash was to locate Leonora and escort her to her home in Brimfield. The Captain said, "Make sure she understands she is not to call Lawrence or go near their home. She is not to take calls from him. Have her turn off the location device on her phone. He's in IT. He'll know how to locate her and he will.

"Both Lawrence and Charlie will be on to our investigation very soon, if they aren't already. We do not have enough evidence yet. I'm hoping they'll do it for us. I want you, Juan, Ted, and Lilly, to set up a watch of Lawrence and Charlie. Which detectives haven't they met yet?"

"I think they've only met Ash and Ted from the first interview," said Lilly. "Lawrence is arrogant from the descriptions and I think he may be a misogynist and most certainly bi-sexual. Send Mason and Petra. He won't even think of them as interested in him, because I believe he would not be interested in them."

"Not a bad idea. You really think he'd be blinded by his own prejudices, Lilly?"

"Aren't we all? And he's such a narcissist; my experience is narcissists see only what they want to see. They see only what's helpful to themselves and Petra and Mason do not count."

The Captain summed up the direction he was moving towards, saying, "We do not have enough evidence. I know these two are my persons of interest; which one is the murderer I don't know. Charlie looks the cooler of the two, but for sure, they are two sociopaths. My guess is Lawrence is the only one who could compete with Eleanora for Josh's affections. Josh was mainly interested in men; his passion for pain kept Eleanora important to him. I think she married him because Josh was losing interest in her for Lawrence. Lawrence has the sadistic side and would use it to control. And from what Leonora has told us all along, Eleanora hated Lawrence.

"She hated him for good reason; she saw herself in him, but there was a difference. He was willing to get out there in the market and help get people. He did not need Josh; she did."

25

Pressure Cooking

The police detectives knew they were normally limited in the time they could hold persons of interest. However, the only one complaining was Judith Wallace who finally found an attorney and it was not Norberto Cull. The Captain explained in depth Judith's precarious situation in aiding and abetting a plot involving murder. Her attorney did what all good attorneys do; he asked for immunity. She was pleased to stay in custody for her safety as he negotiated with the district attorney for complete transactional immunity.

Beauregard received a report from Norbie Cull on his repeat visit to the Oxford Martini Bar. Norbie said, "Rudy, Emmet said the Cabal is in disarray. Lawrence and Charlie were there while I was having a drink. I brought along Jim Locke, Petra's husband, so I wouldn't stand out as a lone drinker. Jim's ears are bigger even than mine. Emmet could only talk with me for a few minutes, because about five patrons were insisting in knowing whether the party was on for the next night. Emmet could only tell them to wait for Charlie Logan and Lawrence Sontin. They wanted to speak with Charlie, since the party was supposed to be at his house the next night. I'm telling you, Rudy, it was as if they were completely stressed out. Whatever this S&M does, I can tell you this group is addicted.

"Then Charlie walked in and assured them the cosmetic party was on, but the later party may be cancelled. They argued and Charlie almost lost control of them, when Lawrence entered. He ended their complaints and told them to come or not come. He didn't give a damn, but they were not to think they could not come one night and be invited back. It gave me the chills seeing his authoritarian control; Hitler at his best."

Rudy said, "I don't have to tell you, Norbie, this info doesn't give us evidence, but it does let us know they'll have to deliver something to these folks soon. Did Charlie or Lawrence ask about Judith or Bart or Eric?"

"Not that I heard, but when Charlie came in, he whispered something to Emmet who shook his head in the negative. Probably was the question; I just can't be certain."

"Do you think they'll hold the party tomorrow night, Norbie?"

"Rudy, I think maybe, but it won't be too daring. Why, what are you thinking?"

"Don't know yet, I'll tell you, Norbie, after the fact."

And Norbie groaned.

At ten o'clock the next evening, two detectives, Ted and Ash, were parked in Charlie's nosey neighbor, Mrs. Solomon's driveway. The view was terrific. They'd watched when a few of the earlier cars left. The remaining cars left belonged to Charlie, Lawrence, Dr. Girandeau which was a surprise, and six other cars, which after a review on the registry's database showed only one belonging to a familiar name, Warren Thomas. Ted remembered him as an employee of Leslie

Hosman, who not only hated her, but had a lot to say negatively about Leslie. He did, at the time of the interview, admit he was into group sex parties, and that Leslie kept him in line. He laughed when he said he was willing to be kept in line.

Ted said, "We should have followed this one up more, but his car was never one of the plates seen at the new parties or the old ones. Now he's at a foray looking for some serious pain. He's a new player for Charlie and Lawrence, but the type they would want to play with because he was able to be kept under control."

They called the info into Beauregard who was parked one street over in a car with Lilly next to a car with Juan and Petra. Their question was, "Should we hold off on the plan, given we may have a new witness who may talk?"

The Captain's answer was a negative. He said, "They're continuing to party and it is past ten. We're on."

They waited until eleven when they saw the lights in the main room dim and some new low lighting in the family room turned on. Their knowledge of the layout of Charlie's home was helpful.

Ted rang the bell, and moved to the left of the side curtained windows to avoid being seen until the door was opened by the newbie Warren Thomas. They both recognized each other. Ted took the off moment to push Warren aside and entered the room to a vision of chaos. Five detectives including Beauregard and four uniforms followed and entered the premises. They were thrilled with the view from the open door. Several people were tied and in the act of being beaten and tortured. The torturer was to no one's surprise, Lawrence, while Charlie sat in a soft chair watching the mayhem. The detectives walked in; no one stopped them. They entered another room with three people involved in torture and there were cigarette burns on one of the women's breasts and one man's scrotum. Blood was on sheets used as protection for the rug and furniture. Most of the men and women involved were on some drug and appeared confused with the exception of Charlie and Lawrence who were angry but not confused.

Lilly immediately had the uniform who specialized in photography memorialize the scenes while Charlie went berserk. Strangely, Lawrence just smiled and started to dress. Charlie immediately tried to make a call but an officer took his phone. Beauregard answered Charlie's demand about a private party and what right did the police have to break in the door. Beauregard did not have to answer. Ted said, "We were answering a neighbor's repeated requests about noisy parties. I knocked at the door and when it opened, I saw all the blood and people bound up."

Beauregard suspected that exigent circumstance possibly may not hold up, but there were enough people here to use as witnesses to the chaos and the blackmail. The murders were quite another thing. He decided then and there to arrest both Lawrence and Charlie for blackmailing, endangering others, acting as illegal drugs suppliers, and for murder. They were both read their rights. Only Charlie reacted, declaring, "You have nothing on me; nothing. I'll sue you fuckers and this city."

The other detectives with the assistance of two uniforms took statements and allowed the participants to dress and call their attorneys. Juan smiled as he said to Lilly, "It is unfortunate and surprising don't you think that the press is outside."

The station was ablaze with staff busy with arrest procedures and handling phone calls. Three hours later Beauregard, Ted, and Mason conducted an interview with Charlie. He refused to speak without his attorney, who'd been contacted but wasn't currently available; he would get there as soon as possible. The Captain shared some but not all details about the blackmail scheme, illegal injection of drugs, Charlie's sole ability to deliver the drugs through injections, his lack of alibis for all the murders, his arguments with Eleanora before she died and with Josh, and his relationship with Judith. He concluded with, "I don't know who the first will be to ask for immunity, Charlie, but I'm talking to Lawrence next."

Charlie spoke for the first time and said, "Lawrence? You realize he's not quite right in his head, don't you? Anything he says is a lie. Check his background. He's gotten away with everything because he's crazy."

Beauregard answered, "And what about your history as a juvenile, Charlie, don't think we don't know about it. It looks to me you think Lawrence will pull the 'insanity defense.' Where does that leave you; the one who is capable and culpable?"

Charlie sputtered, saying, "My records are all sealed. You can't use any of it against me."

Beauregard on leaving the interview room said, "We'll see. We'll see just how the dice fall. Lieutenant, please have Mr. Logan brought back to his cell."

Two minutes later the Captain, Ted, and Mason met with Lawrence Sontin, who, now dressed, looked the rugged country squire gentleman. Mason thought, *Charlie Logan looked smooth both naked and dressed; this guy did not look smooth naked. He looked evil. Now he's the epitome of the best dressed macho guy. He's dangerous. He changes completely depending on the situation. Nope, I think I'm wrong. Charlie's demeanor appears to be the same despite the situation; that always indicates more danger. The Captain has two of his sociopathic psychopaths here today.*

Lawrence had called his attorney, but unlike Charlie, Lawrence was talkative. He relayed a story, an unbelievable story, about his attempt to save his marriage by joining the sex parties. He stated Eleanora told him, if he wanted to keep Leonora, he would have to become more adventuresome. When the Captain confronted him with evidence of Eleanora's rejection of his entre to the forays, he brazenly stated, "She wanted me to be her second in command. I'm second to no one."

Lawrence corrected with new information every detail the Captain stated from their interviews with him and others. He would invent a new scenario to explain everything from his arguments with others, new alibis, his bringing new marks into the parties, and particularly, his relationship with Charlie Logan. He stated, "Charlie's just a good old boy with some medical knowledge. He thinks he's in charge; he's never been in charge. Eleanora got rid of him, replacing him with the idiot doctor. That should tell you something about Charlie."

Beauregard asked, "We have a shoe print at the scene of Eleanora's murder. It is a match to yours."

Lawrence said, "How could you get my shoe without a warrant?"

He then answered his own question with, "That bitch, Leonora. She let you into the house. She probably put the shoe print in the house that night to frame me. You'll never get me with that one."

"Unfortunately for you, Leonora has an alibi for that night, Lawrence."

Lawrence lost control and two uniforms cuffed him as he banged his fist on the table in an attempt to reach over to grab the Captain. Beauregard said, after Lawrence settled down, "We have you, Lawrence. We have motive now. We have opportunity. We have your history. We have witnesses to your blackmailing scheme. Tonight, we have a group of witnesses we did not have before. Think about it. Do you think Charlie Logan is going to take this fall; he's going to hang you. Now is your opportunity, before I offer this deal to Charlie. I'll take a walk. You think about it. Call me back in when you decide."

Outside the room, Mason queried, "Captain, what's with giving him time to think? That's a no-no. His attorney will be here shortly who'll tell him to shut up. You could have kept up the pressure; it was working."

The Captain answered, "No, I think Lawrence thinks Charlie's going to talk first and get away with all of this. Lawrence is a sociopath and so is Charlie. There's no allegiance and unlike my readings on other murders committed by sociopathic partners, these two have no respect nor generally any real need for each other. He's going to call me back in; he's going to deal. He has to deal. We have nothing on Charlie with the exception of his medical expertise."

Ash approached the two and said, "One of the witnesses said some things which might help."

The witness, Warren Thomas, said Charlie Logan was involved in the blackmail scheme with his boss Leslie Hosman. Charlie organized the scheme originally, not Alison or Leslie. All three had one common trait outside of the sex stuff and it was greed. The Captain asked Mason to get Charlie's financial records; they had enough for a warrant to search his home based on Warren Thomas' statements, Charlie's medical expertise, and his arguments with Elenora and Josh before their murders.

Lawrence Sontin was not a man who dealt with quiet. Not twenty minutes after the Captain, Ted, and Mason left the interview room, he was yelling for their return. The Captain reread him his rights and had him sign. He asked for immunity.

A call was made to the District Attorney. He asked for public counsel saying he didn't have the funds to handle this situation.

Two hours later, Lawrence's version of the facts was memorialized a nd signed.

In the other cases, lawyers occupied the interview rooms, one by one, with their clients. Some made statements to avoid arrest, but understood they were witnesses. Those who did not were arrested. Charlie Logan's attorney met with him, and then asked for a conference with the District Attorney. The ADA in charge asked for a confession. Mr. Logan refused.

When the Captain had initially told Lawrence, any immunity was in the purview of the District Attorney, the Captain pointed out, over and over, all evidence pointed to Lawrence and not to Charlie. Without his story, Charlie would walk; meaning Lawrence would take the fall for the murders. Lawrence's anger was not as explosive as before. Now it appeared to be a burning inside him. He said, "I want immunity. Charlie's not even interested in sex. He loves to watch beautiful people being demeaned. He likes their doing it to each other. He's worse than Eleanora and has an even higher level of enjoying crushing others; he's also minus the sex side, just like her. I've never seen him have sex with anyone."

Lawrence's confession included, "Josh pushed Charlie. Josh was in love with him. Charlie loved watching Josh grovel, but he hated him. I didn't do the murders; I don't need to murder for my high. Charlie enjoyed murdering Eleanora and Josh. The other two women just knew too much. I felt bad about his killing Leslie. I could rely on her. I understood her. As far as Reggie, I don't know if he killed Reggie, but I didn't. I don't do murder. I like sex and I like to give pain, but I don't kill. I did help him move Eleanora's body that night, after he injected her. I thought he was just going to have sex with her when she was out. Kind of a way to later control her with photos. He took photos. But, he then strangled her and laughed. It was too late for me to do anything then. I cleaned up the place and left her panties outside by the water just to create confusion. No one saw us leave. Our cars were down the street.

"When I went there that night, I thought we were going to negotiate the price of the drugs and the amount of the cost of entre to the forays or for blackmail. Our lists were getting bigger for getting money, but Eleanora said it was too dangerous. She wouldn't budge on money and Josh wasn't there to protect her. I think Josh knew Charlie was going to kill her, and it was okay with him. She was interfering with his relationship with me and Charlie."

Later, Beauregard explained to his detectives, "Charlie Logan does not play well in the sandbox. A partnership is not his preferred setup. He's typically a sole proprietor. He gets away with things. Getting to him is like chasing mercury. You simply can't grab it. For starters, search his house for all financial records and photos. Bring his computer in. Mason will handle any passwords. Lawrence insists Charlie took pictures. Find them. They will support the confession. Search Reggie's house again for photos connected to Charlie or the bar. I want all cell phone activity for the dates and times of the murders. Maybe Charlie got careless about turning off his locator. For certain, an IT guy like Lawrence would not forget; but you never know."

26

Questions???

Days later after paperwork, arraignments, Press Events, and the District Attorney's Office's conferences with victims' families, West Side MCU's detectives sat together to review motives.

Petra, who'd been discussing the psychology of the two perps with her psychologist husband and MCU former detective said, "No matter what Jim says, I don't get it. These guys had everything. They even had situations in which they could express their deviant control issues. Why murder?"

Juan interrupted, "Enough is not enough when you're addicted. In this case, what was the addiction? For Charlie, it's greed and control and the joy of witnessing others' suffering, and he was not in control of Eleanora, nor would he ever be. I think Lawrence has the sex addiction mixed in with the greed and control and other stuff."

Ted impatiently said, "Charlie did not have to murder Eleanora. He and Lawrence were making inroads, particularly with Josh. Eleanora thought she had to marry Josh to keep him in line; makes me think she knew she couldn't continue to control. She gives Charlie a hard time. She screwed up on that one. Josh had needs and he liked men more than women and was addicted to risk. Charlie could have developed his own foray using Lawrence and Josh, and leave Eleanora out in the cold. Instead, he killed Eleanora. Why do murder, when it opened up all kinds of additional problems?"

Ash and Mason fought for the floor. Ash won, saying, "They say that the sociopath who covers up is a psychopath. I think they are both psychopaths. I can't know the difference. In this case they were both superior in covering up their deeds, but could not stay away from the forays. How stupid were they to think continuing to blackmail and enjoy these parties wouldn't bring them under our scrutiny? And to answer your question, Juan, they're both risk takers who believe they'll never be caught, and impulsivity is also a common trait for psychopaths."

Mason said, "I thought we decided they think the police and most others are stupid. Those pictures found in Reggie and Charlie's homes did it. Charlie was stupid."

The Captain said, "Sociopaths create disorder to allow themselves to control. One aspect seen often when two sociopaths, in this case psychopaths work, is for one of them to outdo the other. Charlie murdered Eleanora. He took control and then had Lawrence clean up the mess. Charlie is in my mind what I would call the 'Alpha' dog of the two psychopaths. I thank God we found the photos of Eleanora and Reggie's murder sites. There again, Charlie couldn't let go of a memory he had of his power over the death of his murder victims. Without those photos, Charlie may have walked and let Lawrence take the hits."

Ted said, "Captain, you know I like details explained; what about the movement of Reggie's body? Lawrence Sontin insisted he knew nothing about Reggie's murder."

"You have just pulled the hanging thread. Could it unravel the whole case if smart lawyers got involved? Reggie was a well-muscled and heavy guy. Did Lawrence help him move him; if not, did someone else? Is Charlie strong enough, if he had a good wheelbarrow and was able to clean his trail, to move the dead body over to Eleanora's house? I don't know. We have evidence of Charlie in Reggie's house, but none of Lawrence. Is Reggie's murder an unsolved murder? I guess that question may offer some wiggle room for the lawyers. Perhaps we have solved only four murders. The District Attorney and the Chief have directed us to leave it to them. There is a novel here for an investigative journalist to write sometime in the future. Do I like this hanging thread? No, but I'm not OCD and what we have is good enough for now. Reggie's murder will haunt my nightmares along with unanswered questions from other murders. My final thoughts revolve around the danger of a focused group satisfying unhealthy ideas or practices. Group psychology often misdirects the vulnerable. You may be able to complain. You may say the vulnerable should know better. However, group thinking has created hell on this earth from war to murder.

"I've had enough of this investigation. I'm going to wash my hands, go home to Mona, and not think too much, unless required. I'd advise you all to do the same."

Acknowledgments

To my husband Joe for his unquestionable
loyalty, kindness, and love.

To my children: The lights of my life.

To my grandchildren: Continue to Dream, Endure, and Prevail!

I am grateful for all technical assistance
I received from my good friends:

Police Matters:
Retired Springfield, Massachusetts Chief of Police Paula Meara
Massachusetts State Police Officer John Ferrera
Retired Springfield Police Officer Michael Carney

Attorneys:
Charles E. Dolan
Joseph A. Pellegrino, Sr. (ret. Justice, Massachusetts Trial Courts)
Raipher D. Pellegrino

And to my editors: I thank you for your
editing, support, and counsel.

To all above: All errors on implementation are solely mine.

More Books by K. B. Pellegrino
Kathleen B. Pellegrino – Author & Storyteller

Evil Exists in West Side Series:
Sunnyside Road –Paradise Dissembling (Liferich Publishing) 2018
Mary Lou – Oh! What Did She Do? (Liferich Publishing) 2018
Brothers of another Mother – All for One! Always? (Liferich Publishing) 2019
Him, Me and Paulie – Drugs, Murder and Undercover (Livres-Ici Publishing) 2019

You can find K. B. Pellegrino's books on all
major online Book Stores, such as Amazon, Barnes
& Noble, kobo, I Books Store, and SCRIBD.

Follow K. B. Pellegrino on her website. KBPellegrino.com

CPSIA information can be obtained
at www.ICGtesting.com
Printed in the USA
LVHW080817250920
667082LV00015B/185/J